D1203973

THAT
GOOD
NIGHT

THAT
GOOD
NIGHT

RICHARD PROBERT

BEAUFORT
BOOKS

THAT GOOD NIGHT

Library of Congress Cataloging-in-Publication Data On File

For inquiries about volume orders, please contact:
Beaufort Books
27 West 20th Street, Suite 1102
New York, NY 10011
sales@beaufortbooks.com

Published in the United States by Beaufort Books
www.beaufortbooks.com

Distributed by Midpoint Trade Books
www.midpointtrade.com

Printed in the United States of America

Interior design by Mark Karis
Cover Design by Michael Short

To all the aging folks out there:
Do not go gentle into that good night,
Old age should burn and rave at close of day;
Rage, rage against the dying of the light.

— DYLAN THOMAS, 1914–1953

PROLOGUE

Lieutenant Jim Dillingsworth was manning the radio when the call came in from NOAA. An EPIRB signal had been received from a vessel, position N 42 20.2; W 69 10.4, approximately 65 miles southeast of Boston. Lieutenant Dillingsworth scrambled Search and Rescue Team 6, led by Captain Sam Harrington. Within minutes, Captain Harrington had the copter airborne with co-pilot Douglas Percy, Petty Officer Jason Berte, and Seaman Tony Corcelli on board. With calm seas, bright skies, and little wind, Team 6 was relaxed, expecting the call to be bogus. Most were. It took less than fifteen minutes to spot the vessel, a sailboat with sails neatly furled. There was no sign of anyone on board. Using his VHF radio, Petty Officer Berte tried to raise the vessel as the helicopter hovered 150 feet on the yacht's port side. No answer. They circled. No movement was detected. No sign of distress. Perhaps it was an unconscious sailor. Hovering on the yacht's port side, Seaman Berte slung the winch cable outboard. Snapped securely in his harness, Seaman Corcelli was carefully lowered to the water. He unhooked and swam ten yards to the vessel. The boarding ladder was down, making boarding easy and without incident. He made his way from the swim platform onto the aft deck and into the cockpit. "Anyone aboard?" Corcelli called out. No answer. He moved toward the companionway. Peering in, he saw only a meticulously clean cabin. Again, he called out. No answer. Going below, Corcelli quickly searched the vessel. There was no sign of life. Seaman Corcelli reached for his handheld VHF radio.

"Captain, this is Corcelli. Over."

"Corcelli, this is Captain Harringan. Over."

"The vessel has no one on board, sir. Vessel appears seaworthy. Over."

"Any sign of struggle? Over."

"Negative, Sir. There is a note addressed to USCG, sir. Over."

"Read it to me, Corcelli. Over."

To my Friends of the USCG:

My name is Charles Lambert. I am now deceased, having taken my own life and buried myself at sea. I ask that no attempt be made to recover my body.

The red-file contains my ships papers indicating that this vessel is fully owned by Adam and Roslyn Burris. Please contact their representative, one Baxter Hymlaw, Annapolis Yacht Brokers. 126 Port Road, Annapolis, Maryland.

Please post the package as addressed to Abigail Tennera and the letter that is addressed to Arden Smith Esq.

Thank you and best wishes,

Charles Lambert

"That's it, sir. Over."

"This is Captain Harrington. Corcelli, remain on board. Can the vessel make port under its own power? Give the systems a going. Over."

"Roger that, sir. Stand-by."

Pause.

"Captain, this is Corcelli. Fuel tanks show three-quarters full. Batteries fully charged, navigation system operable. Bilge clean and dry. Engine running, all gauges showing positive. Over."

"Roger that, Corcelli. I'm sending Berte down to assist. Monitor Channels 16 and 22. See you back in port. Oh, Corcelli, water and food on board? Over."

"Fit for a king, sir. Over."

"Have a good voyage. Captain Harrington out."

"Corcelli standing-by on 22 and 16. Out."

INTRODUCTION

Dear Reader,

I met Charlie Lambert in Boston. I was there on a photo shooting assignment for *National Geographic*, working on a study of Boston's waterfront. Let's just say at this point, that Charlie saved me, my camera, my self-esteem, and much more.

During my few days with Charlie, he told me very little about his past. Mostly we talked about his sailing and my photography. We had discussions more suited to young lovers than two mature adults.

What follows is an account of Charlie's determination to live his final years as he wished. From escaping the confines of a nursing home to courageously, singlehandedly voyaging on a sailboat, this account of self-discovery at the age of eighty-four is written in his own hand. Upon his death, he had his writings sent to me accompanied by the note printed below. I contacted a friend at the *National Geographic,* who put me in contact with Jared Bevins, a freelance editor. Jared was able to transform the musings of Charlie's aging mind with its vacillating ebb and flow of present, past and future into a coherent narrative while maintaining the blossoming re-emergence of Charlie's spirit from the confines of nursing home life to the freedom of wind and water. There was also a digital recorder that Charlie sent to me which belonged to an insurance investigator by the name of

Justin Roberts, who was hired to locate Charlie after he escaped the nursing home. Using the memos that Investigator Roberts entered into the recorder, Jared edited, and added dialogue to the recording to offer the reader a clearer picture of Charlie's continued battle to live life as he wanted to live it.

I trust that you, the reader, will discover that aging, with all its trials and tribulations, can be and should be the most rewarding and adventurous part of life. I've included below the personal note that Charlie sent to me.

Sincerely,
Abigail Tennera

Dear Abigail,

I am sending you my musings from my sailing venture aboard That Good Night. *When I was in the nursing home, I started to keep a journal, but once on the water, I spent quiet evenings expanding my writings into what I hoped would be a book. Do with them as you will. I am also including in the package a little black box that looks and acts like a belt buckle. Actually it's a digital recording device that belonged to an investigator that dogged me from the moment I landed in Maine. The post on the buckle operates the recorder. You'll catch on, it's really simple. I had hoped that my voyage would have taken longer, but death had other ideas. At least I died the way I wanted to and not in some purgatorial nursing home.*

It was wonderful to have you as such a sensitive last love. You brought spring to my winter.

Love,

Charlie

FRIDAY, JUNE 22

Shelia, the night nurse's aide, just squished by, her rubber cross-trainers compressed by overload. Hippo sized, she wears a god-awful smock done up in pinks and blues, imprinted with lambs and kittens; it's draped around her bulk as if Cristo turned fashion designer. White fluorescence skims along the terrazzo floor, sneaking under my door like a thin sheet of crackled pond ice. A low incessant hum lies like fog, blanketing anything familiar. This is nighttime, every nighttime at Sunset Home. I hate being here.

My name is Charlie Lambert. I'm 84 years old. Currently, I'm a resident in this wretched place. Really, it's more like a repository for old folks; there's little left of anyone's personality here. In an attempt to keep myself sane, I've latched onto the idea of writing down my thoughts using a notebook I found in Howard Denner's trash the day he died.

Howard lived and died in the room next to mine. I'd visit him every morning just to chat. Dementia had torn a hole in his memory leaving behind snippets of his life: a farm boy, a runner in college, an engineer, a love for American Beauty roses, a woman named Clara. Howard's deceased wife's name was Doreen. Dementia is sometimes like a heavy dose of truth serum. In Howard's case, his love affair with Clara came out in what was dubbed as "My Story Time." Using volunteers, Sunset encouraged clients to join together to talk about their former lives. Marianne Suchance, a well-meaning but entirely inept volunteer in her thirties, led the session, which was offered once a week. When it came time for Howard to tell a story from his life, he began by describing in great detail his secret love life with Clara. I wasn't there, but the word through the grapevine was that ol' Howard's confessional was very graphic—none of those romance novel euphemisms for him. The sordid details of Howard's affair turned deep-seated boredom into smiles and tears as clients vicariously dug into their own hidden memories. Hidden thoughts and desires become prey to the beasts lurking in demented minds, ever ready to pounce, dignity notwithstanding. For those in nursing homes there is no future, only the past, as sketchy as it may be.

The notebook that Howard left in his room was blank except for the first page. Scrawled there were the words, *My Darling Dear.* That was it; the rest of the page was empty. I tore it off and put it on Howard's bedside stand next to his nursing-home-issued plastic, pale-green water carafe. Maybe *Darling Dear* would somehow find it there, but I doubted it. People living here seldom had any *Darling Dears* other than in distant echoes.

I've been in this place for six months. My life is whitewashed, my memory bleached. I miss the simple things. Common things like the sound of my refrigerator, or my squeaky front door, or the motor gearing up on my home's heating system, the growl of the sump pump, the bark of a neighbor's dog, a car going by. All replaced by raspy coughs and mournful groans, a hacking, old, wheezing ensemble improvising its own requiem. I lie in bed, lights out at nine, the exception being the hallway's cold light sneaking under my door. And the ever-present night light—bright enough for nurse Shelia to check on me, like I might sneak off to some place for a beer or to get laid like an old alley cat. I think back on these six months like a felon recalling his time in the joint. Only my crime was getting old. Judge and jury were my two boys and their co-conspiring spouses. What the hell ever happened to extended family? You bust your ass, raise kids, and they take it all like they're entitled from birth on to have everything you have and more.

My two boys and their greedy wives began taking notes of my "dementia" shortly after Lori died. Lori and I were married for fifty-two years. She was my childhood sweetheart. We loved, we struggled like everybody else, we overcame day to day bumps in the road, we built a wonderful life, and then she was gone. And it was sudden. We all prepare for death when we get old, but let me tell you, when it happens, it can come on as fast as a firing-squad bullet. Or linger, withering us like forgotten fruit on the vine. Old folks in homes like Sunset await death. There is no next day or the next month because planning ahead is a futile exercise. Visits from family and whatever friends are left, happen less and less as time goes by. There is definitely no living for tomorrow. It's more like hour to hour—long, unforgiving hours of waiting for the Grim Reaper and his stone-sharpened scythe.

I met Lori in high school. She and I were on a team collecting scrap metal for the war effort, WWII, that is. Who the hell remembers that these days? Lori was five-foot-two, had blue eyes, had a great ass, and could lift fifty pounds of scrap metal like it was nothing. I'd watch Lori bend over to grab hold of a chunk of rusted steel, and for the next week and a half be in a terrible way. I didn't need pin-ups to stir my adolescent yearnings, I had Lori. Courting back then was different than it is today. It might take a week or more just to get up enough courage to kiss the girl. And even then, first-tries were summarily rejected. There were all sorts of expected courtesies in those days, like opening doors, carrying books, being a down and outright slave and, of course, getting the approval of the parents before even thinking about taking a walk together. Is it better today with getting sex as easy as picking fruit off a tree? I'm not so sure. But I think when you come down to it, romance has always trumped sex and I hope that it still does.

The boys said that maybe I was depressed and needed help. Are you kidding! Of course I was depressed. Sad perhaps describes it better. Damn sad. How would they know what my days were like? After Lori's funeral, off they went. One to North Carolina, the other to Kansas. "C'mon and live with us for awhile," they offered half-heartedly. Sure, tear me away from the familiar just when I lose the most familiar. And since when does living with your kids lift one out of depression? And what is *for a while* supposed to mean? Until one or the other of us can't stand it anymore! Anyway, they didn't mean it. A gesture, at best. "You want to do something," I wanted to say to them, "then call me once in a while. Maybe invite me on a vacation like on some Disneyesque cruise ship or rafting down the Colorado. But don't ask me to come and live with you for awhile. No, let me alone to figure it all out." To me, it made no sense to visit anyone, sleeping in a strange bed, being an interloper in someone else's routine. But apparently, my desires weren't anyone's priorities but my own. My adjustment to post-Lori was quickly noted as going off the deep end. I hate to admit it, but I'm convinced my kids had a plan: get power of attorney, commit the old man to a managed care facility, and take whatever they want. I know that sounds like paranoia, but they built a case, hired a lawyer and hauled me before a judge.

Enlisted as watchdogs by my *caring* kids, my neighbors reported that I only went out after ten at night. When Lori was still alive, we were asleep well before that time, so my late night forays were seen as a sign of instability. The truth was I enjoyed going out late to buy groceries and other things. For one thing, there was less traffic. For another, there were no screaming kids and their hectic moms clogging the aisles. I liked night people more than day people. Things were more relaxed. What the hell do people expect? You're married for half a century and then in an instant you're single. What? I'm supposed to be unchanged, go about life like everything's rosy-pink? Well, it isn't. Major changes in life are just that, major and the older you get the more anxiety comes with it. Did my kids or neighbors or the minister expect my life to simply go on as if nothing happened? One neighbor pimped me the idea of hiring her cousin as a live-in. Can you believe it? Replace Lori with a *live-in*?

Another item on the indictment was leaving the stove burner on. I admit that this can be a serious matter, but I was pretty careful and only slipped up now and then. And what's supposed to happen? If the damn pot burns, the smoke alarm would scream like a nervous Banshee and the fire-department shows up. That only happened once. A little smoke damage and it's as though I planned to burn down the neighborhood! And if there was no pot on the stove, the house would just get a little warmer.

There were other things that raised suspicion that I was losing it. Like on one of their spying visits, my daughters-in-law found jelly pieces in the mayonnaise, or me wearing two different socks, not always zipping my fly, not shaving every damned day, and the clincher, banging the back wall of the garage with my car that put a little bulge in the living room wall. Hell, it's my wall. Okay, there were two other things, both of which included getting lost. Who hasn't in their life gotten off track? Heading north instead of south is no big deal. You turn around and go back. The first time it only took a few hours to get home. The second time it took almost two days. But I did get home. That's the main thing, isn't it?

At first the judge seemed to be favoring my side. He told my kids that their observations were more typical of depression than dementia. The judge asked me if I felt in command. I replied, "Sure I am."

He went on, "Mr. Lambert, the evidence before me seems to indicate that your life will straighten out, given time but before I rule on the matter, would you be willing to submit to a psychological assessment?"

I guess that I should have bowed my head and said yes, but hell if I was going to have some shrink dig into my grey matter. It's none of anybody's business what goes on in old Charlie's brain. Back in my elementary school days, I was caught in the girl's bathroom. For that infraction of exercising pubescent curiosity, I had to go to counseling. What a waste of time. I swore then that no shrink was ever going to get me ever again. So, I told the judge, "No, sir. I will not submit myself to that foolishness."

The judge looked at me like the principal did back in elementary school. "Mr. Lambert, your denial of my request, which was made entirely for your benefit, places a considerable burden on the court. On the one hand, I understand your reluctance.

On the other, your welfare trumps that by a large margin. Are you sure that you want to refuse a third-party evaluation?"

"Yep, I'm certain. All I want to do is go home and be left alone. Left to live my life where I've always lived it. My bed, my rugs, my stuff. Just let me get on with it, Judge."

After some more discussion, some of it rather heated, I could tell the Judge was sliding in favor of my kids. I blurted out, "Just wait your honor, your time's coming."

"Is that a threat?" he asked me.

"No sir, just life talking. You're on a downward spiral. You'll understand someday." With that, I walked out of the court.

Can you believe it? At eighty-four years old, me, myself, and I ceased to collaborate. I was admitted to a retirement village. What that means is, if you're not on death's doorstep, you're assigned to *assisted living*. Essentially, that means that they watch you like a hawk and not because they have your welfare in mind. No, it's because if you fall or hurt yourself they become liable. And no car. That was one of the worst things, losing my car. I'd been driving for over sixty years with a only a few scrapes and a less than a handful of tickets and by damn, they took my car away from me. They might as well as have cut my legs off.

At first, I had a two room apartment in the Senior Living section of Sunset Home. I was able to "decorate" with some things from home. But not any furniture, or my bed, or any dishes utensils, cookware, or just about anything that might taste or smell like home. I brought my and Lori's favorite pictures and a few things from my dresser. Hell, I had more stuff when I went on business trips. The thing that was so goddamn depressing was this: there was no going home. This was not home. This sanctuary of the living dead could never be home.

There is no way in hell that all the new sounds, colors, toilets, sinks, linens, pillows, chairs, smells, or whatever could possibly be home. Bullshit!

Connected to Senior Living is what I call Senior Death. If you get sick, which I did, you graduate to a room in the nursing section, which is like moving from a larger coffin to a smaller one. It wasn't like my kidneys failed or my heart stopped beating. I got the flu. The flu put me in the nursing home, isolation to start with. That was two months ago and while I'm out of isolation, I'm still on death row. Apparently, when I was *temporarily* moved out of my two room suite, they let somebody else have it. My little bit of home stuff was put in storage, probably in a damn shoebox stuffed in the janitor's closet. I'm told it might be a year until I can get back to the living section. My guess is that they get bigger cuts from Medicare by having me in the nursing home.

Soon after Lori's funeral, the kids started visiting me at home once a month for three days. After day one, coveting would begin. Table tops would be stroked, vases caressed, paintings studied, chairs patted, corners of rugs turned to check the weave, silverware hefted, linens fingered. "Do you watch *Antiques Roadshow*?" one or the other would ask. A lamp might get, "Where did you and Mom get this? I've always liked it and would just love to get one." All of the sudden, my boys took great interest in my gun collection, even though when growing up they wouldn't dream of shooting poor Bambi. Who the hell did they think they were kidding? After a few of those visits, I had pretty much decided to change my will so all my earthly goods went to the Salvation Army. And I suppose the kids guessed it, because here I am and all my and Lori's stuff is theirs.

Notice, I haven't mentioned their names. I will not write or utter their names ever again. At first I felt guilty about all this as if I had done something terribly wrong; or that maybe Lori was a poor mother. But, no, we raised these kids, we loved them, nursed them, nurtured them, wiped their butts and their noses. We paid for college, bought them cars. We gave them life and what did we get in return? Not much.

The boys got what they wanted, their wives divvying up the spoils like victorious Vikings. My house was sold with the proceeds going into a trust established for my care. My social security check goes to the nursing home, as does my annuity check. My eldest son has Power of Attorney and control of my assets. I had sold my machinery business for a couple million, so his control is no small thing. Legally, I don't exist. My rights are gone. I'm in a place I don't want to be with people I don't want to be with. But I have an ace up my sleeve which I'll pull out when the time is right. The old man isn't dead yet. But first, I have to get out of this place.

Officially known as an Electronic Home Monitoring Device, I wear an ankle monitor like criminals wear when they get sentenced to home confinement. The penalty for two foiled escapes, I wear it like a badge of honor. The first try was spur-of-the-moment. I was lingering around the lobby when a family group was leaving. I simply walked out with them as if I belonged. Out front is a bus stop sign that read "Bus to Downtown." Next to it was a very inviting bench. A flower pot with geraniums sat to the right. I nervously sat down, convinced that a neat little bus would appear to whisk me away from this place. But that didn't happen. Like everything else in this place, it was a fake. Within a few minutes of sitting down, I had two white uniformed men sitting on each side of me. The damn bus stop sign was a baited trap for unwitting old people trying to go home. Devious bastards.

My second escape was pre-meditated. I tried leaving with the food delivery truck—a stowaway who boarded via the kitchen's back door. At the next stop, the deliveryman discovered me hiding behind some Del Monte carrot crates. The Sunset van was summoned and I was returned to the home, like a truant that skipped school. I was called a "bad boy" and fitted with a security strap fixed around my left ankle. The device was programmed to alert staff if I ventured into what they called *unauthorized places*. I told them all to go screw themselves, which only got, a "Now, now, let's not go potty-mouthed on us." The staff's use of language hovers somewhere around the first grade. I'm an eighty-four year old man, for Christ's sake, not a six-year-old boy. Whatever sanity I had left coming into the place was quickly eroding. A few more months of this crap and *senile* would be a justifiable term. And, I'm afraid to admit, even welcomed.

The ankle monitor is no-nonsense. Shiny black, it had a fastener that cranes could use to lift girders. Go out a door or into an unauthorized space and Security is on you like ugly on an ape. For fun, now and then I stick my leg out a door and run for my bed where Security finds me smiling. Rather than annoy the guards, it only enhanced their quasi-military pea-sized brains. Since being fitted with the damn thing, I've turned all of my attention to getting out of the place. Escaping is really no end in itself. It needs to be a part of a plan, a cog in gears that mesh, turning slowly with power and grace, like a torque converter.

My escape would be masterful, like Clint Eastwood's in

Escape from Alcatraz. Perhaps it'll become a legend, inspiring others to try. The old WWII movie *The Great Escape* joined *Escape from Alcatraz* as my inspiration: Heroic Americans befuddling overly pure-gened Germans by digging a tunnel right under their stinking feet. If prisoners of Alcatraz and a bunch of unfed POWs could do it, so could I. And like them and countless others who slipped past prison guards and barbed wire, crawled through claustrophobic tunnels, scaled walls, out-witted sophisticated electronics, and made fools out of experts, I, Charles Lambert, would find my freedom. And I could afford it, too. What I mean to say is that I have a bunch of money hidden away. That's the ace up my sleeve. It would rot in safe deposit boxes before I'd let it get into the hands of my kids.

I began making lists of where I wanted to go and what I'd do when I got there. Home was out of the question. There was no home. Friends? Listen, when you're old and your spouse dies, friends and neighbors disappear. You become a loner. And it's not just because your friends don't want you around, it's also because you get bored being with them. It's just no fun. Everything changes. Your personality changes, reverts to some hidden part of yourself that you either hate or admire. You go out and can't wait to get home. You get home and there's nobody to talk to about the day's events. It's an endless cycle of gloom and doom. Death begins looking good. It's the going home together that matters. Without that, life sucks. Or at least it did for me.

I think that I would have adjusted if just one person would have taken an interest in me not out of pity, but rather out of love. Lori and I had been members of the Emmanuel Lutheran Church for over forty years. We took our kids there, we gave money, we helped pay for a new organ, we even bought choir robes for the choir. The minister buried Lori. And what happened after that? I had two visits from the creep, one to inquire if I'd like to give a gift in Lori's name to the church's endowment and the other asking if I was interested in setting up a trust. I got a fruit basket from the men's Bible study fellowship, and an ugly afghan knitted by the ladies sewing circle with a note that read "To warm body and soul." I got pity, enough to overflow a baptismal font. But not one drop of love.

I thought about going on the road. Bumming around in a camper. Maybe get a dog and write about my travels like John Steinbeck did in *Travels with Charley.* Perhaps I'd write about old people trying like hell to live in a world going so fast that they wobble around just trying to stay upright. But there's not a lot to observe doing 70 mph down an interstate. And back roads aren't much better. Ah, I hate driving anyway. It's like the killing fields out there. In my day, I rested my elbow on the frame of an open window letting country air filter through the car, never going more than fifty miles-per-hour. I bet people today drive coast to coast and never get a healthy whiff of good old cow shit. They eat at fast-food conglomerates and keep the kids entertained with some crappy cartoon flashing its junk through the onboard video system. If I did escape to the open road, I figure that I'd get caught right away like I did on the bench waiting for the bus that never came. I'd have to retake my driver's exam, get a camper, get the vehicle registered and insured. Hell, I might as well paint a line leading to where I was. I wanted to disappear. Just vanish. Maybe make it on the Most-Looked-For-Senior-Citizen list.

The idea of where to go once I escaped came to me while I was chatting with a woman named Emma. Emma is a darling old lady with azure eyes, crystal clear like blue ice. Her hair is thick and pure white, no blue rinses for Emma. She's one of the few women in this place who still has a shape. She doesn't wear smocks or those God-awful Velcro tabbed sneakers. She dresses in a neatly pressed blouse and a nice skirt with leather pumps. You can tell that she was absolutely stunning when she was young. She stirs an old man's memory. I'd like to have known her back then. Her mind is a bit addled, but then that's consistent with things here. She was wearing earrings in the shape of tiny sailboats. I commented on them. "I wear them every June, for the whole month," she informed me. Then, whispering to me like she was telling a secret, she said, "Damon gave them to me when we reached the Azores."

"When was that?" I asked, leaning close to her. I noted a hint of lavender.

"I was seventeen, so that would make it sixty-two years ago this month," she said smiling. Her eyes glistened with youth.

I said nothing. She continued, "I just graduated from high school. Damon just got out of the Army. It was sparks from the very first moment. He told me he wanted to be a sailor, but the only service that would take him was the U.S. Army. To make up for it he bought a sailboat the day he got out. A tiny little thing but big enough for two. We took off together, Annapolis to Corsica." Fumbling with her right earring, she added, "With a stop at the Azores." She leaned even closer, spoke even softer, "We had sex right across the Atlantic Ocean." Her eyes glossed over, she withdrew back into her chair and fell silent. The movie was over. The book closed. Snippets of memory like Emma's pervaded the nursing home. Like photo albums opening and closing, loops of audio tape repeated over and over. Sweet secrets, regrets, anger, love. Dusty tapestries. Woven with each birth, folded with each death. All pretty much the same colors.

I sailed once upon a time. Up and down the east coast. To Nova Scotia, Newfoundland, Maine, the Chesapeake. I was damned good at it and sailed mostly solo. I eventually gave it up. I loved it, but it wasn't Lori's thing. I never got lonely sailing solo, but sometimes at anchor tucked away in a remote cove, I'd long to have someone onboard to share the mystery of it all: great sunsets or watching an osprey dive needs to be shared. I have great memories, but few to share, a tiny corner of my own tapestry, perhaps. I used to envy sailing couples like Emma and Damon. All told, I guess I sailed on and off for about twenty years. I managed some terrible storms. Was a whiz at navigation. And I never got seasick. Why not go back to it? No trail to follow—I'd like to meet a tracking dog that could sniff out a boat's wake. My plan took on meaning. All I had to do was get the hell out of here and that thought, the idea of getting out of this place filled me with energy and purpose.

SATURDAY, JUNE 23

Sunsets follow sunrises. *Sunrise, sunset,* like the song says. Endless hope followed by endless rest. The great cycle of life. Well I wasn't ready for the endless rest part. It might make sense poetically to equate death with rest, but it doesn't make any sense to me. I figure that death is it. Nothing afterward, no matter what the Lutherans, or Shirley MacLaine, or anybody else says. No flying up to heaven or morphing into something else. As far as I'm concerned, it's over. I'll take the hope of morning any day. Give me light over dark. And the sea over land. At sea, sunny or stormy, it's all about light, how it dances and cavorts with swells and waves, changing every second: blues and grays, reds and purples, misty greens and yellows. Take unimaginable beauty, mix with turbulent winds and threatening seas, and it turns into a dynamic force that sings songs of life and death and courage and faith and hope. Not like fluorescent white or institutional green that speak nothing to the spirit while robbing the heart of hope. God, I need to get out of here.

My plan was simple enough: Escape, buy a yacht, and sail until I die. I wondered if Frank Morris (Clint Eastwood's character in *Escape from Alcatraz*) had such a simple plan. Probably to start with. Escape is usually fantasy. Carrying it off though is pure reality. For Morris, it entailed making a raft out of raincoats, digging a hole through the cell wall, making a fake head to stick on his cell pillow to confuse the guards, scaling a wall, jumping over some rocks, swimming through ice cold water, and overtaking the meanest currents on the West Coast. Freedom is a real taskmaster. Escaping Sunset might be easier than what Frank Morris had to contend with, but it was an escape nonetheless. And it did require planning. It relied on luck and demanded creativity. And, for sure, a co-conspirator.

There wasn't a single person in the entire nursing home that I could trust to keep a secret. Secrets are commodities in nursing homes; they gain value with each telling until something new comes along. Sex is a big gossip item. And truth be told, there's lots of it. New couples pop up every day. Yes, old people can still cuddle, stroke, kiss, and make love, and why not? Why suppress what little lust remains? If anything, it should be encouraged. It's fun to talk about sex and all that. But what gets the most attention in the gossip mill is when staff members cross the line and have sex with patients. (Officially, patients are referred to as clients here at Sunset, which I think is nonsense.) Oh yes, it happens more often than you know. Then, of course, there is stuff going on between staff members, between visitors and patients, and between visitors and staff. And who knows what goes on in the kitchen? But trumping sex in the gossip mill are escape stories. A missing patient is the worst thing that can happen to a nursing home. Insurance companies go crazy over it. Government overseers swarm the place like locusts. Nursing homes blame it on senility as if it is some grand surprise. The press loves escapes: *Old Man Escapes Nursing Home to Find Better Life.* "*I just wanted to go home,*" says *tearful eighty-nine year old.* Who wouldn't read an article with headlines like that? "*Disappeared, presumed dead,*" would work just fine for me.

Getting rid of the security strap was first on the list. This was no delicate matter. The bright black plastic must have been made by some devious packaging specialist. I kept picking away at the battleship-tough plastic with a fork I lifted from the cafeteria. No use. Google told me that buried in the plastic were thin wire cables, probably wound from piano wire. I gave up on the idea of cutting the damn thing. I tried using bacon fat that I saved in a napkin from breakfast to try and slip the thing off. No good. I rubbed my ankle raw with a piece of sandpaper I took it from the hobby shop (no electric tools or any sharp objects; how the hell were you supposed to make anything?) hoping that they'd take the damn thing off to let me heal. Nope. I got to wear it on my other ankle. Dan Forteneau (I called him DF—you figure it out), head of security, told me to stop fooling with the strap or I'd get billed for damaging property. I wanted to kick him in the nuts.

After a whole lot of angst, hours of planning and fretting over my escape plans, it dawned on me that I needed help, somebody on the outside I could work with. At my age the list was pretty short. I used to run a company that machined parts for the defense industry. Any one of the guys in my machine shop would have had that strap off in two shakes of a dog's tail. Not a one of my old workers is left. And the company's gone, too. And that's how it went. Everybody was either dead or as far removed from my life as a waterfall is from a desert.

It was Emma again who triggered a thought. We were sitting in the sun room, a closet-like space with one small window facing south. Emma was telling me her sailing story again. She did so word for word with the same pauses, inflections, and sexy little smiles as before. Emma lived only in her memory. While

Emma was telling her story, I began visualizing a memory of my own that took me back to a day many years ago. That morning I had weighed anchor early, to starlit skies and light winds. My plan was to sail from Gran Manan, an island between Nova Scotia and Maine, to a small inlet named The Cows, with an ETA of mid-afternoon. But, as I approached The Cows, I just couldn't relinquish the helm: the sky was too blue, the water too green, and the winds just right. In other words, I just couldn't stop sailing in such perfect conditions. About an hour later, all hell broke loose. A fast moving storm swept in from the Atlantic with high winds. The seas became a witch's brew with sharp foamy waves. I reefed sail, and did what any sailor does in a storm: pray. Things were going well, until my idle prop found an errant net floating just below the waterline. The boat struggled to make headway. The seaway had her in its grips. Trimming the main, I was able to bring her into the wind which had every intention to rip the now flapping sail to destruction. Fiddling with a boat hook, I was able to free the net from the prop and off I went. It was after dark before making the small Down East harbor of Corea, Maine. I dropped my hook in a tiny, well-protected cove, grabbed my bottle of scotch, and swore that I'd rather sell the damn boat than venture out ever again. I either lost my confidence or gained my senses. Either way I was ready to forsake my unrequited love of the sea. A few hours later, I was awakened from a sleep of the dead, by a boat that came up alongside. Hailing me, the guy wanted to know where my hook was so he wouldn't drop his over mine. Now this kind of query can only come from a careful and courteous sailor. I had quite a bit of rode out (anchor line) and felt that a change of wind in such a small cove would inevitably lead to trouble. So, rather than take the chance, I invited him to tie alongside. He accepted. While he prepared his lines for the tie-up, I busied myself setting out some fenders. In minutes we were two boats on one anchor. Some coffee on my boat and a few shared war stories later, a friendship was born.

A Mainer through and through, Bob Liscome was a hell of a sailor. Which means besides knowing how to tackle the wind, he knew how to fix things. Sailboats are always breaking down. There's just too much that can go wrong. And the engine on these things can be as reliable as a drunken janitor. Bob was a fixer. An independent Mainer who built his own house, cut his own wood, fixed his own trucks, and didn't give a rat's ass what people did, said or thought. Each summer thereafter, we'd meet up and do some serious sailing. It was because of Bob that I regained my sailing legs. The shaking legs of storm-tossed sailors might come from fright, but they build muscle.

If he's still alive, he'll be living right where he always did, Bickles Island, Maine. And I'll bet my life (not worth a lot these days) that he'll come and get me out of this place. All I have to do is make a few phone calls—not an easy thing in a nursing home that locks its phones up like wise daddies lock up their guns.

SUNDAY, JUNE 24

Visitors are always welcome at Sunset as long as it's between the hours of 4 p.m. and 7 p.m. on weekdays and between 1 p.m. and 7 p.m. on weekends. Patients gravitate like a huddled mass toward the lobby about an hour before the posted times. Some desperate for a visitor, others just to watch the passing parade. Emma never sat in the lobby; Damon was always with her. I was a watcher. I couldn't venture past the red line taped on the floor or I'd set off my alarm, so I took a chair back near the receptionist's desk to watch the world go by. My favorite place was next to a plastic fig tree, leeward of the creepy eyes of DF, who hung around the reception desk like he was about to thwart an attempt to steal state secrets.

I was sitting under my plastic fig tree when I noticed a young family pass by: quintessential American foursome—mom, dad, girl, and boy. The boy was fidgeting with a shiny black rectangle. How the hell that boy didn't bump into anything and everything was beyond me. His eyes were glued to the thing like he was witnessing something miraculous. And, maybe he was. They signed in at reception and disappeared down the white hallway. I followed. The main hallway is an affront to any sane individual over the age of two. The best way I can describe it is by comparing it to a Sunday school corridor where pastel images of biblical scenes are pasted to the walls. Lots of lambs and stuff like that. Only here, the cardboard cutouts reflect whatever holiday is in vogue. Halloween is particularly offensive to anyone who has ever had to bear nursing home life. Further down the hallway there's a bulletin board showing pictures of clients playing games, sewing, dancing—if that's what you call limping around in a circle, a few mug shots of forced smiles. What you don't see are photos of people picking noses, puking and drooling, or spilling food.

I followed the family to room 128, then strolled a bit more down the hall, turned and went back to the lobby and parked back under the plastic fig tree. Soon enough, the boy with the black plastic rectangle walked by to flop down in a chair just past the red line.

After observing him for a while, I asked curiously, "Hey, lad, what is it you have there?"

No response. I repeated myself. He looked up. "A phone," he said.

"Why are you looking at it?" I asked.

"I'm playing a game."

"On a phone!" I exclaimed. "Are you winning?"

"I always win," he said with a grin.

"Can I see it?"

"Sure," he said, not getting up.

"I can't come over there," I explained. "If I cross the red line, it sets of an alarm." Lowering my voice, I said, "Just like in prison."

That was enough to get the boy to get off his ass.

Heightening the drama, I whispered, "They can't see us over here," motioning toward the fig tree. In stark contrast to his parents and sister, each dressed in their Sunday best, this kid was dressed in baggy black pants, had on a T-shirt with more graphics than a comic strip, and his hair was a color I hadn't ever seen before, hues of iridescent purple, pink, yellow, and maybe some orange. He had it all spiked up like he'd grown a nuked sea-urchin on the top of his head. He wore some pretty heavy chrome chains, too. I have no idea what they were connected to, if anything. But underneath his wild façade was Boy. Whatever these kids wrap themselves in, they're still kids. I judged the kid to be insecure, and why not? He's probably pressed on all sides by parents, teachers, peers, religious folks, and anybody older, bigger or in any way possessing a bit of real or perceived power. Let's just call it social coercion.

When I was a kid, we didn't live in a pressure cooker like today's kids. But we had our rebellious moments. I remember my father kicked my butt like there was no end to Sunday when I came home with a buzz cut. And God forbid if he caught me smoking *before* I was sixteen. This kid had access to every evil out there: sex in any number of guises, drugs aplenty, access to guns, movie heroes that survive explosions that would take down the Eiffel Tower, cars that take off with g-force, and the threat of being shot on his way to school. Hell, in my day sex was so taboo that the word *pregnant* was never said in front of a kid younger than twenty-one. And my boyhood hero, The Green Hornet, wouldn't have a snowball's chance in hell of beating off a missile toting titanium robot. We seldom shot each other, too. This kid was probably fifteen years old with acne ready to bloom like huckleberries in August and scared out of his wits. Not to mention hormones making more racket than cats having sex on a hot tin roof. But he was a boy and that meant he was curious, inherently against authority, heroic, and clever as a fox. At least I hoped that he was.

"Like, what's the black thing on your ankle?" he asked.

"It's called an ankle monitor. It sets off the alarm," I said, gesturing toward the red line. "I tried to escape," I explained. "Twice."

"Awesome!" he exclaimed, giving me a high five. At first I ducked. But then I got it and connected with his palm on the second try. I'd never been high-fived before.

"What's your name?" I asked.

"Catlin," he answered quietly.

"Great," I said. "Do you have a last name?"

"Giffords, but you can call me Cat, everybody does."

"My name's Charlie Lambert. You can call me Charlie."

I looked left and right, and then whispered, "Cat, I need a favor."

"Go for it, Charlie," he said without hesitation.

"I'm trying to reach an old friend up in Maine, but I don't know his phone number. Hell, I don't even know if he's still alive." Pointing to his black shiny gadget, I asked, "You think you can find him for me?"

Cat raised his black shiny gizmo like it was a wizard's wand and proclaimed proudly, "It's an iPhone, it can find anything."

"Wow! I've heard about those but I never saw one." Then asked, "How do you use the damn thing?"

Cat swiped the face of the phone with a finger. It lit up like the screen of a spaceship. "Name, location," he asked authoritatively.

"Robert Liscome, Bickles Island, Casco Bay, Maine." I responded.

Cat put his face to the phone. His fingers worked like those of some of the ladies in the home when they tatted: quick and sure, geographically precise. No sound, just fast movement. In no more than a minute, he handed me the phone, "Try this. It's ringing."

I took the phone without a clue of which end was which. It was a foreign object, something so far into the future that my imagination collapsed. Cat quickly took it back and held it to his ear. "Is this Robert Liscome?" he asked politely. I didn't hear the response. Cat placed the phone to my ear, "Take it," he said. I hesitated. "Like, c'mon, man you'll lose it. Talk now," Cat urged.

I did. "It's me, Charlie Lambert," I said.

"Yup," came a familiar response. Bob's rather taciturn.

"We used to sail together," I said, hoping to jar his memory.

"I know," came the reply. "What are you doing now?"

"I'm in a nursing home."

"Why?"

"Because my kids put me here," I said honestly

"That's not good," he said.

"No, it's not. You want to go sailing?" I asked.

"Sure, I'd love it. What kind of nursing home are you in? Do they have a marina?" he asked incredulously.

"No, Bob, no marina," I laughed. "This is a bad place," I said, turning serious. "I got to get out of here. I'd like to talk to you about that but I can't go into detail right now, can I call you back tomorrow?" I asked, and then said, "Hold on a minute." I held the phone away from my ear.

"Cat, can you come back tomorrow, maybe after school, so I can talk more to Bob. It's really critical. The whole mission depends on it."

"After school? Like, summer's on man. I'm free to roam,"

Cat said. "And don't tell my parents. And what mission?"

"I'll explain tomorrow. And I won't say a word to your parents or anybody else."

Back to Bob while eying Cat, I asked, "How about around three-thirty, tomorrow?" Cat gave me thumbs-up.

"A.m. or p.m.?" Bob asked, as if it was a perfectly logical question.

"How about p.m.?" I asked sardonically.

"That'll work," Bob said then added, "I cut wood in the a.m."

"Jesus," I exclaimed, "You haven't changed."

"No need to. Talk to you tomorrow." The phone went dead.

I handed the portable space station back to Cat. "Thanks."

"Yeah, no problem," Cat said. "Like same place, tomorrow?"

"Tomorrow's Monday," I replied, "The lobby's dead quiet on Monday. Can you come to my room? 136."

"Like no problemo, man" he said. Then Ashley walked by. Ashley's a teen volunteer who has every old man in the place thinking dirty and every old lady remembering bygone days. Laser-like, Cat's eyes zeroed in on Ashley's sexy to and fro motion. I looked too, but my thoughts were of what used to be; Catlin's surely was on what might be. Cat aimed his phone at the vanishing figure then turned the device's screen for me to see a well framed photo of Ashley's cute bottom. "I'll share this with my buddies," he said like a trophy hunter showing off his latest kill. "You want to see my collection?" he offered. I declined.

Cat turned to leave, "See ya then."

"Wait," I said. "Wanna see something cool?" Cat nodded.

I walked to the red line and stuck my leg out. Almost instantly a bell rang and a red light on the wall flashed. The two white-clad goons appeared, one taking my left arm, the other my right. Marching me past Cat, the lad mouthed silently, "Like, way cool." I went back to my room with a light skip in my step.

MONDAY, JUNE 25

Cat was right on time. He just shrugged when I asked how he got past the receptionist and security. I closed the door to my room. Cat handed me the iPhone. "It's ringing" he said.

Bob answered with his characteristic "Yup." I asked him about how his life was going. He told me that his wife Jennifer died eleven years ago, that he was living in the same house he built fifty years ago, that he's lonely, that he thinks the government is too busy in people's lives, that heating with wood is the only way to go, that his German Shepherd was killed by a pack of dogs left over from bear hunting season, that the tides are still working like they always work and that winter in Maine is just damn cruel and inhumane.

He ended by saying, "So what's this about going sailing?"

I took some time to fill him in about my being stuck in the nursing home and that I needed his help to escape. When I told him about the security strap, all he said was, "Damn government." Bob is a Conservative. Not a nut case one, but one who adheres to the idea that if you can't make it on your own, you have no business holding out a hand asking for help. He doesn't protest or go to tea parties or bang the Bible like it's a gong announcing Armageddon. He just does for himself and expects everybody else to do the same. He willingly accepts Social Security and Medicare, understands the threat of global warming, supports women's choice, and believes that evolution might just be true. Bob's world is definitely not flat but it's not completely round, either.

While we talked, Cat lay on my bed fidgeting. Without the electronic wonder to keep his hands busy, he played with his keys, ran his fingers along the shiny chains, twisted the peaks of his spiked hair, and just acted overall like a six year old in church. I tried not to pay attention.

Bob and I came up with a preliminary plan. He'd drive down from Maine; he saw no problem with cutting off the security strap. "I'll bring some tools," is all he said about that. We can escape in his truck. That is the plan. He asked me what kind of sailboat I had. I told him that I'd have to buy one. All we had to do was stop at a few banks for me to get the money. He told me he wasn't into robbing banks. I told him that I had the money put away. We set the date: Saturday, June 28, just three days away. Directions to Sunset Home would be sent to him, courtesy of Cat. Just before we ended the conversation, Bob asked, "Where are you anyway?"

"Upstate New York," I told him.

I could see Bob's frown over the phone. "What's Upstate New York?" he asked.

"It's like Down East Maine, I answered, "only up."

That seemed to satisfy him. Before we hung up, I gave him the address then added, "What's your ETA?

"I'm leaving in the morning. I'll call when I'm near," he said, and then hung up the phone. Cat took his phone back and held it to his heart like a good Catholic clutching a treasured Rosary. We hung out for awhile. Cat fiddled with some game on the phone while we talked. He called it multi-tasking. We agreed to meet again to discuss the escape plan. I had no idea how to involve Cat other than I was rather certain that he'd be needed. But first we had to get him out of the home undiscovered. He suggested we practice for the escape. "I bet that your ankle monitor has a GPS unit in it. Probably tracks wherever it is. I'll hide in the bathroom while you wander off somewhere to set off the alarm."

"Good idea," I complimented his genius. "But why not just do it here. If I stick my leg out of the window, they'll think I'm jumping."

"Cool," he said. "You stick it out the window; I'll hide in the bathroom. When the goons come, I'll slip past them."

"What if you get caught?" I asked.

"I won't!" he declared. I was impressed with Cat's moxie.

The window raised only about eight inches, but I managed to stick my leg out far enough to trigger the alarm. The goons came. Cat disappeared. Great rehearsal.

Besides Ashley and now Cat, there were no young people at Sunset. Oh, there were the sing-songy waitresses and other help, who were probably in their thirties or forties, but they acted more like zoo-keepers than anything else. I mean, there were simply no opportunities to develop relationships with young people. Observing a changing world through what the boob-tube offered only excited resentment and confusion among Sunset's clients. The frame of reference here was sepia-toned memories rather than the simple fact that while the trappings of life change, little else really does. Take Cat, for instance. His chains and hair, baggy pants and loud T-shirt, were my two toned shoes, zoot-suit, and Brylcreamed hair. He seemed to know a lot more that I did when I was his age, but I sure as hell remember how confused I felt in the ninth grade about the blossoming of the girls in my class and why I couldn't find the courage to ask one out on a date. I wonder if I would have been taking lewd photos if I could have done it without a flashbulb. At Sunset, my world had stopped spinning, Cat got it turning again.

When I worked selling highly specialized machine parts to the defense industry, there were untold ways to make a few extra dollars. Let's just say it was something like building bridges to nowhere only the bridges might be for some Senator's precise need for a folding toilet for his mirror-polished black Chevy Suburban, or a personalized bathroom fixture, or whatever the guy wanted to feel bigger and better than anyone else. Fat kickbacks helped. I figured whatever was requested didn't concern me. It kept our shop in business, which meant employment for our workers and bonuses for investors. I rationalized further that the more money we paid our employees and the more our investors pocketed the more taxes they paid, which gave politicians more money to give out in the form of earmarks. Everybody was happy. The only rub was that I couldn't really pay taxes on my *cash incentives*, which I preferred to call them. I did give to charity, though, especially to the foundations that preserved nature. I figured that most earmarks went to screwing the environment in one way or another, so I tried in my own modest way to make up for it. I don't think a judge would buy it for a second, but that's what I did and I feel good about it. The results of my accepting these *cash incentives* were safety deposit boxes in a number of banks where I did most of my sales, which ran a corridor from Syracuse, New York to Annapolis, Maryland. Fortunately, I paid my three-year rental fee just before my kids tossed me in here. Maybe my mind was a bit addled, but I sure as hell remembered that.

I didn't keep track of exactly how much I had stowed away, but I wouldn't be surprised if it neared or topped the million-dollar mark.

TUESDAY, JUNE 26

Thinking about the escape gave me real purpose. I was talk-ative, nice to the staff, backed off of cursing too much. I could taste freedom. Just a little maybe, but that's enough to give anybody hope.

Let's say Bob shows up, cuts off the ankle monitor, we run like hell for his truck, peel some rubber and get caught two blocks away. That's not the headline I'm looking for. As I was pondering all this, discouraged over my lack of creativity, Cat strolled in. And right behind him was Ashley smiling like a dog that just spied the biggest, meatiest bone in her entire life. "Hey, what's happenin?" was the best I could muster.

Cat gave me a high five. "You know Ashley?" he asked, smiling back at the only thing in Sunset that qualified as a hot chick.

"Yes," I replied. "I've been helping Ashley with her homework."

Turing to her I asked, "How's the trig coming?"

"Great, thanks to you Mr. Lambert," she answered smiling. Looking over to Cat, she added, "Catlin's thinking of volun-teering. I'm going to give him a tour."

"Oh, he'd be good at it," I commented, then fell silent without anything else to say.

"I'll be back as soon as my *tour* is over." Cat's smile oozed with all manner of teenage fantasy.

"I'll be here," I said. "Nice meeting you Ashley," I said as they left.

The second they disappeared, I felt jealousy, unadulterated envy over their youth and my age. Everything was in front of them. I teetered on depression. What the hell was I thinking, that I could just escape this place and go sailing? My confidence in the whole idea burst like a soap bubble hitting a fan. Maybe Bob was on his way, maybe not. Maybe he was too old to help. Maybe my son found out about the money and got his hands on it. Maybe I was too goddamn old to do a damn thing other than eat, shit, and die in this living purgatory. I lay down and cried a little, hugging Lori in the form of my pillow. The idea of escaping slipped into folly. How the hell was I going to carry this off? I drifted off. Around seven o'clock, nurse Sallyanne came by with a tray of warmed-over food. Lightly tapping my shoulder to awaken me, she said, "We missed you at dinner Charlie, are you all right?"

I nodded, "Just a little headache, I guess I slept through it."

"Well then, sweetie, here's some nice broth and biscuits to scare the nasties away," Sallyanne sing-songed. I thanked her and she left. I fell back asleep.

WEDNESDAY, JUNE 27

I already had breakfast and was standing staring out of the window when Cat came in. He was out of breath, something rare for Cat. "Hey, Charlie, you got a call from Bob. Said you should call him back right away. It's ringing," he added pushing the phone into my hand.

"Charlie, I'm coming up 81. My GPS says I have thirty minutes before arriving at your place. What do I do when I get there?"

Depression scattered in all directions. "Come into the lobby. I'll be waiting there."

"Good enough," Bob said before hanging up.

"Bob will be here in a half hour. For god's sake, I'm down to the wire and I don't have a clue how to make it out of here."

Cat shuffled around the room, his chains making light metallic sounds with each step. He turned toward me. "The tour I was on with Ashley—she's hot, don't you think?—she gave me a good look at the place. Pretty standard, like maybe Days Inn designed it. It's not going to be easy. But I think I might have an idea. Like, maybe it includes a few dogs or something like that."

"Dogs!" I exclaimed. "What the hell do dogs have to do with it?"

"I'm not sure," Cat said moving toward the one chair in my room. I sat on the edge of my bed while Cat flopped down on the chair, taking on a posture that might be comfortable for an octopus. "Ashley said it would be neat to have a dog in the home. Like one that could meet and greet, you know, give the folks some petting time. Maybe a black lab. You old guys like that kind of stuff. So, it got me thinking. Like, maybe we could get a dog to help us."

I asked, "What the hell would we do with a dog?"

He whined, "I don't know. Just a thought."

I looked at my watch. "Bob will here soon. I better get out to the lobby."

"Chill man, we've got time. Like, rushing out there's not the best idea. Do you want me to come to the meet and greet with you?" Cat asked.

"Ah, maybe it's best if you wait here. Security might get suspicious. Besides Bob is, well, he's kind of conservative. I'd like to prime him."

"Say it straight," Cat said, getting up from the chair. "He'd think I was a freak. That's how a lot of old people see me. Like, why don't I just disappear and let you two adults chat about your favorite Lawrence Welk video."

"Hold on, Cat," I stood to confront him. "Let me do what I do and you cool your heels. Go chase after Ashley for a while. Then come back here and let things evolve."

"Yeah," Cat said. "Maybe I'll come back, maybe I won't." His eyes went to his iPhone, his fingers danced, and he was out of the room, missing the door frame by a fraction of an inch.

After about ten minutes of sitting under the fake fig tree, Bob appeared, swinging open the double glass doors like John Wayne entering a saloon. Bob looked around like he was sizing up the place. I hadn't seen him in over a decade but I recognized him instantly. Topping six feet with thick curly white hair, he was lean with wide shoulders and long arms. His hands were bigger than bear paws. A woven bracelet dangled from his right wrist. Tan plastic clogs completed an outfit of loose fitting dungarees and a T-shirt that read, MAINE MAN. So much for the John Wayne image.

I stood and came slowly out of the shadows, apprehensive that he wouldn't recognize me. His eyes met mine and he said, "So you want to go sailing?" I looked around to see if his comment aroused suspicion. Besides the bored receptionist whose face was nose close to a paperback and a few visitors sitting with clients, we were alone. We walked toward each other. We hugged. Or I should say he squeezed the breath out of me producing a series of clicks and clacks that came from somewhere along my spinal column. I hadn't been hugged for over a year and despite the fact that my body went into survival mode, my heart and mind cherished the feeling. We stepped back.

"You have to sign in at reception," I said. Bob went over to the desk and scribbled something. Without looking up from her book, the receptionist said, "Thanks."

As we walked toward the hallway, I whispered, "Did you sign your real name?"

Bob gave me a slight shake of the head as if to say *stupid question*, then said, "I didn't sign anything. That lady didn't look up so I just pretended to sign."

I gave a thumbs up. "Follow me," I said, leading him to my room down the hall. I closed the door behind us. Bob paced the few steps it took for him to cross my room. He stopped to look out the window which had a great view of the maintenance garage, trash bins, and a beat-up old dump truck with a rusty plow stuck to its front.

"Not a whole lot here," he commented.

"No kidding," I said. "I just want to get the hell out of here. It's no place to live."

Bob turned from the window to face me. "Or die, either," he said, walking to the chair to sit down. I perched on the edge of the bed. "So that's the security gizmo," he asked, eying the shiny black strap on my ankle. He motioned with his hand for me to lift my leg so he could have a closer look. Like an orthopedist, he cradled the heel of my left foot in his hand, turning my ankle left and right carefully examining the security device. A few moments of guttural sounds from Bob and he let my heel go. My leg dropped like dead weight. "I brought my hydraulic shears," he said with pride. "We'll have that thing off in no time."

"That's good, I said. "The problem is, the minute we cut it, an alarm goes off. We'd have maybe a minute or two to get out of here. Not enough time."

Bob sat back in his chair. His hand went to chin. "How about we throw the damn thing out the window, maybe make it to one of those bins out there?"

"Oh, that might work," I said. "But you'd have to toss it like a Frisbee. The window doesn't go up very much. Besides," I said, "I stuck my leg out a few days ago and the guards were here in minutes."

We returned to silence. There was rap on the door. "Can I come in?" Cat asked. I nodded. Cat opened the door, caught sight of Bob, and froze.

Bob did a double take, his eyes focusing on Cat's iridescent spiked hair. Cat's eyes went to Bob's rubber-clogged feet. Bob leaned forward, squinting his eyes like reality had just taken a nasty turn: Earrings, chain necklace with dragon pendant, black shirt opened to mid-chest, jeans with more rips than a hurricane-roughened flag, chrome chains everywhere, red sneakers. "I'll be damned," Bob uttered under his breath.

Cat's head withdrew like he smelled something bad. His eyes scanned Bob bottom up: white socks with plastic clogs, nondescript full-cut dungarees, belt buckle with embossed bulldozer, Maine Man T-shirt, smoothly shaven chisel-featured face, neatly combed wavy white hair. "Holy shit," Cat whispered to himself. It looked like a gun-fight in the making, a stand-off between age and youth. No one said a word until I interrupted. "Bob, Cat; Cat, Bob."

Their eyes met. Lips curled in distain. Eyes narrowed under furrowed brows. I thought I detected some subtle snarls.

Slowly entering the room, Cat turned to close the door. He was shaking his head. Bob grimaced at me with a *what the hell is that doing here* look. Great beginning for an escape plan, I told myself.

Cat sidled over to sit beside me on the bed. I filled Cat in on Bob's plan for getting the strap off, that we were in a what/then mode.

"I got it down," said Cat with utter assurance. "Like, remember me talking about the dog? Well," he went on, "how about we get a dog in here. We cut off the damned thing, put it on the dog and let him run lose. Maybe let him out of the maintenance door in the basement which I found thanks to my tour with Ashley. And, like, here's the good news, baby," Cat proclaimed spinning his index fingers heavenward, "because the basements door's always locked, there are no alarm sensors. Cool, huh?"

I looked over toward Bob. "Yeah, that's good work," he said, giving Cat a slight nod.

"What about the thing going off the second we cut it?" I asked, looking from one to the other.

"Hey, I found the route and I'll get the dog, you figure the rest of it." Cat said.

"A shunt," Bob said. "We put a shunt on it."

"What's that?" Cat asked Bob.

"If we connect the wire embedded in the plastic with another wire before we cut it, we wouldn't interrupt the current."

"Phew, the dude knows his stuff," Cat said, eyes directed upward.

I chimed in. "Okay, I'm with you on the shunt. Back to the dog with a few questions. First, how do we get the dog in here; second, how do we know that the dog will take off and not run back into the building? And finally, will we have time to get to the truck and out of here?" I leaned back on the bed to listen.

"This feels like an oral, man," Cat said. "Don't sweat it. I'll bring the dog in through the outside basement door. Then I'll come up the inside steps and let you in. Like the rest? What am I, an escape artist or something?"

Bob let out a big breath. "The kid's got a good idea," he admitted. "Maybe I can meet the kid…"

Cat interrupted, "The *kid's* got a name and that name is Cat."

Bob drew back his lips. "Okay, maybe I can meet *Cat* at the outside door with my tools. You get there the best way you can. And one more thing, I have a Rent-a Wreck. A rental I picked up in Utica. I left my truck there."

"Not a breakdown, I hope!"

Bob sat back in his chair. "This is an escape, right?" he asked nonchalantly. "Well, I figured a car with a NY plate is better than a Maine plate on an F150. If that security guy you talked about has anything at all in his head, right now he's out checking out my car, which he won't find because I parked it about two miles away on a tree-lined street in a residential neighborhood where it blends with all the rest of the ugly cars out there." Cat's eyes were like saucers. Bob noticed. He continued, "Tonight, I get a motel. There's one a few miles from here, a Budget Inn with a Bob Evans next to it. I'll be registering under the name Clement Jones from Peoria, Illinois. So where's this basement door you're talking about, *Cat*, and what time do we meet?"

"You're beyond, dude, man. You're awesome. I mean, like talk about blowing the stereotype thing." Cat slapped me on the back, "This guy's amazing."

We sat and talked over the plan. In truth, it was really Bob and Cat that did the talking. They cajoled, partook in repartee, even high-fived once. Unlike me, Bob connected with a loud assuring smack. Their outer shell belied the fact that these two seemingly very different characters had a common gift for scheming that rivaled Steve McQueen in *The Great Escape*. I felt safe in their hands.

We planned the escape for tomorrow morning, Bob insisting that the sooner we were away from this place the better. Bob and Cat arranged to get together to figure out the best way to get into the basement without being seen. The plan was that at nine-thirty, I'd go to the hallway basement door, where Cat would meet me to unlock the door from the inside. From there it was a matter of cutting off the strap, letting Cat and his dog take off with it while Bob and I make our escape. It couldn't be simpler, except for one thing: innovative disruption. I first heard this slick-sounding term when I lost a contract to a competitor who'd undercut my bid by twenty-five percent. I couldn't beat his price because he bought a computer driven lathe that could operate with some kid punching in numbers. Forget employees. I had Herman, George, Pete, Helmut, Cliff, and Archie, all seasoned machinists. Each was paid a fair wage with benefits and knew how to handle a four-jaw chuck on an old but fine South Bend lathe, or deal with any of the other well-used machines in my shop. The computer-driven wonder didn't need a seasoned machinist. You put a chunk of stock in the thing, hooked it to a computer, and that was that. Either I had to retool or I was out of business. I took another option, I sold the business. My help retired along with me.

Innovative disruption came at five o'clock. I was sitting, leafing through an outdated copy of *Popular Mechanics*, feeling on top of the world—tomorrow, I'd have a future again. Mrs. Gerard, a handsome looking nurse with hands bigger than mine, showed up with a cart loaded with all sorts of medical paraphernalia. She looked like she lifted weights. Heavy ones. DF showed up right behind her. "You've got your wish," he declared, "the ankle monitor's coming off."

Nodding to Mrs. Gerard and her overflowing cart, I asked, "So what's she going to do, cut off my leg?"

"You never stop being the wise guy," DF said. "No, I'm unlocking the security strap and Nurse Gerard is going to replace it with something new." He leaned forward like some hack actor delivering a punch line, "An implant!"

I got up from my chair, arms clamped over my chest. "An

implant! No way. I'd rather wear the damn ankle monitor than have an implant, whatever the hell that means. Besides, it's almost bedtime. Why now?"

"Because," DF answered.

"Because why?" I shot back.

"Because I said so." DF looked at Nurse Gerard. "Explain it to Mister Smart Mouth."

Nurse Gerard gave DF a stare that could make steel melt. Carefully, she took a packet from her cart; she was calm and soft spoken. My name was written on it in black Magic Marker; "In here is everything I need to insert the implant. It's a tiny thing, about the size of a capsule, you know, like a pill. We put it right under your skin on your right upper forearm. It won't hurt much at all. Just a pinch maybe."

"So, why do I need it?" I asked flatly.

Mrs. Gerard answered, "Because it stores all your medical information and in case it's needed all we do is scan the implant to get it. It might save your life."

"Plus," DF interrupted, "it has a locater built in and a sensor to set off the alarm should you have any ideas about getting out of here. Pretty slick, huh?"

"Slick, my ass," I exploded. "I don't want it. I'd rather keep the collar. And as far as saving my life goes, what the hell good is life anyway? Just prolongs the agony of being in this place of the damned. You're not going to get my permission to invade my body with some idiotic Flash Gordon gadget. Now get out of here, both of you."

Nurse Gerard, remaining calm, gave DF a stern look. "I'm asking you to leave," she said. "Mr. Lambert is my patient and I will see to it that he is respected. Do you understand? Now get over here and remove this hideous black thing."

"No, Nurse Gerard," DF chimed in glowering at me. "Mr. Lambert, we don't need your permission. We need your son's permission, and we have that. Signed, sealed, and delivered. And no, I will not leave until we're done doing what we came here to do. Curse and carry on all you want. Cooperate or," he said, waving his Motorola walkie-talkie like it was a Taser, "I'll call for help."

Nurse Gerard walked over to DF. "Out," she demanded. "Get that thing off of Mr. Lambert's leg then leave and close the door behind you. "

"But…"

"No buts about it. Get out and take that collar with you. Not another word. Just do it!"

In a huff, DF removed the collar then went to the door, "You'll see," he said before slamming the door behind him.

My thoughts were like scattered pieces of a jig saw puzzle. The escape plan dimmed. What the hell were Cat and Bob going to do, cut off my arm? Let me bleed to death. I took a few deep breaths and calmed myself. I needed information.

I turned to Mrs. Gerard, apologized for my outburst and thanked her for getting DF out of my room.

She smiled and said, "You're welcome. Now, as I was saying, the insertion of the implant will be a painless procedure. The most uncomfortable thing will be a pinprick from the needle I'll use to inject the anesthetic and perhaps some soreness later on. I'll leave some mild pain medication in case you need it. Before I begin, are there any questions?"

"I have a few," I said earnestly.

She nodded, "Yes, dear?"

"Once you insert the implant, can it be taken out? I mean

if it needs servicing."

"That's very unlikely," she said. "It should last at least five years."

"What if I'm not dead in five years?" I laughed.

"Oh, forgive me. I didn't mean that," she apologized.

I went on, "What if the thing breaks, let's say next week or next month?"

"Well," Nurse Gerard explained, "We'll give you another injection of anesthetic, make a small incision and remove it. It's not brain surgery, you know," she chortled like she'd just thought of that worn out metaphor all on her own.

"What kind of anesthetic?" I asked.

"The same thing I'll give you today, a local anesthetic," she answered, lifting a small syringe from a row of syringes labeled "Lidocaine." "It's preloaded all ready to go."

I acquiesced. Nurse Gerard readied herself for the procedure. I rolled up my sleeve. Nurse Gerard sat opposite me on a folding stool she had slipped from a bracket on the side of the cart. Resting my arm on Nurse Gerard's muscular thigh, she gave me a shot of the anesthetic. "There now," she said. "Let's give it a few minutes for that to take hold." She gave me a motherly smile. "May I get you anything?"

I pouted, "May I have a glass of water, please?"

"Of course, dear." Nurse Gerard replied. "I could get you some orange juice if you like?"

"That would be great," I answered.

"I'll be right back," she said. As soon as Nurse Gerard left the room, I quickly nabbed one of the preloaded syringes and, like a seasoned card-shark, slipped into my pocket.

Ten minutes later, the implant was inserted, and I was alone, my hand caressing the pocketed syringe like it was the key to a lost kingdom. The staff at Sunset could certainly learn a lot from Nurse Gerard. I was a patient to her, nor was I client; I was person in need of professional and even loving care. I hope that she doesn't get into trouble for a missing injector. My guess is it won't be missed. And, I want to believe that she'll say a little prayer for me once I escape.

THURSDAY, JUNE 28

At precisely nine-thirty a.m. on June 28th, I was standing outside the basement door. "You there?" I heard Cat say from behind the door. I gave a light knock.

A metallic click and the door opened. Squeezing past Cat, I quietly descended the darkened metal staircase. Cat hung back to relock the door. Meeting me at the bottom of the staircase, Bob led me through a maze of workbenches, storage shelves, boiler pipes, refrigeration compressors, lockers, a tool crib, and finally a stack of grey metal boxes that looked an awfully lot like coffins, then to an open area next to the outside exit door. Tethered to a post, a large black dog jiggled and squirmed, greeting us like long lost buddies. "Meet Kingdom," Cat said, coming from behind to unleash the dog. My few pats on the dog's head were returned with leaps and licks.

Bob reached into a tool bag he had placed next to the basement door, withdrawing a large hydraulic cutter capable of taking down the Brooklyn Bridge. "Leg up," he commanded. "Let's get that strap off."

With Cat listening in while kneeling next to the ganglia-driven, over-enthused dog, I told Bob, "The strap's gone." Rolling up my sleeve, I removed the bandage and showed them the ugly black and blue area on my arm which was the size of a silver dollar.

"You get vaccinated?" Bob asked. "What the hell for?"

All Cat said was "Like way cool."

"It's an implant," I said, "and it has to come out."

I reached into my pocket and withdrew the syringe of *Lidocaine*. "Let's be real quiet," I said. "We have to get this thing out fast before some goon checks the GPS locator screen."

"Worry not," Cat chimed in, "Ashley's baby blues are a lot more interesting to security than some computer screen."

"Great," I said. I had no idea that Cat had recruited Ashley into the escape plans. I injected the anesthesia, capped the syringe and put it back into my pocket.

While we waited for the bruise on my arm to get numb, I told them how Nurse Gerard tossed DF out of my room and how she had inserted the implant. After a few minutes, I tapped the area around the insert. Feeling partially numb I said, "I'm not waiting any longer, it's time to get rid of this thing."

"Let's do it then," Bob said, pulling out his pocket knife. He flipped open a razor sharpened blade, its edge glittering menacingly in the dim light.

"No, no, no, no," I repeated. "We don't need that, it'll come right out! It's been in less than a day." A bit pouty, Bob reluctantly closed the blade and put the knife back into his pocket.

"Like, what about Kingdom? Do we still need him?" Cat asked

"I don't know," I answered. "I haven't thought that far. Let's just get the damn thing out."

Using my thumb, I began nudging the implant out of the small opening Nurse Gerard used to slide it under my skin. The implant stuck, so I nudged harder. Pop! The damn thing flew out like a watermelon seed squeezed between a thumb and forefinger. Shaking free of Cat's arm from around his neck, the dog made a mad dash around the grey boxes. "No, Kingdom," Cat called out chasing after him. But it was too late. The dog lapped up the capsule the moment he found it. "Shit!" Cat yelled leaping over the grey boxes, "Don't die on me boy! Oh, Kingdom, man, like you're the best dog. Such a good boy." Cat wildly petted the happy black dog.

"Don't worry about it, Cat," Bob consoled the boy. "The dog'll just crap it out in a day or two. It's nothing to worry about."

"Yeah, thanks, man," Cat said sincerely. "I sure hope so. But, boy, my uncle's going to be real pissed when he finds your alarm thing in a Kingdom turd. Dad will ground me for the rest of my life."

"Your uncle? Who's that?" I asked.

"I call him Uncle Dan," Cat said sadly. "You call him DF."

I stood there astonished, not able to say a thing. Bob broke the silence. "Let's beeline the hell out of here."

Back in escape mode, Cat herded Kingdom toward the outside exit, "I think I need to get old Kingdom outside. Like, forget letting her loose upstairs. See you guys. Give a call sometime." He turned to leave, but caught himself. "Hey, dude," he said, handing me a folded note. "My cell number. Use it!" Cat and Kingdom quickly disappeared up the outside basement steps into the sun.

Bob grabbed his tool bag. "Where's your stuff?" he asked.

"In my pocket," I answered. The only thing I wanted with me was a picture of Lori and me posing in front of the carousel in Central Park, taken during our last vacation together. "Now, let's go!"

Once outside the basement entrance, we walked nonchalantly across a grassy area to the parking lot to where Bob's Rent-A-Wreck, a dark blue Camry was parked. In a matter of minutes, we were heading to Interstate 81 south. Next stop, HSBC bank, Syracuse, NY.

The air was crystalline. It was like I was breathing for the first time. Big deep breaths. Pure spring air. A feeling of freedom, as if life could go on forever. What little hair I had left twisted and twirled in the rush of wind. I hadn't felt wind on my face for months. The brush of wind seemed to erase years. I was a kid screaming down a steep hill, my Monarch's 28-inch tires revved to the hilt. In my mind, my hands clutched the handle bars like there was no tomorrow, which at the time, there wasn't. I stuck my hand out the window using my palm as an airfoil like I used to do riding in my 1930 Ford. My body reveled in its magnificent return to childhood. Any thoughts of Sunset Nursing Home were washed away by the high tide of boyhood recollection. I looked over at Bob. He gave me a thumbs-up. We were two kids playing hooky. Damn, everybody should be lucky enough to feel this way when they're in their eighties. Then I thought of Emma. Her quiet smile. Her withdrawal to her lover and a yacht. Maybe her escape was as real as mine. I turned around to look at the empty back seat and pictured her there, smiling.

Bob interrupted my reverie, "Any cops back there?" he joked.

"No," I answered, "only Emma."

"Who?"

"Never mind, Bob, not important."

Nearing Syracuse, I gave Bob directions to the HSBC branch on Harrison Street. My memory was right on. We parked next to the entrance. I took off my right loafer, lifted the insole and withdrew a long thin key. I held it up to show Bob. "I'll be right back," I said.

Is this what it's like being reborn? Decades tumble away. Your step is livelier. Things are new again. I wondered how old I looked. Baggy pants, a wrinkled shirt, unkempt hair. Did it matter?

By-passing the line at the teller windows, I made my way to a cubicle occupied by someone identified as Charlotte Keats-Emory, Assistant Branch Manager. A middle aged woman with short brown hair wearing a white blouse sat bent over a computer keyboard. The keys clicked against her manicured fingernails, longer than I've ever seen. They were painted red with swirling white lines running from cuticle to tip. I knocked lightly on the side of the panel. Ms. Keats-Emory looked at me and said cheerfully, "How may I help you?"

My request to get to my safe-deposit box was answered by her request for some form of identification. From my shirt pocket, I withdrew a leather fold-over. On the inner right side was the picture of Lori and me with the Central Park Carousel in the background. On the left side in a concealed pocket, was my passport which I withdrew and handed to Ms. Keats-Emory. She looked at the photograph, then to me, then back to the passport. "It's about to expire," she observed. "You've got a few months left."

"I hope I have more than that," I quipped, which got a smile but nothing more.

Handing the passport back to me, she stood and said, "Follow me." I secured it back into the leather fold-over and put it back into my shirt pocket.

Ms. Keats-Emory led me to box 1443 in a tidy vault located in the basement. She inserted the bank key and turned the lock. Then I inserted my key and the box was in my hand. Leaving the vault, we entered a small ante-room where Ms. Keats-Emory left me behind a locked door. I set the box on a small mahogany table and sat down in a comfortable upholstered arm chair. Offering a peaceful respite from the turbulent escape, the softly lit room was elegantly decorated with flocked light green wallpaper, dark woods and soft brown carpeting. My stomach was fluttering with a flock of butterflies. No, make that dragonflies. I mean, I was really shaking. My life was in that dark green metal box. Gingerly, I lifted the lid. Inside was a note that I wrote to myself. It read, *You son-of-a bitch. I hope life's good.* Signed, *Your loving self.* I smiled. "It sure is," I chuckled.

Under the note was a stack of bills: One-hundred-six-thousand-dollars in denominations of hundreds, fifties, and twenties. I reverently placed the tidy stacks on the small table. I closed my eyes. This was my secret. Lori knew nothing of it. My kids would never get it. The people who had given it to me were either dead or too old to care. At the bottom of the box was an envelope containing four labeled keys: Binghamton, Scranton, York, and Annapolis. I folded the envelope and put it in my pocket and closed the empty box.

A stack of bills amounting to over a hundred thousand dollars was larger than my pockets could hold. I didn't bring a briefcase or a gym bag, or anything to put it in. I couldn't leave the self-locking door and I sure as hell didn't want to use the intercom to ask for help. Even with my pockets stuffed full, I still had a lot of bills to deal with. With no other apparent solution of how to deal with them, I took off my pants, slid off my boxer shorts, tied them into a makeshift bag, and stuffed them with the remaining money. I had a bit of a time scrunching it all together, but in the end I was able to jam it under my arm and exit the bank without a wisp of impropriety. I had to rap on the car window to get Bob's attention—he could fall asleep at the blink of an eye. He hit the unlock button. I slipped into the car seat, underwear dangling from my left hand. "Have an accident?" Bob asked, eying the bulging boxer shorts.

I spread the elastic. "Does this look an accident?"

"Holy shit!" Bob exclaimed. "Did you rob the place?"

"I thought we already talked about that," I answered. "Of course I didn't."

"But Charlie, there's a lot of money there, that is if it's not all ones or fives."

"One-hundred-sixty-thousand."

"I'm glad I'm carrying."

"Carrying what?"

"A 38 special. Under the seat."

I shook my head. "I should have guessed, Bob. But, I don't think we'll need it."

"Never know."

"Okaaaay," I said, "let's leave that subject for later. Next stop, Binghamton, sixty miles, south."

"Negative," Bob declared, taking on CB radio lingo. "Utica, to get my truck."

I had forgotten about his truck.

Bob's F150 made the nondescript Camry look like a Bentley. Think rust. Dents just about everywhere. A faded green bed-cap with a ladder rack bolted askew to the truck body, a rear bumper fashioned from a hand-hewn log. Some wire dangling underneath. Complete with a coat-hanger radio aerial. I knew this truck when it was new. That was over twenty years ago. Picking out the one positive thing, I said, "New tires."

"No sense running down here on the bald ones," Bob said proudly.

Rent-A-Wreck paid, we hopped into the truck. Though worn, the cab was clean and orderly, the one exception being strands of dog hair clinging to the grey velveteen covered seat. He explained that the hair was to remind him of Faithful, his dead German Shepherd. Bob inserted a worn key into the ignition. Expecting a coughing rumbling roar, I was relieved to hear instead the quiet power of mechanical perfection. My recollection of Bob's engineering prowess assured, I fastened the seat belt, set the underwear bag of money between us, and asked, "Can we take the path less traveled by?"

"No interstate! That'll be a pleasure." From under the seat, Bob retrieved his Garmin. Expertly fiddling with a few buttons he programmed our route to Binghamton—two-lane back roads except for a few miles of interstate as we neared the city. After clicking the GPS into a bracket that was suction cupped to the windshield, Bob slid the shifter into Drive. *Turn left in 300 feet,*" a monotone electronic female commanded as we pulled out of the parking lot.

FROM RIBS TO WRANGLERS, announced the roadside billboard, *JUST SOUTH OF DOG HOLLOW.* We were about midway between Syracuse and Binghamton. "Time to get you some underwear," Bob suggested.

"And a few other things," I agreed.

Fat Joe, the clerk's preferred moniker, led me from shoes to pants to shirts to socks to underwear. Choice of Hanes and Carhart and of course, Wranglers. I traded geezer wardrobe for farmer/construction worker/truck driver. Bob picked up an army surplus duffle bag. "For the money," he whispered. A rack of succulent ribs completed the deal. I handed Fat Joe two one-hundred dollar bills, my first contribution to small business, courtesy of the graft and corruption associated with our deep-pocketed defense industry.

Let me tell you what the taste of freedom is really like: Chewing on a smoky rib after months of nursing home food, that's what it is. With Bob driving, I tore into those ribs like a hungry hyena. My hands and face were covered with BBQ sauce. Bob said I looked like a high-chaired kid eating a bowl of spaghetti. And I suppose I did. I sure felt like one sitting there belted into that pick-up's seat, a stack of napkins to my left, a tub of ribs on my lap and a smile a half-a-mile wide. Eyeing the accumulating mess, Bob suggested that we pull off the road to eat. I informed Bob that if we were to make the banks in Binghamton and Scranton, we had to hustle. He agreed, although to Bob that meant going the speed limit instead of five miles slower.

Unlike my clear recollection of HSBC's location in Syracuse, my geographical memory of the Key Bank of Binghamton's location was nonexistent. Bob wasn't one to ask for directions. The Garmin was no help. So we cruised downtown Binghamton. Granite blocked fortress-like bank buildings anchored corners like stentorian guardians of bygone prosperity. They weren't banks anymore. They were restaurants, discos, clothing stores and in some cases, just empty shells. We found a Key Bank in a ranch-style building that looked more like a drive-in restaurant than a secure place to keep money. Jeremy Gettinger, the appropriately necktied and suited bank-manager spent a few minutes on the phone before directing us to a branch office just south of downtown. With the exception of the olive-drab duffle bag replacing the polka-dot boxer shorts, the procedure for getting my money mirrored Syracuse: this time two hundred fourteen thousand dollars, again in denominations of hundreds, fifties, and twenties.

Retrieving the money from Scranton was easy once we found the bank. Thank God for extended banking hours. In my day they closed at three. The Scranton First National had morphed into The Bank of America. We hit the bank just before closing where I added another one-hundred-eighty-six-thousand dollars to my kitty. Buying a good boat was looking better and better. We stayed overnight in a dingy motel near Wilkes-Barre. Dinner was a Big Mac. If they served these fat-laden things at Sunset, clientele turnover would triple. On the other hand, why not? Why the need to regulate every damn morsel of food? To keep us alive? How many weeks or months would any one of us give to have tasty food?

The motel mattress was thin and lumpy, the linen clean but threadbare. My first night out of Sunset and I actually missed the bed. But by damn, I didn't miss anything else.

FRIDAY, JUNE 29

Unusual for Bob, he was sound asleep when I awoke at six. Bob was embarrassed that I had to wake him, as if sleeping in was a mortal sin. His MO would have him traipsing all over the place by 4 AM making enough racket to wake the dead. At least that's how it happened when we sailed together. Over breakfast, Bob apologized for *not getting up in time* whatever that meant. "Been a bit tired these days," he explained as if any explanation was necessary. I simply responded by telling him that older people are allowed to sleep as long as they liked. He seemed to accept that.

On the road by seven, we headed for York, this time via all interstate. Let's just say that Bob's driving was by the rules. If the speed limit was 65 MPH, then we went 65 MPH, no matter that cars passed us like we were standing still. If a car pulled in front of us that Bob thought was too close, he braked hard and called the guy a bastard. Then, slowly, he'd get back up to speed. We spent half the time reading lettering on the back of semis. Between playing road hazard and stopping at nearly every rest stop, we arrived in York just before noon.

After getting my money out of York Savings and Loan, I had a nest egg of eight-hundred-thirty-thousand dollars. With that much money, I could buy a solid boat and live out my days enjoying the good life of a sailor. And there was still one bank to go. On our way out of York, we stopped in a Wal-Mart where I bought a disposable cell phone. I never had nor needed a cell phone so I was entirely captivated by the device. When I was a kid, we'd use two Campbell soup cans connected by a taut string. Jerry Pearsall, my next door neighbor, and I talked between our adjacent bedroom windows like we were spies behind German lines. Damn, with this cell phone anything was possible. It was like having a Dick Tracy two-way radio watch. I called Cat.

"Hey dude, how's it goin'?"

I filled Cat in on our adventure, sans the stops at various banks. I asked about what happened after our escape.

"I hate to tell you, man, like nobody wanted to call in the cops or anything. Everything was hushed up, like the other inmates don't even know it. Maybe they think you're dead or something. I guess they called one of your kids, because like some lawyer guy came to Sunset this morning raising all kinds of hell. Talked about closing the place down."

That didn't surprise me one bit. I could see my junior name-sake turning the loss of his dad into financial gain. Suing Sunset was right up his alley because my disappearing would tie up my estate. No body, no pay. So my guess is that he'd try to get me declared dead. That'd take a while. Maybe years. In the mean-while, he had my money to play with, especially since he'd be relieved from paying the nursing home eight-thousand a month.

"What about the implant?" I asked.

"Dude, you're going to love this. I took Kingdom home and like gave him some Ex-Lax. I mean that poor dog. He like crapped like you wouldn't believe. The implant showed up in a turd, like it was packaged. Kingdom left it next to Uncle Dan's back porch. They fingered me, but I'm not cooperating. I think my uncle just wants to forget all about it."

Laughing harder than I had in years, I exclaimed, "You've got to be kidding!"

"No man. I'm telling it like it is. Anyway, Kingdom is fine. Like, it's not like you made America's Most Wanted. Anyway, tell the Maine Man I said peace. I'm off to a skateboarding rally. Happy day. And good luck." Cat clicked off. After telling Bob about Cat's phone call, I sat in gloom. Why in the world would my firstborn's first reaction to my missing be to sue the nursing home? Why not mount a campaign to find me? Both Lori and I grew up with extended families where grandmas and grandpas and uncles and cousins were within an easy Sunday's drive. Back then extended families were the norm. You were born, raised by a tribe of relatives, nurtured into old age by loved ones and buried in the family plot. I remember my grandparents dying: first Grandma, then Grandpa. No nursing home for them. They died at home, both in their late seventies. We were all there. Grandkids, aunts, uncles, cousins. Right there when they died. My parents got the same treatment, though there were far fewer family members around. Then our generation came along. As we got old, extended families were pretty much a thing of the past. The new way is to hire out, let somebody else deal with the old.

Bob's sudden braking of the truck kicked me out of my dark thoughts.

"Squirreled," Bob said. "Better than a moose, wouldn't you say?" Bob laughed. "So where have you been for the last half-hour?"

"Your kids," I said. "Do you ever see them?"

"All the time. They come out to the island near the end of

every month. When their bills are due." He continued, "Maybe that's not fair. They try. My youngest boy works two jobs. He works his ass off. But with three kids and a wife with MS, he's strapped. Writing a check to him is an investment. The other kids don't need the money, but by God, giving it to one seems to empower the others to demand the same. But, I don't give it to them. The louder they holler, the less I listen. What about yours?"

Sparing Bob the details, I just told him that my kids are ingrates and I've pretty much written them off.

Nearing Baltimore, Bob's driving became more and more defensive. His white knuckled fingers gripped the steering wheel like he was just waiting for screeching tires and the crunching sound of metal. Seldom did he exceed fifty miles an hour. Traffic blew by, horns blaring, middle fingers stabbing the air. This was no place for a Maine Islander. As we neared Annapolis, Bob gave me the word: "I have to get back," he said quietly.

"How about we make the last pick-up, find a place to stay, and you can be on your way tomorrow morning," I offered. Bob nodded his assent. Visiting The United Bank of Maryland completed my pick-ups. I was surprised at how much I had hidden away. I guess it was time to get it back into the economy. I can tell you, I was damned nervous about having all this cash with no safe place to put it.

Bob and I had talked earlier about my plans to buy a sailboat and head off into the unknown. He wasn't convinced that at eighty-four I would be strong enough to single-hand a boat. I wasn't so sure myself. Whatever stress and strain might be in the offing though, sailing into the sunset was far better than dying in Sunset. We discussed hiring crew—there were a lot of young people wanting sea time. I wasn't averse to the idea. It might be fun; having some young people around is always a good thing for an old man. But, then again, it scared me to think of myself as an observer. I'd go to bed early, lie in the stateroom, and listen to youth out in the cabin having a good time. I feared being on the outside looking in, peering under the tent rather than being ringside. I didn't want that. I'd rather go it alone.

Bob and I checked into the Annapolis Marriot Waterfront. Our entrance into this grand and luxurious hotel dressed as we were with Bob carrying a grubby gym bag and I with an army duffle slung over my shoulder caused a few stares. Even so, the staff was courteous and very helpful. Not having a credit card, I was asked for a fifty-dollar-a-day deposit for any charges I might incur. "How long will you be staying," the desk clerk asked. I told him that I was uncertain, maybe a few days. I'd let him know tomorrow. I handed over two fifty dollar bills.

Over dinner of tenderloin steaks finished with a demi-glace sauce, I tried to convince Bob to join me, maybe sell the truck and head out to sea, but he declined. He was hell-bent to get back to Maine as if his damn island would float away if he wasn't there to keep it anchored.

"It's summer," he told me. "Time to get my wood in, else it'll be a damn cold winter." I countered that there's no cold winter in the Caribbean, but he didn't buy it.

"A cold, snowy day reminds us how lucky it is to be alive," he said. I looked at him like he was nuts.

SATURDAY, JUNE 30

The bedside alarm jangled me awake at 2:30 a.m.

"Go back to sleep," Bob said. "I'm off. Going to beat the traffic." The last words I heard were "Good luck." Bob was gone—terse goodbyes were another hallmark of Maine Man. I heard the door click shut but wasn't sure whether I was awake or dreaming. Bob said nothing about leaving this early before we went to bed. But that's the kind of thing Bob did. I had been dreaming about walking on a path I couldn't see or feel. I was lost, alone and there was no sound except the squishing of rubber clogs scuffling along a terrazzo tiled floor. Bob's interruption had me sweating. Where the hell was I?

I lay awake and listened. I wanted to be certain that squeaky clogs or moans, or wheezes, or the hum of fluorescents, or other dreadful sounds of Sunset were residual, not reality. Do freed prisoners have echoes like this? I couldn't say, only guess that they did. Surely, I wasn't afflicted with PTSD. No, not that at all. It was more like needing to be sure I was where I was. I reached over to the other side of the bed. Feeling the rough canvass of my duffle bag gave me assurance that I was who I was and where I ought to be. Comforted, I fell back to sleep.

Earlier when I had flashed my passport to the Marriott receptionist, it struck me that my identity had to be proven. It felt good. At Sunset, no one asked for a credit card, or a driver's license, or anything else to prove that I was really me. I was a stranger to no one. There was never a reason to prove to anyone that I was who I said I was. Sometimes I felt like I was already dead. No one knew my history. During my first few weeks at Sunset, I must have told people who I was a hundred times over. I soon realized that it did no good. What really counts is people knowing who you are, not needing to be told who you are. And at Sunset, people just didn't know each other. There simply was no history to any of us. New patients would often be seen clutching a purse or having a back pocket bulge with a wallet. They were ready to show their identity. But no one ever asked, and in time the wallets and purses were left in dresser drawers. That's where I left mine. I never thought I would need it. How wonderful it is that now I do. The irony is, since I'm a missing person who wants to keep it that way, hiding my identity is important. I can't just walk into a bank and deposit my money. I have no idea about registering the boat. If I get sick or need help, my cover would be blown. Even so, the suspense of the possibility of being discovered is far better than living in limbo.

When I was running the machine works, I'd escape the tensions of managing the business by solo sailing, usually going away for three weeks or more. No cell phones back then, only pay phones when you could find one on shore. Single handing a sail boat leaves little time to fret about being alone, but at an anchorage or snugly tied up in a remote harbor, that was a different story. I wanted to share the sunsets, the cry of the gulls, a soaring eagle, starlit skies. After a week or so of self-pity, the stabs of loneliness lessened. When not at sea, I spent my nights plotting the next day's course, writing, reading, and sitting above decks for hours watching stars slowly dance across the sky. When my cruise was over, I had as much trouble citifying as I had in gaining my sea legs.

I awoke to a sliver of sunlight sneaking around the drawn curtain. With Bob gone, the room felt empty. Following my ablutions and a solid breakfast of eggs with bacon, wheat toast, coffee and orange juice, I had a taxi drop me off at Annapolis Yacht Brokers. A silver Mercedes sat to the left. To the right, was a Beemer sports car, roof down. The brokerage was housed in a grayed cedar shake building overlooking Annapolis Harbor. A yard-armed flag pole with a fluttering U.S. flag accompanied by pennants stood neatly on a manicured patch of grass to the right of a brick walkway bordered with red and white geraniums. An iconoclastic rusting anchor sat stoically at the base of the pole which was encircled by white painted rocks.

Duffle bag slung over my shoulder, I grabbed the brass dolphin-shaped door handle, swung the door open and strutted into the lobby. To my right was a wall covered with photos of full-suited sailing boats, each seemingly competing for how far they could heel before wind slammed them into the ocean. To my left were two large windows framing the boat-filled harbor. Between the windows was a navy blue wall on which were hung two old bronze ports, with mirrors replacing their glasses. Below the ports stood a shiny brass pedestal complete with compass, iron-ball magnetic compensators, and a brightly varnished wooden-spoked ship's wheel befitting a square rigger of which there was none among the high-masted, shiny fiberglass fleet resting in the harbor. I was approached by a gorgeous, healthy young woman.

"I'm Kristen. How may I help you?" she asked smiling.

How I wished I could tell her that she already had helped, just by spilling youth like warm honey. If she only knew how her appearance struck deep into my carnal memories. *Crabbed age and youth cannot live together, youth is full of pleasure, age is full of pain, Youth I do adore thee, age I do abhor thee.* My mind sang Shakespeare as she awaited my answer. I wanted to tell her about Suzy Mae, my first girlfriend. I was twelve years old. About Lori and how we danced to the marvelous and joyous rhythms of youthful romance and marital bliss. About the myths of sex and age. Instead of all that, I said, "I'm here to buy a yacht."

More appropriate to mucking out stalls than visiting a yacht brokerage, the loose fitting Wranglers, T-shirt, and Wellington boots that I purchased at Fat Joe's hardly matched the standard yachty look of khaki, polo shirt, and Docksiders. Add to that an army drab green duffle bag draped over my shoulder, I signaled either being incredibly rich or incredibly nuts, or maybe both. Kristen didn't seem to care which. With a courteous wave of her hand, she said, "Follow me."

"With pleasure," I responded.

Ascending an open staircase bracketed by banisters of taut, stout manila ropes, my eyes centered on the sweet swing of Kristen's youthful hips. Flickers of lusty memories flitted by too quickly before an annoying crick in my left knee interrupted them. Kristen led me to a quietly appointed conference room done up in maroons, browns and, of course, navy blue. Like a jewelry display case full of glittering baubles, a large bay window looked down on the boat-filled harbor. Leather-covered captain chairs surrounded a polished mahogany oval table which reflected a blue sky dotted with puffy white clouds. "Someone will be right with you," Kristen said. "May I get you a cup of coffee or perhaps a Coke?" she asked. I declined and she left the room, adding "Baxter will be with you shortly."

Baxter Hymlaw entered the room looking more like a tugboat salesman than a yacht broker. He was big—more movable ballast than helmsman. My guess is that he carried two-hundred-twenty pounds, on a six-foot-plus frame. He had a massive amount of self-determined red hair. Thick, black framed eyeglasses magnified his light blue eyes. Probably in his early thirties. Following a shake of hands accompanied by a quiet introduction, he motioned for me to take a seat.

I sat my duffle bag on a chair and slowly pushed it close to the table, treating the action as if I were seating my partner. In a way, I was. Baxter's cocked head, his blank stare signaled *nutcase*. I wasn't so sure of him either. He had a name fitting a yacht broker and the khaki/polo shirt/loafers to boot. But nothing else fit. Mutual uncertainty. We sat opposite each other, me facing the framed window overlooking the bobbing boats below, Baxter looking at me.

"What can I do for you?" he asked politely.

During our journey from Upstate New York to Annapolis, Bob and I had spent hours talking about the ideal boat for a single-handed octogenarian. Bob thought a 32-footer would be ideal. I disagreed. Forty or more was what I had in mind. Our list of must-haves included full keel, sloop rigged, auto every-thing, a substantial dodger and bimini with detachable cockpit curtains, a short mast, powerful engine, lots of room below, and built like a brick shit-house. That's the description I gave to Baxter. He wrote it all down on a legal pad. "Add a generator, cabin heat, a fully equipped galley including refrigeration, a no-nonsense navigation station, and radar," I stated.

"Power winches, perhaps. And power furler for both jib and main?" Baxter asked, working his Montblanc.

"Yes," I answered, adding, "and a powerful double acting windlass. I want to avoid going forward up on deck as much as I can; it can be dangerous up there. And one more thing: leaving port you know the weather that you're heading into, sea conditions and all that. What you don't know is how the weather will be on the return, especially if you're out cruising. What I need is a boat that'll get me back, that'll know what to do if caught in a storm. Battleship built with the amenities of a Fifth Avenue penthouse. That's it," I concluded.

Baxter took a moment to finish writing before looking up. He sat back in his arm chair and asked seriously, "How much are you willing to spend?"

"You tell me," I answered.

Baxter slowly laid his pen on the yellow pad and sat back. "Let's start over. How about telling me what you want to do with this boat. With this changing economy, there are a lot of options out there. Many that fit everything you just mentioned. But finding the right one is what's important here."

We talked for over an hour. Besides talking with Bob, this was the first real conversation I'd had since selling my machining company. Forget all those one-sided conversations with my kids and the judge and all the nonsense at Sunset. I was back in the saddle making a deal. Baxter was a good listener. I talked way too much. I prattled on like a kid overflowing with dreams and wonders. How I needed to run before the wind, feel the sting of salt-spray, watch sunrises and sunsets, view the stars, enjoy ports of call, and eat boat food. I told too many tales of my previous sailing days. Of Fundy tides, Atlantic swells, tricky harbor entrances, storms at sea, seeing whales and porpoises, and meeting other sailors. I even turned to Masefield, quoting his famous line: *I must go down to the seas again, to the lonely sea and the sky.* With nods and smiles, Baxter was right there with me in the cockpit through it all. *Boat food* got a big grin. A kindred spirit. Sailors can spot them a mile away. When I ran out of steam, Baxter puckered up his face and said with kid-like enthusiasm,

"Come over to the window." He stood and turned toward the harbor. "Let's look at some boats."

I came around the table and stood next to him. "Take a look around and point out to me the boats that catch your eye."

I looked down at the docks with a kid in a candy-store smile of anticipation and delight.

"That one," I pointed, "the third dock from the end."

"What do you like about her?" he asked.

"Great sheer, coach cabin, substantial, I'd trust her. And, by her looks, I'd say full keel with a skeg rudder."

"It's a Morris. Good call but not for sale. Keep looking."

I scanned the docks, my eyes jumping past the pretty. I wanted handsome. Traditional.

"There," I said, pointing to a boat tied up to the finger dock of the furthest pier to our right. "Solid boat, powerful rig—I bet she'd tame a seaway."

Baxter said, "An Island Packet 460. A lot of boat. And it'll get you through a storm. Good eye and she's for sale. We might need to add a few things, though. Wanna take a look?" I grabbed my duffle bag and off we went. The boat sat quietly at the end of the pier, patiently waiting for the right sailor to board her and sail to places unknown. Baxter lagged behind, giving me an unobstructed view of the boat. He didn't need to sell the boat, that would take care of itself. He knew that I, just like most sailors, was buying far more than a boat. I was buying an extension of myself, a place to house my soul. I was buying adventure.

My first boat was about seven inches long. My brother whacked it together from pieces of scrap wood. He gave it to me for my seventh birthday. He cut a point on the front end as the bow and nailed a smaller piece on the top to represent a cabin. There was no helm, per se, but he did hollow out a small depression near the stern to represent a cockpit. The hull was a shiny blue, the cabin a bright yellow and a red stripe was painted along the gunnels. As kids, we lived on the top of a mountain. No lakes up there, but when it rained the drainage ditch in front of our house became a raging river hell-bent on getting down the mountainside in quick order. With all that running water, I'd get out there and float anything handy down that maniacal sluice. And I did just that the day after my birthday when a thunderous storm swept through. I set the boat into the water and mentally cast off for parts unknown. The unknown turned out to be a storm drain that swallowed my little boat in one mighty gulp. And that was that. But the memory of sailing to far-off places lingers, not the disaster. The rush I got seeing that boat take off stuck with me. No matter that I was born and raised on a mountain top, I was a sailor from that day forward. And now, here I am, eighty-four years old about to jump on that boat again for another go around, avoiding storm drains the best I could.

Hardly a week earlier, I had no dreams, no future, my identity quashed, waiting for death. And now, with a duffle bag full of cash slung over my shoulder, I was walking ever closer to boarding my little boat and rushing off. I heard myself utter aloud, "Emma," as if the name was a prayer of thankfulness.

Approaching the boat, I turned right and slowly walked toward the stern. On the way, I knuckled the hull like a car

buyer would kick a tire. I let my fingers drift along the teak
gunnel, more caress than inspection. Every few yards I stopped
to turn and look forward to admire the gentle sweep of her
sheer. I walked beyond the stern to inspect her backside, a
wide, no-nonsense transom with a convenient boarding platform. The boat's name was done up in italic blue: *Carpe Diem*.
I couldn't count the number of boats I've seen with that cliché
of a name. It sounds like a bad cup of coffee. That would have
to go. There's a myth out there that changing the name of a
boat brings bad luck. I don't buy into that. A boat is part of
the owner's being and *Carpe Diem* certainly doesn't fit a thing
about my being. When it comes time to naming her, I'll give
her a proud soul-catching name, a unique handle that captures
what I'm all about and her as well. She'll like that. I turned and
walked slowly forward. Forty-six feet is a lot of boat. I got a stab
of nervousness thinking about solo sailing this behemoth into
or out of a crowded harbor. I thought maybe I should look at
something smaller. I caught myself. *No way! Let's stick to the
plan.* In a seaway, bigger is definitely better.

My mind had already settled on buying this boat and if
Baxter was the kind of salesman I took him to be, he knew it,
too. Time to set romance aside, I had business to do.

Baxter drew alongside. "How about we take a look on
board?" he said. I agreed.

It had been over a decade since I'd been on a boat. The bow,
the stern, the helm, the deck, stanchions and life lines, chocks
and blocks, traveler and sheets, winches and rigging, all that was
pretty much the same. But that's where familiarity ended. Years
of warp-speed innovation caught me up short. "What's that?" I
asked, pointing to a curved boom growing out of the foredeck.

"A Hoyt boom. It's got a self-tending staysail," Baxter answered. He knew enough not to lecture me on something I should have known.

I gave him a "hmmm" and moved behind the helm, setting my duffle bag to starboard. Baxter watched me studying the gadgets and gizmos, switches and screens attached to the helm in a sweeping panorama. I was used to a gimbaled compass and maybe a toggle switch or two, not a flat screen television set. And what the hell was a joystick doing next to it? In fact, why a joystick in the first place? Baxter excused himself, "I'll go below for a minute to switch on the electronics," he said with a bit of pride.

The screen lit up like Christmas. Icons appeared: radar, depth, boat speed, wind speed and direction, angle of heel, water temperature, navigation. "Go ahead, touch one," Baxter said. I touched navigation. Popping up on the screen was the marina with the boat icon clearly nestled at the end of the pier. "Touch the plus-slash-minus button," Baxter instructed. A few hits and there was the harbor entrance, buoys decked out in reds and greens. I was looking at a chart complete with depths, landmarks and aids to navigation. I must admit, I was rather astonished. Then again, I remembered how my shop was forced out of business because of computer aided machines—CNC's, Computer Numerical Control. Overnight, everything about machining changed—video games turning out gears.

I nodded my approval to Baxter. "Let's go below," I said, grabbing my duffle bag.

I wished Bob could've been with me. Our old boats were comfortable but in a rugged sort of way. We got by with one head; this boat had two. We kept our wine in the bilge; this boat had a wine rack. We had to pump up our alcohol-fueled stoves instead of hitting a propane switch, and the ice box was just that. A freezer was something we had at home.

I say all this as if I wasn't impressed but I was and Baxter knew it. Placing my duffle bag on the starboard settee, I moved aft to examine the engine compartment. For me, a new engine is beauty to behold. Baxter pointed out the bells and whistles including easy changing fuel and intake filters, no small convenience. It's a rare sailor that doesn't rely on a good engine. We moved forward to the owner's state room, plush and inviting. I stretched out on the berth, imagining resting at anchor with stars glinting through the overhead hatch. While I whiled away, Baxter situated himself on the port settee letting me sell this boat to myself. Romance coupled with the lure of the sea is a powerful salesman. I got up, went into the main saloon and sat opposite Baxter with my arm around the duffle bag, my faithful companion.

"How much?"

Baxter gave me the spiel: "This boat has the optional generator, electric furlers and winches plus the high-end electronic system. Less than a hundred hours on the engine. The owners are asking five-ninety-five."

"How much?" I asked again.

The spiel: "That's the asking price. Now, this boat is a gem. The price is much lower than if you went ahead and bought a new one. Did I mention the thrusters?

"So what are you talking here?"

"I think you can get it for five-seventy-five."

"I'll think about it," I stalled.

"Will you need financing?" Baxter asked, trying to put some

energy back into the negotiation.

"You mean do I need a loan? The answer is no. And who in their right mind would loan an eighty-four year old a bunch of money to buy a boat?"

"People do it, Charlie. Mortgage some property. Whatever. There are ways."

"Let's just say that I don't need a loan if the price is right."

"And what price would that be?" Baxter asked.

"Let's start with some basics, Baxter." I explained that I'd prefer the transaction be confidential and discreet—even though this was decades-old money it was still a bit warm.

"Charlie, look, I'm just the middle man here. I represent the seller, though to be honest, I try to be upfront with the buyer. You want the boat; the seller wants to sell the boat. I'm here to make it happen. Keeping things confidential is not in my hands, it's in yours. Once you own the boat, you can do what you want."

All I wanted to do was buy a boat and get the hell out of there without sending up a flare to alert the authorities that nursing home escapee Charlie Lambert has taken to sea. And the money, well, that could cause all sorts of nastiness if I had to explain where I got it. Sizing up Baxter, I decided to do a bit of truth editing. I told him I left a nursing home without my kids or anybody else knowing where I was and I wanted to keep it that way. "If the authorities started snooping around," I told him, "I'd be back in purgatory as fast as a bullet train can move ten feet."

Leaning forward with his left elbow planted on the table and his hand gently stroking his chin, Baxter uttered a long *Hmmm.* Moving his hand to his cheek he quietly said, "You've got a lot on your shoulders, don't you?"

"I suppose that I do," I answered. We fell quiet. Baxter could easily have old Charlie right back in Sunset. "Well," I said, breaking the silence, "are you still willing to sell me a boat?"

Sitting tall, a slow widening grin grew from ear to ear, "If I could, I'd give you one," he said. Standing, he offered, "What I can do is buy you lunch."

"Lead the way, good fellow," I declared, slinging the duffle over my shoulder.

I ordered a tuna fish sandwich with a chocolate milkshake—I still couldn't get over how wonderful it was to order things I wanted. If I had asked for a milkshake at Sunset, at best I'd get soy milk with fat-free ice cream laced with, if I was lucky, a single teaspoon of chocolate Ovaltine.

Baxter told me that the boat I was buying was put up for sale by a couple whose dreams of sailing into the sunset were dashed by losing most everything they owned to some scam. "They sold their home and business to buy the boat and live as sailors. They owe a few hundred thousand on the boat, so any deal to sell it could save them from the streets."

"How much *do they owe?*" I asked.

"Three-hundred-twenty-five K," he answered.

Eyeballing Baxter, I said, "Doable!"

"Is that an offer?" he said, sarcastically. "They'll never go for it, Charlie. They could sell it tomorrow for five, why accept three-twenty-five? They might be hurting, but they're not idiots. They are good people, actually. They got screwed by investment brokers and I'm not about to see them get screwed again with a distress sale. I could take them an offer of five-hundred, but no less."

Our food arrived. We sat in silence; pondered with every bite, Baxter gnawed on his club sandwich with a pissed-off look in his eye. He was right. Of course, the boat would sell at a much higher price than I offered. I could afford it, but wasn't about to give in without some haggling. I finished my sandwich and was sipping on my milkshake when Baxter asked, "So, Charlie, what do you want to do? Make a reasonable offer, go back to the marina and take another look or call it a day?" He put a twenty on the table. "My treat," he said abruptly.

Wind had been taken from my sails. I sat becalmed, looking at the half eaten pickle on my plate. Damn, were my negotiating skills rusted out? There was a time when I could sell a pit bull to a daycare center. Buying time, I looked up and said, "Does that twenty include coffee?"

Baxter hailed the waitress, "Two coffees," he said, as she cleared the table. A long minute or so passed before she was back with two mugs.

"What are the consequences if I buy the boat, don't register it, avoid the taxes and sail away?"

Baxter took a sip and chuckled. "Look, Charlie, I'd like to help you here. I mean anybody that escapes a nursing home and wants to end his days sailing, well, hell, what sailor wouldn't want to rush to the rescue. But, to answer your question, if you get stopped—and with all this terrorist stuff and homeland security rushing all over the place, that's a distinct likelihood—you're going to lose the boat. The coast guard will impound it and you're probably going to spend a few nights in the hoosegow. In other words, you're nuts to even consider it." He paused for a bit, and then added, "But there might be a way."

"I'm listening."

"Let's say you lease a boat. There are some to be had. People are stretched to make payments these days. Leasing gives them the chance to keep their boat until things get better. I have one in the yard, a thirty-two foot Cape Dory; a go-anywhere boat. Think about a six-month lease. If you like it, you might want to make an offer. Gives you lots of options and there's no need for you to do anything but pay the price. Want to take a look?"

Years back, one of my clients said to me, *everything's negotiable*. Whatever deal satisfies all concerned is what drives the business world. So, I said to myself, old Charlie, do whatever it takes, but get that Island Packet 460.

"Too small," I said. "How about the 460 couple. Would they consider a lease?"

"I doubt it," Baxter replied.

"So, what you're saying is, it might be possible."

"Might be. What do you have in mind?

I sipped my coffee and said, "I lease the boat for a three year period for the amount they owe. Three-twenty-five, I think you said."

"How about insurance?"

"You tell me."

"Their policy probably will not allow them to rent the boat and remain covered. To do that, their rate will probably double, maybe even triple."

"How about naming me as an operator of the vessel."

"Charlie, you're eighty-four years old, right?"

"Eighty-four, that's right."

"I could see the underwriter having a problem with that, especially single-handing."

"Is that a bridge we can cross later?" I asked.

"Yeah, okay, but it might be a pretty long bridge."

"So, we agree then. I offer your client three-twenty-five plus the cost of insurance and I have a boat for three years."

"We agree that I take the offer to my client. From there, it's up to you and them."

I reached over the table for a handshake. "Make the call," I said.

Roslyn and Adam Burris were living in a one-bedroom flat in a skuzzy neighborhood just outside of Annapolis. Their white Lincoln Navigator, already keyed on both sides, was a pronounced incongruity in this neighborhood of lost dreams. They welcomed me as if I was their benefactor, their angel of mercy. Being old enough to be this retired couple's father, caused a raised eyebrow or two, but with their future at stake I could have had three heads and it wouldn't have mattered.

I guessed the Burrises to be in their mid- to late fifties. Casually dressed, they looked liked they belonged in a Florida condo, not this rundown apartment. The furnishings were upscale, probably left over from the house they sold to help buy the boat.

Actually, I felt sorry for these two dreamers. Roslyn, an attractive woman with blonde hair and greenish-blue eyes waxed poetically about visiting exotic ports. Adam told stories of bygone days of day-sailing and chartering, how he had spent his lifetime selling shoes all the while imagining never wearing them as he trekked warm sand beaches on some remote Caribbean Island. He was wearing sandals. No socks.

"One of these days, somebody with guts is going to set the bankers straight. All my working life, whenever the economy went bust it was because of the banks. I'm damn sick and tired of it. The bastards!" I nodded my head in full agreement.

"Now dear," Roslyn said, placing her hand gently on Adam's shoulder. "We all know you're right, but now's not the time. Let's hear what the gentlemen have to say and go from there."

All that Baxter had told them on the phone was that he had a client interested in the boat and asked if we could come over to talk. So the Burrises were surprised and a bit taken back when Baxter brought up the idea of leasing. Seated around the kitchen table, the Burrises looked at each other like the garbage stank. Adam said gloomily, "Gee, that's not what we had in mind. I don't think that we can do that." Roslyn, eyes cast downward, slowly shook her head.

Ever the salesman, Baxter laid out the advantages and disadvantages: they would retain ownership and in three years their financial picture would brighten. They could still live their dream. No more boat payments. On the other hand, they would have to get by on what they had, hope for a sale with thoughts that things might brighten up. It was in their hands.

The couple looked at each other, this time there were no wrinkled noses. "Could we have some time alone?" Adam asked. They got up from the table, went into the bedroom, and closed the door.

Baxter excused himself, "I need to make a call," he said, leaving to go outside.

I sat alone at the table, my fingers crossed. I wanted that boat and was eager to do what I had to do to get it. I figured in addition to the lease price, I would need a good bit more for the extras I wanted installed.

Adam and Roslyn emerged from the bedroom looking

ready for business. I've seen that look before. In countless sales meeting, prospects would suddenly switch from doom and gloom to calculated maneuvering. It meant that a deal was in the making. Baxter returned from making his phone call and joined us at the table.

Adam led the discussion with questions aplenty, starting with, "What about your commission, Baxter?"

"Same as before, fifteen percent."

Turning to me, Adam asked, "Are you willing to pay that?"

"I'll pay half," I countered.

"All," Roslyn leaped in like a fullback. "Plus," she added, "Fifty-thousand held in escrow for any damage not covered by insurance."

"Sixty-five percent on the commission and twenty-five for the escrow with the proviso that I can change the name of the boat," I offered, adding, "There will also be some insurance costs which I am willing to pay." Baxter told them that a name change would only require a slight addendum to the commission papers, that it was no big deal and he would help them through the process as well as draw up the papers for the deal. The Burrises finally agreed.

Before we shook hands, Adam hesitated, "Ah, this may be a touchy subject, but what if you, well, you know, you expire before the end of the lease?"

I laughed, "You mean if I die out there, what happens to the boat?" Adam nodded his response. "Then," I said, "You get the boat back and I go to heaven." Laughter all around.

"I'm sorry to butt in," Roslyn said, "but there remains the question of insurance." Looking at Baxter, she asked, "Do we need to call Janet, our agent?"

"All settled, Roslyn. When I went outside before, I called her and she gave a thumbs-up. It'll be costly, but Charlie's paying so I wouldn't worry. Janet's faxing over a retainer as we speak."

With more handshakes all around, Roslyn offered wine for a toast to seal the deal.

"Paperwork?" I asked Baxter.

"Why don't you and I go back to the office? I'll have the papers drawn up, you can write a check. A few signatures later and the deal is done."

Quite frankly, I was anxious to get this deal done. A handshake might legally seal a deal, but only if you go to court to enforce it. I didn't want anything to do with that. I said, "How about I pay for the boat here and now. A cash deal. Write out the particulars on a piece of paper, we'll sign and be done with it."

"Cash!" Roslyn exclaimed.

"Cash," I repeated. "No checks, just hard U.S. currency."

"That's rather unusual," Baxter said.

I said calmly. "There's nothing illegal here, just an agreement between two parties. You get the money; I get to use the boat."

Adam asked Baxter if the deal was legal. "I don't see why not. Two parties agree to terms, money changes hands and that's that."

"Do we have to report it to the IRS?" Roslyn asked.

Baxter answered with, "You might want to consult with an accountant."

"Or," I interrupted, smiling, "you can put in into a safety deposit box."

Adam and Roslyn smiled back and forth to each other. "Deal," Adam said.

I excused myself, grabbed my duffle, went into the bathroom, counted out the right amount and returned to the table. I set the stacks of bills in front of me; a check would have gotten a glance and a smile. But stacks of hundred dollar bills brought glee.

The Burrises looked at each other, with eyes the size of dinner plates. Adam looked over at Baxter and asked, "Is this for real? I mean, have you ever done a deal like this before?"

Baxter shrugged, "To be honest, no. But I don't see anything wrong with it."

"I guess we're okay then," he said to Roslyn, but she was too busy counting the money to pay him any attention.

We signed the agreement, which was written in longhand by Baxter on a sheet of composition paper. Handing it to Adam, he said, "Copy this exactly as I have it written. Both of you sign each copy and that's that."

I paid Baxter my part of his commission plus the escrow which he agreed to hold in an interest-bearing account.

On our way to Baxter's car, he said, "I thought you had clothes in that bag, Charlie. This is a first for me."

"Me, too," I replied.

That night, I slept aboard.

SUNDAY, JULY 1

The hefty full-battened mainsail was furled in the boom, raising it was as easy as pushing a button. This, of course, meant that I had no need to go forward to winch it up, a great plus for safety. Both jib and staysail were handled by furlers as well, each with a dedicated electric winch. I felt a bit guilty about not having to heave-ho halyards like I did when I was younger, but not having to go forward was far safer than trying to manhandle sails.

For sea trials, winds were perfect at 10 to 15 knots gusting 20 out of the west. Once we cleared the harbor, Baxter led me through the process of unfurling sails, first the main, then the jib, a 120 Genoa. We left the staysail furled. With sails pulling, I killed the engine. The boat's keel bit into the water, heeling us ten degrees so before settling on a steady course. Sailing a boat for the first time is like going on a first date; it either works or it doesn't. This boat worked. We rounded the harbor entrance buoy, trimmed the sails, and headed north toward William P. Lane Bridge. The knot meter registered 8.3 knots, a good speed given these wind conditions and sea state. This was no racing yacht. She was built for unpredictable weather and unforgiving seas. It's the kind of boat that prefers open waters to endless days tied to some godforsaken dock. God, was I happy. My smile came from well below my own keel, a satisfaction as deep as the briny sea. Baxter couldn't help but see my joy. It radiated like beams of light. He asked, "Do you have a name for her yet?"

"I sure do," I answered purposefully. "She's to be *That Good Night*."

Pausing, Baxter frowned slightly. "Dylan Thomas?"

"Yup, again," I answered.

A tacit understanding descended on us both as we turned our attention to the swish of salt water breaking from the bow. Our world was in agreement.

We spent the day taking *That Good Night* through her trials. At Baxter's urging, I singlehanded her through all points of sail, reefed her down, then finally lowered her sails and headed back to port. I put her dockside with nary a touch. *That Good Night* was mine.

Late in the afternoon, I borrowed the marina's loan-a-car and went shopping for supplies. I never had a boat with a deep freezer, a refrigerator, a wine cooler and the storage capacity of a moving van. Nor did I ever have to buy groceries bottom up. Lori saw to that. After she died, I got along buying exactly whatever I ran out of; empty cans and bottles defined my grocery list. Now, faced with a clean slate, I was at a loss. I walked the aisles of the grocery store tossing this and that into the cart. Lots of canned stuff, especially soup and fruit. When I returned to the boat to store my goods, I was astonished that I didn't have things like sugar, salt, pepper, milk, juice, lunch meat, bread, mayonnaise. What the hell was I going to do with Fruit-Loops, Tamarind sauce, and a bag of Rye Flour?

I was pondering what to do when I heard a tap on my hull. Topside, I peered down at the dock to see a young couple eyeing my boat. "We're admiring your boat, sir," the young man said. "Ours is just down there," he continued, pointing to a neatly trimmed and painted wooden boat.

"We're live-aboards," the young lady said proudly.

I thanked them for the boat compliment and congratulated them on their youthful determination. "Don't see many wooden boats these days," I commented.

"That makes them cheap. And this is as solid as it gets, Mahogany planking, bronze fasteners. Real good shape."

I gave a thumbs-up and said, "How about coming aboard to celebrate your adventurous lives with a glass of wine?"

Down below was a mess of groceries but that didn't deter the young couple from taking in the luxury of *That Good Night.*

Evan and Carol Emory were recent college grads, Carol with a degree in political science, Evan a biologist. "We're rebranding ourselves as vagabonds," Evan declared, his arm snugly around Carol's thin waist. "Live-aboards. We sold our cars, used graduation gift money, and found some part-time work. Bought an old but solid woody."

Carol jumped in. "Lots of our friends are jumping right into the job market. Getting an early start on career tracking. But not us." Looking at Evan, she continued, "We have loans to pay, but we'll make it somehow. How about you?" she asked.

"Doing the same I guess, only on the other end of things. You two are on a life track and that sure beats a career track which sounds like a little slice of hell to me. How about that wine?" I said, avoiding the subject of my personal life.

Back in the cockpit sipping wine and enjoying the quiet of the early evening, Carol observed that I must be an exotic cook. "Baking your own Rye Bread and Tamarind sauce, that's pretty high-class cooking," she observed. "But, Fruit loops, that somehow doesn't fit unless you're expecting grandkids."

I laughed at her remarks, confessing my ill-conceived trip to the grocery store. "Do you have the receipt?" she asked. I nodded. "Well then, let's go back to the store and get this all settled." We sipped our wine while these young vagabonds assumed the task of making sure that I had adequate stores. Carol was full of questions: "What do you like to cook? What's your favorite dish? Do you have any allergies? We like Dinty Moore Beef Stew, do you?"

My head was spinning. Refilling my wine glass, I gave Carol assurance that whatever she picked would be fine with me and that was that.

Back from our successful grocery buying spree, the Emorys helped me store the goods after which we went shore side for a delicious dinner of crab cakes with all the trimmings. Anyone who has ever voyaged knows the immediate kinship that can occur among sailors. Passing ships in the night, perhaps, but always memorable, always welcome.

Before going to sleep, I called Cat. He answered on the second ring.

"Yo, dude, what's up?" Without going into the details, I told Cat that I was in Maryland ready to put to sea. "Well, like you better hurry up," he said. "You were on my list to call. Like there's a bloodhound snooping around looking for you. An insurance investigator. Hired by the nursing home after your kids hit it with a lawsuit. Like the guy grilled me like a hot dog. I didn't tell him a damn thing, but he's onto you going sailing thanks to old Emma. Like, he's got a lead on Bob, too. I don't know how he got that."

"Did he mention my kids?" I asked.

"Not to me, but hey, I'm not like what you'd call privy to

the inside scoop. Like, what I do know is that this guy belongs on *Law and Order*."

"Does he have a lead on where I was going?"

"It's secondhand, man. From Ashley. She told me that Emma like told the guy her story then at the end she said that you went sailing. Maybe looking for sex in Annapolis," Cat laughed.

Paying no attention to Cat's sarcasm, I said, "Cat, give me a call if you find out anything else." I gave him my phone number, but Cat told me he already had it stored in his iPhone. He used the words, *coded in my phone.* "And thanks for the heads up," I added before hanging up.

I poured myself a glass of Scotch. I have two boys. You'd think my going missing would arouse enough curiosity for them to come looking. Instead, there's an insurance company out there wanting to prove me alive or dead by suicide. So, my kids go after Sunset instead of searching for me. What do I get from my gene pool but a fucking bloodhound? I downed the scotch, poured another, and called Bob.

After filling him in about my purchase, I told him about the investigator.

After a pause, Bob said, "So, get out of Maryland. And if he makes it up here he won't get very far. We don't like snoops." Bob changed the subject. "Have a sail plan, yet?"

I went into detail about the boat, its systems, and how she handled. "I could go anywhere in the world," I said. "I was thinking of coming up to Fundy, meet up with you, and then decide from there. How about it?"

"When?" Bob asked.

"I plan to leave tomorrow but I can't say when I'll arrive in

Maine. I'd like to take it slow."

"Take as long as you like," Bob said, "I'm not going any-where. But don't take too long."

"What's too long?"

"Long enough for me to die."

"What the hell's that supposed to mean?"

"Just come," Bob said. "And if that investigator shows up, well, let's just say that he'll enjoy a special blend of Maine's hospitality. Call me when you get close," he said and hung up.

PRIVATE INVESTIGATOR

Adapted from the digital recorder of Private Investigator, Justin Roberts. July 1, 1625 hrs.

I've been assigned to a missing geezer case in Upstate New York. Finding an old geezer is not on my A-1 list of exciting investigations. Most of these cases are solved by hunters or bird watchers when they trip over a rotting corpse, not by a full-blown investigation. It's all about money. This guy Lambert has a ton of it, or at least had, and his kids aren't going to get their hands on it or a settlement from Sunset until he's either found dead or declared dead. That can take a few days or a few years. Things get messy real fast. Lawsuits, insurance claims, sibling rivalries, you name it. A missing rich guy's death stirs the money pot. Marqued Insurance is the nursing home's insurance carrier. They hired me to find Lambert, dead or alive.

I've decided to record this crazy odyssey by using my BBDRD, (Belt Buckle Digital Recording Device) courtesy of my former employer, the FBI. As an agent, I had access to the most advanced gadgets imaginable. Take this BBDRD for example. It has a waterproof case sheathed in space-age carbon-fiber, a battery that can last for weeks under heavy use, and it is fashionable enough to wear with just about anything. Years back, gathering evidence was a piece of cake compared to today. What we reported was taken as fact. Today, an agent has to have airtight evidence to convict even the worst of the lot. Facts have replaced good old intuition. Things like the BBDRD help us gather and retain the material needed to convict. I don't think that this old guy Lambert is a crook, but you never know.

A search by locals found no trace of the guy. Either his corpse is hiding under some leaves somewhere or he's off having the time of his life. If it's the latter, we'll find him. Old guys on the lam cut a pretty wide swath. I started my investigation interviewing Dan Forteneau, head of security at Sunset Home. He was defensive. As well he should be.

"Let me get this straight," I said. "This old guy who has a Subcutaneous Tracking Device sneaks out of your nursing home and you don't know it until you find the device wrapped in a dog turd in your backyard? You want to tell me about this again?"

"It ain't as bad as it sounds," Forteneau responded. "Lambert was a pain in the ass since he came into the home. We put the ankle monitor on him after he attempted to escape two times before. He wasn't the only one that got fitted. When clients and their families started to complain about the monitors, the administration got the brilliant idea using these subcanus gadgets."

"You mean subcutaneous, right?"

"Yeah, whatever. Anyways, there you have it."

"And the turd?"

"Well, there you have an embarrassment. We think he took it out himself. We put it in only the day before so I guess he just popped it out."

"And the turd?"

"We don't know how Kingdom, that's my dog, got a hold of it. Lambert probably fed it to him."

"Look, Mr. Forteneau," I said. "With all due respect, if security was on the monitors, then wouldn't the alarm go off the minute

Lambert left the building?"

"That's embarrassing, too. Scott Ramsden, he's my second in command, he was being charmed by this high school kid. A girl named Ashley. She flirts a lot and you know how that is."

"No, I really don't. This is a nursing home, right? How can security be such a big deal?" Forteneau shuffled his feet like some kid caught with his hand up his cousin's skirt. I let him off the hook, "Forget it. Is this Ashley girl around?"

"Probably, she comes in around three-thirty every afternoon. Want me to get her?"

"Never mind, I'll track her down. And Forteneau, I'd like to talk to Ramsden."

"I'll tell him. Come on back after you talk to Ashley and he'll be here."

I left the security office. Maybe this Ashley girl had some answers, maybe not. Getting started with an investigation is the hardest and most important part. The tiniest lead is like a bloodhound getting the first scent. I found Ashley in the sunroom giving a light shoulder massage to an elderly, well-dressed woman.

"I'm sorry to interrupt, young lady, but I wonder if you could answer a few questions for me?"

Ashley looked up. Blonde, blue eyes, jailbait. "If you're looking for a patient," she said, "you'll have to go to reception. Did you sign in?"

"I'm all set," I answered. "Actually, I was hoping you could shed some light on Mr. Lambert's disappearance."

"Me? I wish. He was such a nice man."

"Was?"

"No, I don't mean it that way. It's just that I miss him. Mr. Lambert, we all called him Charlie. He knew, like, so much about things. He even helped me with my trig homework. He was awesome."

"Did he ever talk about getting out of here?"

"All the time. He hated it here. He said he didn't belong. I think he was right, too. I mean, he was in good shape. But what do I know about those things? Maybe he was really sick, but his mind was really good."

The elderly lady looked up and said quietly, "Damon was really good, too. He was a good sailor. We sailed to the Azores together. I was eighteen."

Ashley said to the woman, "Emma, I bet that you had a good time."

"We had sex, is what we had, dear." Emma fell quiet.

"Emma's always talking about that sailing trip. I guess I don't blame her but it gets a little embarrassing every once in a while. Like, I'm supposed to know these things."

I was about to launch into a birds and bees story, but I held my tongue. "Did Mr. Lambert ever say where he'd go if he got out of here. Maybe to one of his kids' places?"

"He'd never go there. He didn't like his family and they never really visited." Directing her attention to Emma, Ashley said, "You knew Charlie, didn't you, Emma? Did you like him?"

"He reminded me of Damon. He was a sailor, too. Did I tell you how when I was eighteen I sailed off with Damon? Oh, my." Emma fell quiet again.

I was getting nowhere. "Well, Ashley," I said, handing her my card, "if you think of anything that might help us find Mr. Lambert would you give me a call?"

"Of course we will, won't we Emma?" Ashley said.

"Thanks," I said and went back to security to interview Ramsden.

Ramsden was short, pudgy and arrogant. I didn't like the guy the minute I laid eyes on him. You can tell a lot by the way a person looks. At the FBI, we had lots of training in how profiling saves time and money. Why waste resources. If it looks like a duck and acts like a duck, it's a duck. Ramsden's a duck. I couldn't imagine Ashley wasting a flirt on this guy.

"Do you have any security videos of this place when Lambert disappeared?"

"Tapes? What do you think this is, Fort Knox or something? We don't do tapes."

"I understand that you were talking with Ashley when Lambert disappeared."

"Did you meet this girl? She's a looker. And yeah, we were talking."

"What about?"

"Nothing, really. She was telling me about a pajama party that she was going to that night. So you can imagine what I was thinking."

"I really don't care!" I said.

"I'd have given my right arm to be at that party."

I ignored his inane comment. I asked, "How long did you two talk?"

"Fifteen minutes maybe. Ashley kept checking her watch. I asked her about that and she said that she had an appointment with one of the patients, so it wasn't that long. Hey!" Ramsden exclaimed, "While you're at it talking to everybody around here, you ought to talk to Forteneau's nephew. He had goo-goo eyes after Ashley and I think she likes him, too. They hung out a lot together. That kid's what's wrong with kids today."

"Hung out?"

"Yeah, he doesn't come in here much anymore. He'd hang out with Lambert; I think he used the old man to get to Ashley. When Lambert went missing, Cat stopped coming around much. Ashley probably wised up."

"Cat?"

"That's what people call him. Catlin's his real name. His grand-mother is a guest here."

I was getting my first scent. "Where do I find this guy, Cat?"

"Why don't you ask his uncle?"

I walked around the place just sniffing here and there. Christ, if I ever wind up in a place like this, I'll cut my throat and consider myself lucky. It's hard to blame Lambert. Deep down, I wish him luck. But, wish as I might, I have a job to do. It's like finding an innocent escapee. I did that once when I worked for the FBI. This guy, actually more a kid, got nicked for a murder rap he didn't do. The investigation team knew it too, but we had no say. A conviction was way beyond our purview. Find the guy and let the courts deal with it. When we caught him, he cried. I almost did, too. He's in the slammer forever. That was the court's decision, not the FBI's. When I find Lambert, I'll let the insurance company deal with it. He'll live out his days right back where he was or not. My job is to find the guy and it ends with that.

I found Forteneau chatting with the receptionist. I interrupted and asked, "Who's Cat?

"Catlin, you mean. He's my nephew. Weird kid."

"Why weird?"

"If you met him, you'd know. Embarrassment to the family is what he is."

"Why?"

"Looks like something out of a freak show. If you see him, you'll know what I mean."

"So, when do I meet him?"

"He comes in here sometimes to visit my mom. Wait around and *you can probably catch him."*

"Look, Forteneau, I'm not here to wait around. Give the kid a call and tell him to get over here."

"Good luck. Nobody, and I mean nobody, can tell that kid anything. If you want Catlin, you'll have to go find him. My guess is that he's at his house messing around with his computer. He lives on the damn thing."

"Tell me, does Catlin have a thing for Ashley?"

"A thing! Who doesn't? Yeah, he has a thing for her. He used to hang around here like a buck in the spring."

"Used to?"

"Since Lambert left, Catlin has been kind of scarce."

"Jesus, Forteneau, give me the story will ya?"

"Okay, here's what I know. Lambert and the kid used to hang out all the time with the exception when Ashley was here. He'd leave Lambert and sneak off with his dream girl."

"Back to Lambert, if you don't mind. When did Lambert and this kid start hanging out, *as you say?"*

"A week or two maybe before Lambert took off."

"And you don't find that curious?"

"No, not really. What am I a spy or something? They'd go to Lambert's room and close the door and whatever they did, they did."

"Before I go looking for the kid, was there anybody else that visited Lambert?"

Forteneau turned to the receptionist. "Mary, honey, check the sign-in for anybody that visited Lambert before he took out of here?"

"I already did that for the police and there were no sign-ins for Charlie. Why don't you guys let the old man alone? Have you ever thought that he might be dead? I pray for him every day."

Forteneau looked back at me. "Nope. Nobody."

"Yeah, I heard her. I'm standing right here! Okay, where do I find the kid? Directions would help."

Catlin was different. Dressed in black. Spiked hair, chains, and studs. The whole rebellious package. I was direct.

"Where's Charlie Lambert?"

"Like, if I knew, I wouldn't tell you.*"*

There it is. The kid knows. *"When's the last time you saw him?"*

"Before he left."

"How much before?"

Catlin scratched his forehead. *"Like a day before, maybe."*

"Maybe?"

"Charlie was here, then he was gone. Life's like that, isn't it? Here today, gone tomorrow."

"Gone where?"

"Somewhere, I guess."

"So Charlie's somewhere. Where do you think?"

"Out into the world. On the deep blue sea. On a mountain top. Like at the Salvation Army. How am I supposed to know?"

Emma mentioned sailing. *"Why the deep blue sea?"*

"Why not? Charlie could do it if he wanted to. He was in good shape. He shouldn't have been in the home anyway."

"Did you help Charlie escape?"

Catlin looked away, then said, *"No, I didn't!"*

"Did Ashley?"

"Like, ask her."

"I will."

I left Catlin absolutely certain that he and Ashley were involved in Lambert's disappearance. But I didn't have a subpoena. Finagling is different from extracting testimony. Catlin was

*not going to submit to interrogation. I went back to the motel and
called Charles Jr., Lambert's oldest son. I asked about Charlie's
old haunts. Old friends. What he enjoyed doing. Anything that
might help. Charles Jr. was helpful once he got past lecturing me
on how to do a proper investigation. This is a guy who thinks he
knows everything. Comes with being a college professor, I guess. He
told me that his father was a workaholic. That he had few friends,
he was anti-social, that he liked to do crossword puzzles, enjoyed
listening to Bach, and went sailing alone. Bingo. Emma, Catlin,
now son Charles Jr. Common thread, sailing. It was a weak link.
But it was a link nonetheless. Charles Jr. told me that his father
sold his boat about a decade ago and hasn't been to sea since. That
his sailing buddy was some guy named Bob. Lived in Maine. The
two of them used to go off together for weeks at a time. Big question:
How many Bobs live in Maine?*

*I went back to Catlin's place. He was sitting on his back porch
diddling with an electronic gizmo. A Black Lab sat next to him.*

"Is that the dog that ate the locater?" I asked Catlin.

*Without looking up, his fingers working like a typist on steroids,
he said, "Like goat, man. Kingdom eats anything."*

"Who's Bob?"

*I watched Catlin's fingers slow to a crawl then pick up again.
"A kid I used to like tease in the eighth grade."*

*Too slick. "Look Catlin, you know something. In fact, I think
that you know a lot. Let's just say that Charlie is out there. He
might be sick, in trouble. Don't you think it best to find him? Get
him the help he needs? It's not like he's going to prison."*

*Catlin stopped messing with his phone. "It's just like prison.
And Charlie can take care of himself. Now leave me alone. I'm not*

going to say one more word to you."

Catlin went back to his electronic wonder and remained mum. I wanted to choke the little bastard but at the same time I envied Charlie for having such a devoted friend. Lambert must be something special. But, a fugitive, nonetheless.

I caught Ashley as she was just leaving. I was direct. "You know something that you're not telling me. Catlin said I should talk to you. Why is that?"

"Catlin's just a friend."

"I really don't care what he is. What I care about is you telling me the truth. Did you help Charlie Lambert escape?"

Ashley turned her baby blues on me like they were two Colt 45's. "I said before, I liked Mr. Lambert. He was a beam of light in this place. If I did help him escape, I wouldn't tell you or anybody else. But, the fact is, I didn't. He didn't need me to get out of this place. So let me alone. I have stuff to do." Ashley turned on her heels and marched away.

The sailing thing bugged me. It didn't make sense. An eighty-four year old doesn't just leap on a boat and go sailing. Maybe on a cruise ship. And where the hell would the money come from?

I went back into the nursing home, signed in, and went to visit Emma. She was sitting quietly in the Sun Room with Ashley. I approached quietly.

"Hello, Emma. Remember me? I'm one of Charlie Lambert's friends."

Without a hitch, Emma started her tale of her and Damon's sail to the Azores. She ended by saying, "We left from Annapolis, like Mr. Lambert." My eyes popped.

"From Annapolis," I repeated back. But Emma's eyes were closed. Story over.

MONDAY, JULY 2 AND TUESDAY, JULY 3

It took only two days to get the boat ready to go: buying charts and a few doodads, a neat folding knife that looked like it could cut steel, an Emergency Position Indicating Radio Beacon (EPIRB), which I would use only in a dire emergency, a self-inflatable vest, foul weather gear, boots, a few strobe lights, a stack of books, and a whole lot of other things. I also made my way to a clothing store where I bought a complete wardrobe of clothes befitting a seasoned yachtsman including some warmer clothes for when I reached Fundy. I took time to become entirely familiar with the boat's electronics, mechanicals, and deck layout. Saving me the hassle of outfitting the boat, Roslyn agreed that I could use the linens, dishes, utensils, and cookware as long as they could be replaced with money from the escrow. While I busied myself, a fellow from the yard prepared *That Good Night* for cruising, including filling the fuel and water tanks, changing the filters, installing a new impeller in the water pump, checking the rigging and just making sure that everything was in order. In addition, at Baxter's suggestion, he installed a well-hidden safe behind one of the starboard lockers.

I spent my last night at the marina joining folks from the marina at a bring-a-plate cookout. I brought a six-pack of cherry Jell-O.

It was a marvelous way to kick off my voyage. I would leave the next day.

WEDNESDAY, JULY 4

I left Annapolis at 0530 hrs on a cloudless day with light winds out of the southwest. I'm celebrating our nation's independence with my own. I could use some fireworks. I woke up that morning like an excited kid ready to go fishing with his grandpa. I brewed coffee, toasted some raisin bread, had a glass of orange juice, made two peanut and jelly sandwiches for later, and cleaned the galley to a sparkle.

"Senile, my ass," I said aloud with the final swipe of cloth over the gleaming stainless steel stove top, all burners off. Old Charlie Lambert was fit and ready to take off. I was no longer in my eighties. I was in my thirties, full of piss and vinegar, determination and hope.

Dutifully, I went down my checklist: stow everything, check engine oil, inspect the water separator, eyeball the bilge for any water, turn off propane, turn off shore power and disconnect power cord stowing same in aft locker, switch on navigation system, auto pilot, radar, instruments, activate VHF and get weather report, start engine and check engine instruments. Who wouldn't be excited?

While I was untying the fore and aft spring lines, Baxter showed up. "It's pretty early for you, isn't it?" I greeted my new friend.

"Yes, it is," he responded. "But I couldn't let you leave without a fair sailing farewell and this," he said, handing me a bottle of Veuve Clicquot champagne. "And don't drink it alone."

"Don't worry," I said, thanking him. "I'll save this for just the right moment."

"I'm sure you will," he said. "Any problems out there, let me know."

"There is one favor I need to ask before heading out," I said

"Go right ahead and ask."

"There's a guy on my trail about the nursing home stuff. An Insurance investigator," I added. "I'm not sure, but he might show up here."

"Your secret's safe with me," Baxter assured me. "Don't worry about it, Charlie, just go sailing."

"Just is case you need to contact me, I'll give you my phone number."

Baxter wrote it down on the back of one of his business cards. We shook hands.

Baxter offered to handle the docking lines while I stowed the bottle and prepared to leave. While I positioned myself at the helm, Baxter cast off the lines, carefully tossing them on board. A nudge of the bow thruster with a touch of forward prop had me clear of the dock and heading for the channel that would take me into the Chesapeake Bay and north, to my first overnight at Chesapeake City, a distance of about 50 nautical miles. With light air, I let the engine do its job pushing us along at six knots.

When I first got the idea of getting out of Sunset, I dreamed of going back north to familiar sailing grounds. I gave no thought beyond that. Get to Maine and maybe to Nova Scotia, then go from there. While the yard was working on preparing the boat, I studied charts. It was simple enough. Sail to Maine via the Upper Chesapeake Bay, the Delaware Canal and River, sail north off the New Jersey Coast, visit New York Harbor, East River to Long Island Sound, transit the Buzzards Bay Canal, stopover in Boston, Portsmouth, Portland, and finally visit Bob. I figured that the voyage would take two or three weeks depending how fit I was to put in long hours and maybe even an overnight. Plus, of course, factor in weather. The navigation was pretty straightforward, with no real hazards to be concerned about, except for inept boaters or being smashed by a freighter as I could be crossing numerous sea lanes. I vowed to just go and enjoy myself.

There was a chart plotter on this boat, a high-tech gizmo that rivals Cat's fancy cell phone. This amazing device is supposed to tell me where I am, where I came from, where I'm going, how to get there and what time I might expect to arrive. With the push of a few buttons, it'll even tell me where the marinas are and what I may expect in terms of locating grocery stores or restaurants. It's a great gadget for a man who goes to get something, and then once he gets there, stands empty-minded. On this first leg to Chesapeake City, I discovered myself looking at the thing like a kid glued to a television set. My choice was either turn it off or discipline myself. I chose the latter. I kept a paper chart close at hand and, as I used to do years ago, plotted a fix every hour.

Sailing a great boat is like the music of Bach; a certain busyness that makes pure sense. Really simple when you get down to it, but very complex, too—still water runs deep so they say. That's how it often was machining precision parts. With specs in the thousandth of an inch, it takes great machinery, expert operators and a respect for materials. Here we have the shape of the boat, the cut of the sails, a few ropes that adjust this and that with wind, and water as friends when you work with them and enemies if you don't.

Having motored all the way, I anchored mid-afternoon in a cut off the canal across from Chesapeake City. A push of a button and the anchor chain rattled out of its locker and in a few minutes I was hooked. No need to scramble up in the foredeck to drop an anchor like I used to. *Used to.* Those two words echoed around Sunset like a mantra. Used to swim, dance, cook, clean, plant gardens, take out the garbage, make love. All those simple and not so simple things we *used to* do and took for granted, or complained about or wished we didn't have to do some of them. But garbage does accumulate, weeds grow, kids scrape their knees, and lust, well, let's just say that *used to* does apply. But then again, I felt a real ache looking back at that gal in Annapolis. I hadn't felt that way for years.

You know, every young adult should have to spend time in a nursing home—sleepovers for the sake of learning that the simple day-to-day stuff is what underscores being alive. What I noticed was that visitors came and went as fast as they could. And I bet a dime to a dollar that when they left, they said to each other that they would never in a million years want to wind up in a place like that. So it's okay for a loved one, but not for them. Now what does that say about love? I admit that people like Emma need a place to be. For her, Sunset is forever being on a cruise ship. But the moans one hears bouncing around the place are real. These soft and pathetic drones are the new underscore of people wound down to their lowest common denominator. They deserve our pity.

I didn't think any of this when I anchored, but let me be clear, my experience at Sunset lies just below the surface of my consciousness, and now and then it bobs up to take a gulp of my freedom. I don't like it, but that's the way it is.

Once the anchor was set, I patted myself on the back for my first day solo sailing. No one knew where I was, no one cared—except the damned insurance company. I was in command of my life and I felt like I would live forever. I went down below, poured a glass of scotch, went back up to the cockpit, and toasted the sailing gods.

I slid back into the old sailing routine of years past: Anchor, switch on or off appropriate electric panel switches; drink a scotch in the cockpit; go below and do tomorrow's navigation; check the weather report; check the boat's essentials; have another scotch; and make dinner. The galley in this boat is full-blown. My other boats had an alcohol two-burner stove top. *That Good Night* has a four burner stove and an oven all fired by propane. A few clicks of switches and knobs and the galley stove fired up, just like at home. Unlike at home, I'm paying particular attention to turning the thing off when I'm done cooking.

I thought about uncorking Baxter's gift of champagne, but decided to wait until I had someone to share it with. Maybe Bob, once I reached Maine. Thanks to Evan and Carol, I was able to select a handsome tenderloin, some canned potatoes that I fried in olive oil, and a can of corn. For dessert, I dug into some fresh sweet cherries. Accompanying it all was a glass, or maybe two, of Cabernet. Cooking, eating, and clean-up took about an hour. I ended my first night sailing sitting in the cockpit watching the sun slip away, then retired down below.

Here might be a good place to describe the head, or

bathroom, as it is referred to on land: vanity, shower, toilet, Corian counter top, hot and cold running water. Did I miss my old boat with a tiny sink, small toilet, cold water only and no shower? No, I did not!

I lay in bed looking through the clear hatch at a star-filled sky. My mind wanted to take me on an anxious ride about being hounded by that insurance investigator. But those dark thoughts disappeared once the fireworks began. Kicking off with booms, cracks, and thunderous roars, lighting the sky with flurries of colorful falling stars, this pyrotechnic show was just what I needed. For old Charlie, for all us octogenarians who can still smell the roses. I missed Lori. Very much. While she wasn't much of a sailor, when she was onboard, she was a great companion to have on board. We'd snuggle after a day sailing, our bodies sharing the stored-up warmth of a sunny day, our minds softened by the gentle rocking of the boat, wearing love like an old woolen sweater. I have my photograph of Lori hung from the starboard bulk head where I can see it every time I come below. I had my wallet sized photo blown-up and framed in Annapolis. Sometimes she appears so distant, so faraway that I have to work at it to get her back. Other times, she's just there, right in front of me, smiling, and content with being together. But we're not together. She's dead and I'm close behind. When she appears to me, I go on as if she's right there next to me. I even talk to her. But the sadness lingers, like a low-lying, soft, dark cloud.

PRIVATE INVESTIGATOR

Adapted from the digital recorder of Private Investigator, Justin Roberts recorded July 5, 1852 hours.

Spending July 4th weekend driving from Upstate New York to Annapolis, Maryland is no way to celebrate our nation's independence. But duty calls. When I get near water, I start shaking. I hate the stuff. Nearly drowned in a YWCA swimming pool when I was eight. Give me a Kansas cornfield any day. But work is work. Annapolis is all about water. There's got to be fifty marinas, thousands of boats, plus the Naval Academy. The big question of the day was how does an old man with apparently no money get to Annapolis, buy a boat and sail off on the briny sea? Or maybe just buy a boat and live life dockside. Many do.

I took a room at an inn in the center of town. I'd let my fingers do the walking. Be it a fugitive or a grandma, there are three things that everyone needs: people have to eat, they need to have clothes and they need to find shelter. Real basic stuff. If Lambert was in Annapolis, he'd have had to stay somewhere. I made a pot of coffee and started calling. Given what his son told me about Lambert's business travels, I started by calling hotels. Third call was a hit.

Charles Lambert and Robert Liscome stayed at the Annapolis Marriot on July 1st. Now I had a last name for "Bob from Maine." Paid in cash. Liscome stayed one night, Lambert, two nights. License plate number Maine 6492 HT. Bingo.

I spent the morning day visiting marinas. Fancy as some of them were, it was boat after boat nestled together like floating house trailers. Living aboard one of these things was not my idea of Shangri-La, but it would be better than bedding down in Sunset. No one so far seemed to know of any Lambert nor did anyone recognize the photograph of him that I got from Sunset. In early afternoon, I visited an upscale marina just off the main drag overlooking the harbor. Inquiring about recent boat sales, I was directed to a salesman named Baxter.

Whatever image I had of a yacht broker did not fit this guy Baxter: overweight, red kinky hair, thick black rimmed glasses and a shoe size that would have given that old woman a place and then some for all her kids. Right off the bat, Baxter started sweating even though the office was air-conditioned. At first he didn't recall the name Charles Lambert. How could he not remember an old man looking for a yacht? We sat in a conference room overlooking the harbor. I took the seat with my back to the water. Baxter was going to drown in his own sweat by the time I got done with him.

"Nice place you got here. Business good?"

"Thanks. And, well, business is not all that bad considering the economy. I mean a lot of folks got it hard, but those with the big bucks seem to be in pretty good shape."

"How about Charlie Lambert? Was he in good shape?"

"I'm sorry. Charlie Lambert?"

"You know, the guy that bought a big boat from you. Seems like folks on the dock remember him."

"Oh, that Charlie Lambert," Baxter chuckled.

"One and the same."

"Got hold of an Island Packet. Great boat. Nice guy, Lambert was. He left though. Do you mind if I get a glass of water. Do you

want something, maybe a Coke or Sprite?"

"Help yourself. I'm fine." Baxter got up from the table to go over to a credenza. He opened one of the doors to reveal a small refrigerator and got himself a bottled water.

"You sure?" he said, turning back to me.

"I'm sure," I answered.

Rather than return to the table, Baxter wandered about the room collecting his thoughts. I said nothing. He walked over to the window, his back to me as if he was trying to hide his eyes from mine. I had already checked online for recent yacht sales but came up with nothing. I suspected that this Baxter had made a sneaky deal and was about to wet his pants. I decided to play my ace.

"Look, Baxter, you obviously are in deep shit here. Selling a boat to an old man, a wanted old man. Now, I suppose that the government might be interested in where all the money came from. And don't forget taxes. And other regulations. I warn you, I used to work for the FBI and I can cause you more trouble than you would ever want to know. Now, make a choice, either come clean, or cover for Lambert and I'll nail your ass to the wall."

Baxter slowly turned around. He looked like he'd gained a foot in height. Through pursed lips, he said as clearly as I've ever heard it: "Go fuck yourself and the horse you rode in on."

In my days with the FBI I'd have this idiot squirming on the ground crying for pity. And if he kept it up, that's just what I was going to do, toss the hulk on the floor, maybe break his arm.

"Repeat that," I challenged.

"You heard me. And while you're at it, pick up the phone over there," Baxter said, pointing to his desk, "and call the FBI or the CIA or the goddamn local sheriff. If you knew anything about what yacht brokers do you wouldn't even be here. All we do is put two

people together that have similar interests. All the details are theirs. I don't owe you or anybody else an explanation or even the time of day. Now get out of here before I'm the one calling security."

Disrespect is something an agent of the government simply can't tolerate. Retired or not, I've earned respect and I was going to get it. I moved on Baxter so quickly that he hardly had time to think. If I hadn't tripped on the rug, I would've nailed him good. As it turned out, this Baxter guy got a hammerlock on me and damn if he didn't toss me out of the front door.

It's amazing what a brick sidewalk can do to a good pair of pants. That son-of-a bitch Baxter will pay for this. It's just a matter of time before I nail that prick to a wall.

I got up and dusted myself off. Storming my way out of the marina, I saw a young couple heading for the docks. I calmed myself before calling them over. "Do you folks have a boat here?" I asked

"We do," the young man said, staring at my torn pants.

"I've been looking for an old friend, a fellow named Lambert. He's quite a sailor."

The couple looked at each other, "No, the name's not familiar."

"He's an old guy. White hair, in good shape, maybe six foot, give or take."

The young woman responded this time. "What happened to your pants?"

"Never mind that! I'm the one asking questions, not you. I'm guessing you know this Lambert guy. Now, where is he?"

"Who the hell do you think you are? Bug off. We're done here," the man said. I apologized to these snips but it didn't matter, they just ignored me and strutted off like two over-indulged kids. Screw this place. Sailors might be courageous and all that, but by damn, they have the minds of criminals with this covering each other's

asses. Bunch of hooligans, I'd say. So, the hell with them, I'm off to follow my next lead: Maine license number 6492 HT, here I come. Like I said, old men leave a wide swath. I'll bet he's off to visit his old friend in Maine.

THURSDAY, JULY 5

Cape Henlopen, a harbor of refuge on the Delaware side of the Delaware River's delta is a perfect anchorage for *That Good Night* in preparation for my run up the New Jersey coast. A harbor of refuge is where you go when you need to duck out of terrible weather, like a hurricane. With a relatively narrow entrance the harbor is surrounded by a sturdy seawall. These harbors are not pretty tree-lined, dock laden places. They're bare bones and mighty welcome when the wind's up. If I wanted shore-lined restaurants, I'd have opted for Cape May, New Jersey, just across the river.

Last night was the first night anchored. A boat is never still. A subtle stir of the wind, or a bit of current or both in consort cradle the hull ever so gently. When trying to find sleep in Sunset, I would try imagining how it felt cradled in an anchored boat as I was last night. More often than not, I would toss and turn, trying to escape the weight of inertia. But, no, it was as if I was bound to that bed, to the rustle of the plastic clad mattress with every turn. I'd lay there dull to what might come in the morning because there would be nothing new, so surprises. But not now, I'm free to think ahead, to plan and wonder what the morrow has in store. Weighing anchor this morning and heading out into the Delaware Canal, my freedom took hold. Every turn of the canal, its sweep into the Delaware, meeting or passing other vessels presented endless ways to celebrate being alive.

Tomorrow, I'm aiming for tucking in behind Sandy Hook where I anchored some thirty years ago. Here I am sailing for two days and I feel one again with the sea. Like riding a bicycle, you don't forget. Though *That Good Night* is full of technological devices, she's much the same as Jason's *Argo*: longer than she is wide, sails to catch a breeze, a rudder to steer her by and an old salt at the helm. The aches and pains I had in Sunset are sloughing off me like outgrown snakes' skin. Back there, you couldn't help but ache. It was all around you. Pain was a commodity, traded from morning until night. Back, knees, elbows, hands, neck, and shoulders all talked about and compared for levels of hurt. If you felt good, no one was interested. Out here, it's wind and water, no complaining from them, some nastiness maybe, but no pain.

Tomorrow's run is straight forward. Winds promised to be westerly so going north should be a breeze, pun intended. But it is, give or take, 120 nautical miles of coastal sailing, plus keeping a wary eye out for the big boys.

I have a rule of thumb for when I first spot a ship on the horizon: I have just eight minutes to determine if we're going to pass or if the behemoth will roll over me like a runaway steam roller. Tracking with radar helps but, in addition, I plan to take sightings; there's nothing like good old eyesight. I plan to leave at daybreak, hoping to make Sandy Hook at dusk. But, as any wise sailor would do, I fixed Barnegat Inlet as an alternate layover.

Just as I was about to go to sleep my phone rang. It was from a woman named Jennifer who asked for her *little turnip*. Obviously, a wrong number. I told her that I was a piece of celery and hung up. Cell phones are great gadgets but not when cruising and certainly not when you need sleep. I turned mine off and stuck it in the bedside table drawer.

FRIDAY, JULY 6

I'm anchored in Barnegat Bay. Assuming that I could sail from Henlopen Harbor to Sandy Hook in one day was biting off more than I could chew. The promised 15-to-20 knot westerly wind turned out to be more like ten knots once it made an appearance at around 1100 hours. Translated, that meant my boat speed was in the five knot range, not fast enough to make Sandy Hook until well after nightfall. When I dropped below four knots, I let the engine take over. I wasn't on anyone's schedule but my own, so I decided on my alternate, Barnegat Inlet. Luckily, I approached the Inlet just as flood tide was making an appearance. I had some late afternoon on-shore breeze but not enough to threaten *That Good Night's* entrance. As it was, I joined a line of weekenders making their way back to port. I had no choice but to gingerly follow not only a narrow channel, but a shallow one as well. *That Good Night's* keel stirred the sand more than once, but we made it through without embarrassment. I found an anchorage in the Bay with nine feet of water. I had been at sea for fourteen hours, which made my nighttime glass of Scotch taste all that much better.

I had just raised the main and unfurled the jib when my eye caught two boats heading in my direction. White foamy water sprayed from their bows. They were coming at a high rate of speed, like they were intent on T-boning me to the bottom.

Moving to avoid one brought me into line with the other. My choices were prayer or get their attention. I chose the latter. I yelled, blew my claxon, cursed, and watched as they bore down on *That Good Night* like laser-guided missiles. My guess is that these guys were either sitting in the back swilling beer or cleaning some poor fish or maybe both, but I sure didn't see anyone at the helm. The presumption is they had their boats on auto-helm: it'd be like driving down the highway on cruise control while playing cards in the back seat. Anyway, at the last minute I swerved *That Good Night* as they barreled past—one to port the other to starboard. The idiots actually waved.

Abusive technology: set the GPS in line with the auto-helm, crank up the RPMs, go have a beer, screw everybody else, and believe that you alone own all you survey. The argument is that it's never technology; its people. Did the invention of the telephone create gossip? Did the invention of the telescope give birth to voyeurism? Maybe not, but they sure did advance the cause of the nutcases. We used to look at a great ass and remember it. Cat clicks a button on his electronic wonder and photographs it. Is that bad? Maybe not, but I think it's a bit over the top. Not like it was years ago.

Years ago—now there's a term. It's like *back when* or *when I was a boy*. Same as *used to,* I guess. After about a week's time living at Sunset, these opening phrases would signal repetition. Not like Emma's stuff. She was stuck; her mind ran a constant loop. I'm talking here about repetitive stories that old people get into. I'd run like hell whenever someone started a conversation with *did I ever tell you the story…?* Yeah, about a thousand times. There was nothing new to build on. Lots of gossip, though gossip isn't memorable. Sunset gossip circulated around errant body functions, so-n'-so's new wig, or sometimes some inane tidbit about Lance Lordell whipping his manhood out at breakfast. Maybe my escape has them talking, hoping, vicariously embracing adventure. If I could give the folks back in Sunset a gift, it would be a tomorrow to look forward to.

There's not much tide in Barnegat Bay, but enough to make the difference between grounding out and floating. My Garmin chart-plotter told me that the best hope of safely getting out of the bay was for me to leave at 0530 hours the next morning. "Fine with me," I said aloud to no one but myself.

Restudying the charts, I decided to enter in a route directly to New York Harbor rather than ducking into Sandy Hook. If things went well, there'd be no problem adding some extra miles.

SATURDAY, JULY 7

In preparing my course to New York Harbor, I consulted the charts for Morris Basin, a place I tied up decades ago. Consulting the chart plotter, I learned that Morris Basin now housed the Liberty Island Marina; a mega center for God only knows how many boats. The good news was that I could top off my fuel and water tanks. The lump in my throat was about negotiating a forty-six-foot yacht—plus three feet for the stern platform—single-handed in a crowded marina. This would be a first for me, other than the rather benign docking in Annapolis, but Baxter helped with that. I thought about calling the marina to ask for some help, but changed my mind in favor of taking it as it comes. I'd go to the fuel dock and go from there.

With making way in and out, ships anchored, water taxis zipping around like swarms of gnats, bright orange-painted Staten Island ferries chugging by with myopic captains steering straight no matter what, and of, course, pleasure boaters meandering here and there without a care in the world, I decided to furl the sails and kick on the engine. I didn't have a chart plotter or radar or a GPS the last time I was here. I did have a compass, charts, and my eyeballs connected to my brain. In other words, I sailed by observing what was going on around me. Approaching New York Harbor, I clicked off my chart plotter, sailed from buoy to buoy, avoided nutcases, treated every crossing and meeting situation according to regulations, and thoroughly enjoyed the controlled chaos of a busy commercial port.

It's hard not to be moved by Lady Liberty. *Give Me Your Tired, Your Poor* built this nation. Just upriver is Ellis Island. I had plenty of opportunity to hire immigrants, legal ones, although I could never be entirely certain. They worked like mules. A sick day to these guys meant they couldn't get out of bed because if they could, they'd crawl to work. Great workers and good people.

Nearing Morris Basin, I looked to my right and saluted. I miss the Twin Towers. Like a lot of folks, I cried the day they went down.

Approaching the entrance to Morris Basin, I headed *That Good Night* into the ebbing Hudson River, kicked the engine to dead slow, set the auto-helm and took the short bit of time needed go forward on deck to prepare the docking lines and attach the fenders. Back in the cockpit I switched off the auto-helm, increased engine speed and headed in. Whatever concerns I had about entering the Morris Basin were for naught. The few boats plying its waters were courteous and fully in compliance. Stopping forward motion, I quickly went forward to kick out the fenders then returned to the cockpit. A nudge of the bow thruster, a prop kick forward and *That Good Night* gently kissed Liberty Marina's fuel dock and that was that. No docking boy, no help. It turned out to be self service. I tossed the docking lines to a fellow who was walking by and eager to assist. He chocked the lines then kindly made sure that I safely made it down onto the dock. I thanked him and he was on his way.

My legs were wobbly and I had trouble walking the few steps to the diesel pump. My instability concerned me until I realized that this was the first time I stood on an immovable surface since leaving Annapolis just four days ago. It felt so much longer. Only ten days had passed since the escape; yet, that felt like it was a lifetime ago. When I was back there, days went by so slowly that time seemed to stop

After topping off my fuel and water tanks, a docking boy showed up. "D-Dock," he said, pointing in a westerly direction. "Slip number six. Four boats in. I'll meet you there, sir, and help you with your lines."

"What's your name, lad?" I asked.

"Elgin, sir."

Current was slight but noticeable as I made my way up D-Dock slipway heading for number six. I'd have to go dead slow into the docking space. The architect that designed this place obviously also designed airline seating. I saw Elgin standing at the end of the dock waving. Easing *That Good Night* into the slip, Elgin grabbed my lines and chocked them down. "You're all set. Is there anything more that you need?,"

I answered, "No, Elgin." Then reached down and handed him a fifty.

"Thank you, sir," he said and left.

"Amazing," a fellow yelled down from a Hatteras Motor Yacht tied up across from me. "Damn good for an old man, sailing solo, to boot," he declared.

To which I replied, "And I can piss a steady stream, too!" He disappeared rather quickly.

SUNDAY, JULY 8

I thought about running into the city, taking a water taxi that berthed just a few docks down, but quickly dismissed the idea. I'd been there enough times, seen the sights, enjoyed the hustle and bustle, gone to concerts, the opera, and went to Broadway shows when actors sang and not yelled, like they do today. I can't get past the need for young people to sacrifice their hearing for the sake of pop culture. Cat's earphones were turned up so high that I could hear the music like he was a human stereo set. I didn't care for the music either, but who's to say. Back at Sunset, people just loved the big band stuff. The Beach Boys were icons. One lady played excerpts from the *Sound of Music* day in and day out. I mean, just how much do, re, mi can a person stand!

I discovered Bach in my thirties thanks to one of my machinists, named Helmut. He might be running a shaper or turret lathe with his radio broadcasting a Bach fugue. In sync with slapping of the machinery, things would just sound right. For fifty years I've been listening to Bach and I hear more stuff in it every time I listen. I used to think that it was Bach's genius at play and to some extent it certainly is. But as I age, I realize that Bach's genius is manifested in the music's innate ability to remain relevant to my changing perceptions of myself and my world. The music grew with me as opposed to sticking me in some time or place. I have to admit here, though, that whenever

I hear "A White Sport Coat and a Pink Carnation," Lori comes dashing forth to join me in a slow dance.

MONDAY, JULY 9

I departed Liberty Harbor Marina at 0430 hours to catch the slack tide at Hell Gate. The East River, which connects the Hudson River with Long Island Sound, can toss a boat hither and yon, especially with the Harlem River adding to the confused current. I used to think that Hell Gate referred to the hellish whirlpools that dip and swirl anxiously at the river's narrows. But I learned from a fellow at the South Street Seaport Museum that in fact the term comes from Helegat, a Dutch term for bright passage. Before the East River became shadowed by skyscrapers, the sun would play on the rippling waters creating sparkling delights, hence the term. Put that on Jeopardy!

The fact is, with power galore, today's crafts can plow through these eddies without a hitch and they do so with abandon. I preferred to pay attention to the rules of nature, so slack was fine with me. Besides, I love sailing according to the tides. This natural flow feels like time slows down. I don't wear a watch anymore; I stopped doing that back in Sunset. What the hell does it matter what time it is when you don't have to be anywhere at any time? I do have a chronometer down below that dings according to a watch schedule: four on, four off. At Sunset, there was breakfast, lunch, and dinner. That was the clock. There was no need for any watch, but every wrist had one, some residents had one on each wrist. Mine was on the top of my dresser. Here, I have no deadline. I eat when I'm hungry, I look for an anchorage when the sun passes through the meridian, I sail according to the winds and tides. Old folks use the phrase, *my days are numbered*. Whose aren't?

Just past South Brother Island, Rikers, the citadel of criminals, lies to starboard. Foreboding to say the least. I wonder what memories lifers have. Guilt and regret, would be my guess or at least I would hope that's the case. When I was in my darkest moods back in Sunset, I envisioned myself as a prisoner. A lifer. And for good reasons. I really didn't have much to look forward to. Life in a nursing home is not much of a seedbed for memory building. I don't think it has to be that way. I was a skilled craftsman but did anybody care? Did anybody ask me to fix things or get involved in any way with things that had to do with my living there? No. I would have enjoyed having something productive to do. People in nursing homes are people first and patients second and people need to feel productive. I just bet some of the ladies committed to Sunset could cook up a storm. Why not let them?

If you had one pleasant life experience that you could live over and over, what would it be? I've searched my memory bank for one and except for having Lori in my life, I came up empty-handed. But now there's the escape, buying *That Good Night* reconnecting with Bob, being here right now. That's what old people need, reconnecting with life. The lucky ones have an extended family where life is a continuum rather than a life disrupted.

Before Lori died, she got into scrapbooking. Every photograph we ever took was neatly glued in place, labeled, and packaged so in the end we could waltz down memory lane with a flick of pages. What shocked me was how many photos didn't include me. There were lots of photos with the two boys and their mother, the boys playing sports, on stage, at the playground, going to church. So where was I? Doing business is my guess. When I bought the machine shop, it became my life. Sales, competition, my workers, regulations, and updating machinery took over my life. Helmut and the rest of the crew were family for me. My clients were like cousins, my banker a buddy. So, is that the epitaph I want carved into my grave stone: Solid businessman, Machinist? Lori's has her name, birth and death dates and the words *Caring and Loving* Mother. I would like something similar, maybe *Devoted Father and Sailor.* It may be that my sons are just pissed off at me for not being there. Still, that's no reason to shit-can dear old Dad. After all, the machining business bought a good life for them. But kids need a dad, not just a caregiver. Maybe I'd have been a hell of a grandpa or can still be. Maybe I need to forgive my kids.

A low-flying jet out of LaGuardia rattled the rigging. Time to get back to being helmsman.

I anchored in a cove just off Manhasset Harbor at around 1500 hours. Entertainment: Watching harbor police in high speed boats trying to catch some kids on jet skis. No contest. The kids disappeared into the far reaches of the Sound while the police boat lumbered along at only about 60 mph. Damn kids. Gutsy, mindless risk takers, emotional blobs. God, I envy them.

TUESDAY, JULY 10

Last night a boat came into the Manhasset Cove and anchored on top of me, that is, they set their anchor over mine. This means, of course that when I raised my anchor in the early morning hours, I got wrapped in their anchor rode. Thankfully, the seas were calm, but still this meant going forward to untangle the mess which I didn't want to do so I blasted my horn until the owner came bleary-eyed on deck ready to do battle. It was 0500 hours.

"Sorry to bother you, sir, but you anchored over me." I said. "I'd appreciate your untangling the mess so I can be on my way." (I was thinking *jackass* and maybe it showed).

Portly to say the least, the fellow was dressed in boxer shorts with tiger imprints, and arrogant. His reply, "You must have dragged anchor. It's not my fault!" Let's just say that I was dealing with a four year old here.

"As you wish, lad," I said, unsheathing my Myerchin serrated cut-any-damn-thing six-inch knife. "I'll take care of it." I left the cockpit, carefully making my way toward the foredeck.

"You're not going to cut my line?" the guy protested.

"Yes, son, that's exactly what I'm going to do."

Joining irate husband on deck, his wife squeaked, "Do something, honey!"

I reached the foredeck. Brandishing my knife, I said, calmly, "Last chance."

The guy sprinted forward, hauled in his rode, untangled his line from my anchor and scolded me. "Satisfied, old man?" Returning to the cockpit, I engaged the winch, weighed anchor, shifted into gear, and motored out of the cove.

I sailed to Long Island's North Shore and headed for West Harbor, Connecticut. On the chart, the harbor looked to be a secure place to drop the hook and, sure enough, it was. The problem was the place was blanketed with mooring balls. On each one was printed PRIVATE followed by the name of the boat to which it belonged. There were plenty of empty ones. Small yellow floats declared, *No Anchoring*. The shore line was an architect's dream and a landscaper's money trough. Situated at the end of the harbor was a modern stone building. A flag pole with a yardarm flew the American Flag, the Connecticut State flag, and a fancy burgee: a yacht club. Tidal waters are up for grabs, money or no money. I decided to anchor. I edged my way back to the harbor entrance, respected the channel, and let my plow find the bottom eleven feet below. I played out fifty feet and secured *That Good Night*. As I had expected, it didn't take long before a launch came shooting out of the yacht club. A white clad youth was at the helm. In the bow stood a fellow dressed in enough gold braid to make Admiral Nelson take notice. The launch drew alongside.

"Excuse me," the Commodore declared, "but this is a restricted area. No anchoring allowed."

Go fuck yourself, according to regulations I am legally anchored off a channel in tidal waters. I played the game. "Yes sir, thank you for that information. Is there a mooring that I could tie up to for the night?"

"As you may have noticed, all moorings in this harbor are

private. May I suggest a nice cove about ten miles to the east?"

"Actually, sir, you may, but I'm not going to it. I'm within my rights to remain right where I am. Have a nice evening."

Commodore Whoever proceeded to give me a dressing down when a well-used dinghy came alongside. A man about my age dressed in raggedy shorts with a t-shirt that read, "Suck" on it in red letters, was at the oars. In the bow stood a Portuguese Water Dog at full attention. "George," the man addressed the Commodore, "what's going on?"

Commodore scowled, "Yacht Club business, Ernest. No concern of yours."

Dismissing George, Ernest turned to me. "Where are you from?"

I had to think about that. At Liberty Harbor Marina, I had given my address as PO Box 126, Clear Valley, Pennsylvania. "Ah," I hesitated, "The Chesapeake."

"Good place to be from during the summer. Hot as a honeymoon down there. Humid enough to drown a barracuda, too. I was stationed in Norfolk. Medical Corp. What about you?"

"Not WWII?" I asked incredulously.

"What do I look like, that I'm in my nineties? Korea, goddammit! Nobody remembers the Korean War anymore, but if you fought at Chosin Reservoir, you do remember it! Did you fight in Korea?" he demanded.

"Not directly. But my company made gun sight parts and other stuff. I lost a cousin to it." I said.

"Pardon me, gentlemen," Commodore broke in, "But you must move that boat."

"George," Ernest said in no uncertain terms, "blow it out your ass." I noticed the young helmsman snicker with *I wish I could say that* written all over his face. "Why not go back to your mahogany-paneled suite and let me and this gentleman figure it out." The Portuguese Water Dog barked approval.

"I'll write you up for this, Ernest. Expect a reprimand." Commodore turned to the helmsman, who at this point was eating his fist trying to still a deep seated urge to burst a gut, "Take me back to the club. And, you will sign a witness statement."

"Yes sir," the young man replied, and then sped off back to the yacht club.

It appeared to me that Ernest was enjoying his waning years being a curmudgeon. Rather than have me subjected to the yacht club's quasi-military establishment, he invited me to tie-up *That Good Night* at his dock, offering me a shower, dinner, drinks, and an evening of, as he said, "Bullshitting."

"Thanks, Ernest," I said, "I'll follow you in."

"Ernest! Jesus god, call me Ernie. That half-wit Commodore's as formal as a goddamned Beefeater. And," he continued pointing to the bow, "the dog is known as First Mate," to which the dog barked, *affirmative, sir.* I weighed anchor and followed Ernie to a pier that spoke of care and pride. After tying up, we walked up a few stone steps to a large deck overlooking the harbor. Greeting us there was Mildred, Ernie's live-in house-keeper, cook, and companion.

After introductions, she asked, "A nice glass of sherry, perhaps?"

I nodded while Ernie said, "Yes, and the carafe, too, please." Mildred walked into the house as Ernie and I made ourselves comfortable on two well padded teak chairs. "Without Mildred, I'd be lost," Ernie offered.

I acknowledged his comment with a smile just as Mildred returned with two cut crystal glasses and a a carafe of dark, amber sherry. "Would some nice strip steaks do well for dinner?" she asked.

Ernie looked to me for an answer. "Medium rare," I said, tipping my glass to Mildred.

She asked me, "Will anyone else be joining us?"

I answered, "I'm sailing alone."

"Oh my," Mildred said. "Then steak will be just the ticket."

I laughed, "Certainly beats frozen dinners." Mildred answered with a cute shrug and pursed lips.

"The usual, Mildred," Ernie chimed in, giving Mildred a warm and generous smile.

Sipping sherry, Ernie and I chatted about sailing, exchanging where we've been, boats we owned, close calls, and the joys of wind and water.

After a dinner of steak and fixings accompanied by a bottle of cabernet sauvignon, Ernie and I returned to his deck, cradling snifters of Courvoisier while Mildred remained behind to clean up.

As much as I wanted to boast about my escape from Sunset, I left it out, instead simply telling Ernie that after Lori died, I sold out and headed to sea. "I expect to die out there," I heard myself say. Since leaving Sunset, I hadn't given much thought about dying, so I guess that consciousness finally caught up with something that had been brewing in my mind for a while. At Sunset, death pervaded my thinking, especially right before sleep. I'd hear wheezing and coughing, dreading that those would be the last sounds I'd ever hear. Once out of that place, it was all about future. So I was a bit taken aback at hearing myself utter the word *die*.

"What are you gonna do?" Ernie asked. "Sail into the sunset, until somebody rams into your boat, all stinking with what's left of your rotting corpse?"

This was not a discussion I preferred to have. "I'll have to give it some thought," I told him abruptly.

"Listen, Charlie," said Ernie, "I didn't mean to be so crude. The fact is I envy you. My days are numbered and I gave some serious thought to taking my Alerion, heading out to the middle of the Sound, and calling it a day. But, that would be suicide and, quite frankly, I'm not into murdering myself." We sat silent for a bit, sipping our brandy, casting our eyes out into the cove. I broke the silence.

"If you were going to commit suicide, how would you do it?"

"Whoa, Charlie, why are you asking me that? Go ask Dr. Kevorkian, not me." He leaned in close with pursed brow, "Are you thinking of it?"

I hesitated before answering, "When I was sailing off the New Jersey coast, it did cross my mind. I had this thought of getting really ill while sailing. The thought of heading to shore, seeing a doc, winding up in some warehouse for the ill, letting *That Good Night* bob away at a dock…suicide sounded like a logical alternative. Do you understand?"

"I do, more than you know. I think all of us in our later years are scared as hell that we might wind up in a nursing home. I dread the thought. But suicide?"

"Why not?" I asked. "There is a reality at play here. I am an old man. I am sound of mind. I do know that I will never ever submit to spending my last days cooped up in some fluorescent lit, sanitized box. So, I ask a simple question, how would you do it?"

Palming his snifter, Ernie gave the glass a quiet twirl, inhaled its delicate aroma before taking a thoughtful swallow. He said, "I'd use morphine. That would do it. It's a painless, soft way to die."

The subject of death was taboo at Sunset. Maybe that's because it was all around us. Beds became empty. The roster changed. It wasn't like people went on leave or some fancy vacation. No sir, it was death. Roommates changed—reminders that all of us were rapidly spiraling downward. Nurses and aides would change shifts, go home to families. We went to the grave. I thought of the gray boxes in the basement of Sunset. Neatly stacked.

"The name of your boat," Ernie said, breaking the silence. He stood and walked over to the edge of the patio. I followed. Overlooking the cove and the sound beyond, he recited:

"Do not go gentle into that good night,
Old age should burn and rave at close of day;
Rage, rage against the dying of the light."

He turned and caught my eye. "Suicide? Is that how you're going to *rage against the dying light?*"

I stood, walked over to him, and pointed to my boat. "That's my rage, Ernie. That wonderful boat out there is my rage. The sea beyond, that's my rage. When death has me in its grip, I will submit. If I'm lucky, I'll just die. Slip off in my sleep. My boat might become a navigation hazard, I might stink it up with my rotting corpse as you suggested, but I will not demand suffering from myself. If I have to, I'll take death into my own hands."

Returning to the deck, Ernie refilled our snifters. While pouring, he said, "Let's take a walk."

Palming our snifters, we left the deck and ambled our way to a brick path that led to a small salt marsh. The tide was in. Bulrushes mixed with other tall grasses were a pleasing break from the manicured lawns that surrounded the marsh. Frogs croaked here. Dragonflies flitted for their catch. A neatly coiled black snake enjoyed the last heat of the day.

"So, you were in the machining business?" Ernie asked me.

I answered, "Precision stuff. After the Korean War, we stayed with the DOD, air force mostly. But we competed in the marketplace, too."

In my heyday, when someone would ask me that question, I could expound for hours about the trials and tribulations of running a business, wooing clients, hiring workers, taking risks, carrying debt, sacrificing for the sake of business. But looking back, there really wasn't much to say. I worked hard, made a good living but I really didn't live much of an exciting life. We were talking about legacy here and I had little to offer. I thought about Lori's photo album, so many photos sans Daddy. One of the rare ones with me in it was of me, Lori and the boys standing in front of a hot dog stand on the boardwalk of Atlantic City. I piped up, "There was this time I took my family to Atlantic City. We had a great time just walking the boardwalk. The kids hit the beach like they'd never seen water before. My wife, Lori—she looked like a starlet in her bathing suit. It was a family day." I choked up a little.

Where had *that* memory been? Were there more? Sure, there must be. Where the hell are they? I felt a strong urge to get back to my boat. Crawl into the cabin and shut out the world. Is that what I was doing, hiding, sailing nowhere? The Ancient Mariner? The Flying Dutchman? Charlie Lambert?

"Are you okay?" Ernie asked. "Hit a soft point, did ya?" He continued, "You know Charlie, the thing about the past is we have a lot of it. Live to be eighty and you have a hell of a lot of past to mull over. There's a lot of stuff in our wake and not a lot of future. But hell, there's always a tomorrow, at least there is for now. Here's to life," he said, proffering his glass for a friendly clink. We toasted in silence to tomorrows.

"So Ernie, what about you—I'd guess medicine?"

"Toothpicks. Can you beat that? I manufactured toothpicks. Billions of goddamn toothpicks. My grandfather spent his life building the business. So help me, Charlie, the old man worked right up to the end. Damn, he even died sitting behind his desk. Anyway, you're right about the medicine part. Fresh out of my internship, I was drafted and served in a MASH unit. Remember that? The TV series?" I nodded. "From the frying pan of working like a dog in the hospital to the fire of wartime trauma. That was Korea. Now, how many people give that war a thought today? Hell, I bet it gets at most a sentence or two in the kids' history books and not a word more. We fought like bastards, Charlie, and for what? When the Korean conflict— they didn't even want to call it a war—ended, I wanted nothing to do with medicine—too much gore, Charlie, too much trying to do the impossible. I lost too many kids. It's the craziest damn thing. Why the hell do we fight like that? Anyway, war wiped out my idealistic view of medicine.

"When I got out, Grandpa had just died so I took over the company. It only took me three years to drive it into the ground. Obviously, I had no idea what the hell I was doing. Besides, old Grandpa had a ton of debt. That's when I returned to medicine. General surgery, you know tonsillectomies, appendectomies, that kind of stuff. Pretty sure bet that patients would survive. There was a real push for me to jump into trauma medicine, but no way was I going to get back into that. Oh, now and then I was called in to the ER when the shit hits the fan, mostly having to do with gang warfare—don't get me started on that."

After a slight pause, Ernie switched gears. "Any kids? Grandkids?"

"Two boys. Both married. No grandkids. You?"

"I had a son. Killed flying a Piper Cub into a bunch of trees. Can you believe that? It was the worst time in my life. I still think of Brad most everyday. He was a good kid. College degree, fiancée and all that. Anyway, my marriage died with it. So, no kids, no grandkids, no wife. It's just me, my housekeeper Mildred, and dog First Mate." Ernie swallowed hard and shook his head as if to dislodge his demons. We walked quietly back to the deck where he pointed to his Alerion. I read the boat's name printed in neat dark blue block letters on the white stern: LAMEKUF. I read it aloud pronouncing it *Lame-cuff.*

"No, no," Ernie said. "It's pronounced, *Lamb-eh-cuff*"

"What does it mean? Is it Swedish or something?"

"No, it's not Swedish. Pure American. Try reading it backwards," Ernie instructed. "Take your time."

I studied it for a bit then said out loud, "Fukemal." I let it sink in. "Do you mean fuck 'em all? Is that it, Ernie?"

Slapping my shoulder, Ernie laughed, "You got it, Charlie. Lima, Alpha, Mike, Echo, Kilo, Uniform, Foxtrot, that's what I named her. And believe me, it's worth every letter. That's the way I see it, Charlie. At our age it works for just about everything." Leaving no time for me to respond, Ernie abruptly switched gears again. "So you're really going to die out there?"

"Die where out there? Jesus, Ernie, I'm still trying to figure out how you came up with naming your boat like that. I mean, why?"

"You know, Charlie, when you get old and all that was gold fades into a cloudy distance; there is a pervasive sense that life is a journey of aloneness. When I left my doctoring career, there was the tried and true retirement party with all the congratulations and tokens that come with it. Retirement is not commencement. It's the end of something except perhaps for a few lucky ones that keep a hand in their work or find some great reward. After retiring, I lost contact with my former colleagues. Now, don't get me wrong, I don't blame them for not calling or coming by; rather, I came to understand that going to the hospital every day had become my life instead of my job. When I left the job, I left my life behind. So when I say fuckemall, what I'm really saying is I prefer to just be me. I no longer want or need to be a part of a herd."

"So there you go. Deal with it!" Abruptly changing the subject, Ernie swept his arm toward Long Island Sound, and asked again, "Are you going to die out there?"

"If you mean Long Island Sound, I sure hope not," I replied. "Maybe on the Atlantic somewhere. What about you?"

Ernie laughed heartedly, "I'm going to die playing with myself. I decided that the other day when I had a rare erection and, of course, used it. My chest tightened a bit and that's when I concluded that I would die whacking my carrot. You still pound the meat, Charlie?"

"Jesus, Ernie, what are we, in junior high school?"

Ernie looked at me like I had a screw loose. "Haven't you joined the fraternity, Charlie? I have exactly one friend left in the entire world. And my guess is you have less than that. So, here

I am offering some old man bullshit, maybe trying to capture some bit of yesteryear and you act like I'm some decrepit old bastard looking for a thrill. Well, I'm not, Charlie. The way you treated Commodore Idiot back there, I took you for a kindred spirit, an octogenarian that could still piss-write his name in the snow. Ever do that, Charlie, piss-write your name in the snow? Or am I getting too personal?"

Unlike my contemporaries back at Sunset, Ernie wasn't regaling me with times past. Ernie was in the present, spontaneous, more pubescent than octogenarian. His Boy wasn't crushed out of him, not like it has been for so many old men. Time for me to let go.

"You're damn right I piss-wrote," I said. "In upstate New York where I was raised, we had farms all over the place. One winter, I was piss writing in the snow. Ever piss on an electric fence, Ernie? Now that's something you don't forget."

Off we went telling dirty jokes, cursing, and carrying on like pumped-up prepubescent boys meeting behind a barn. We laughed, drank, and farted with abandon until we petered out just after midnight. Just before heading back to *That Good Night*, Ernie invited me to hang around to crew for the West Harbor Yacht Club Anniversary Race. "It's tomorrow," he commented, then added with a grin, "We'd make a hell of a pair."

I agreed. What was one more day?

WEDNESDAY, JULY 11

I'm not much of a racer. Years back, I crewed as a mainsail trimmer for races on Lake Ontario. Racing skippers are another breed entirely. If they have a lot of money, their boats are bedecked with every conceivable electronic gizmo on the market. They'll buy sails worth more than a modest house. Their wives seldom go with them. Racing sailors yell a lot. And as far as safety goes, they might as well have their crew walk a tight rope over alligator pits. After a few of those races, I promised myself never to go near those nutcases again. But, I have to admit, more often than not, they know how to handle a sailboat.

From what I had observed so far, Ernie would be more collected and respectful of crew, boat, and wind/water conditions. As it turned out, he was, except for one thing: he appeared to literally hate every other skipper out there.

It wasn't a matter of winning for Ernie; it was more a matter of belittling every other sailor. Ernie knew tactics like a navy admiral and used them to out maneuver his competitors. Like at the start of the race. Once we had the five minute warning, *Lamecuf* went into stealth mode, zipping among boats like an Australian sheep dog, herding the boats into an ever tightening pack; adhering to rules for racing sailboats becomes much more difficult in close quarters. Ernie enjoyed the mayhem he created.

Once the cannon roared to announce the start, Ernie held

back, letting his competitors crunch across the starting line. As the pack broke loose, old Ernie trimmed *Lamecuf's* sails and off we went on a journey of harassment. Ernie's favorite was to saunter up to a boat's stern, hang there a second then go windward around the boat, stealing his wind. And never did we go by a boat without Ernie saying something sarcastic and, at times, giving a one finger salute. At the end of it all, Ernie neither won nor did he ingratiate himself to any member of the club. It was enough for Ernie to let everyone know that he *could* have won the race if he had wanted to.

I shared crewing duties with a young fellow named Steve McIntyre. Steve ran the foredeck which essentially meant setting and managing the spinnaker. He was a good guy, nimble and very focused on his job. Steve, thirty-five years old, was a fireman with the West Harbor Fire Department. Ernie handled the helm, I trimmed the main and Steve did all the rest. I envied his agility; Steve just zipped and zagged around that foredeck like a cheetah chasing an antelope. I, on the other hand, had painful spasms in my neck from looking aloft to find the right sail trim. The three of us left the Yacht club right after dinner in time for Ernie to avoid the award ceremony. We took a slow walk back to Ernie's place, sat on the deck, drank beer, talked and waited for dusk and the annual yacht club fireworks. Steve bid adieu after the last boom. Ernie broke out a bottle of Sandeman Founders Reserve Port.

"I've been putting something off," Ernie said, pouring some of the garnet red liquid into my glass. "Yesterday, when I told you about naming my boat LAMEKUF, I didn't mention that after retiring, I kept an old couple on as patients. I've been doctoring Doris and Ivan Heller for over fifty years. Late last night, Doris called me to tell me that Ivan passed on."

"I'm sorry to hear that," I said. "Did he die at home?"

"He did. Nice way to go. In fact, he's still there. Doris called to ask me if I could arrange a burial at sea. Are you interested?"

"Wait, you mean to tell me that this old woman is staying in her house with her dead husband?"

"Damn it, Charlie. What's so wrong about that? I went over and took care of things. Now are you interested or not?

I wasn't certain what *interested* meant. "What do you have in mind?"

"Ivan was in the merchant marines. He lost a lot of friends in the war. Picking off Liberty ships was like shooting skeet to the U-Boat guys. Anyway, Ivan had a streak of guilt a mile wide. He was one of these guys who just couldn't understand why he was spared and his friends weren't. I guess he wants to join his friends."

"So, what do you mean by *interested?*"

"Your boat. We can't take *my boat*. Too small for a few overnights."

"Overnights?"

"What are you thinking, that we can bury the guy in Long Island Sound? We need to take the body out into the Atlantic."

"I assume that you've looked into this. And why not cremate the guy and scatter the ashes?"

"Ivan was very clear. He specifically said that he did not want to be cremated. He wants to join his buddies for a game of cards and Ivan didn't believe that ashes can play cards. And, yes, I have looked into burial at sea: At least three miles out in water no less than six-hundred feet deep. The closest spot is off Long Island Sound by thirty miles, so I'm guessing three overnights."

"And you want me to do this on my boat?"

"It's the perfect boat. Doris will come along. That makes three, four going out if we include Ivan."

"Whoa, Ernie. Slow down. Why Doris?"

"Why not," Ernie answered. "This is a funeral. She needs to have closure. For God's sake, Charlie."

"Ernie, you are a true pain in the ass."

What the hell. Go with the flow and yes, pun intended. That's what sailors should do. Anyway, I had no schedule to keep.

"Conditions," I declared. "First, his body must be prepared by an undertaker for an at-sea burial, weights and all. Second, he's got to be in a box and kept on deck. Third, the box must be padded on the outside so it doesn't scratch the deck. And last, you're in charge of Doris—I don't want to have to take care of a grieving widow."

"Agreed, except for one thing, the box. Ivan wants to go over the side like his buddies did."

"Look Ernie, what are we supposed to do, fling him overboard like tossing a kid in a swimming pool?"

"Maybe. Why not?"

"Because I don't want to. Simple as that. You solve the problem."

"How about we flip over the box. You know, just dump him overboard."

"How much does he weigh?"

"No more than eighty pounds—he was pretty far gone when he died. And when the mortician gets rid of the fluids, he'll be down to maybe seventy or so. Plus, don't forget the weight needed to take him to the bottom."

"We can do that from the stern platform. Did good old Ivan

express having a problem with being dumped off the stern?"I asked sarcastically.

"He never mentioned it. Sounds good to me. Can we leave tomorrow?" Ernie asked with the enthusiasm of a four year old about to get his way.

"Depends on the weather," I replied.

"I've already checked: Southwest wind 15 to 20; high pressure for the next four days."

"We need to take on stores."

"Mildred is making up meals for three days."

"Jesus, Ernie. You had this all planned out. Why didn't you bring this up yesterday?"

"Because you weren't ready."

"What does that mean?"

"C'mon, Charlie, let's just do this and enjoy ourselves. When Doris called, I was looking over at your glorious boat and thinking that Ivan deserves to go out in style."

"My boat looks like a Cadillac hearse?"

"Hell no. It's a magnificent sailing vessel that speaks of pride and love of the sea."

"Ernie, you are the biggest bull-shitter I've met since leaving Sunset."

"Sunset?"

"Forget it. Okay, I agree. We leave tomorrow at 0930 hours."

Acquiescing to Ernie's plea came rather easily. There are but few opportunities for old folks to find new friendships. So many of the old ones have disappeared either through death or illness or just moved on. Meeting Ernie was like a visit to the fountain of youth.

Sinking Ivan in six hundred feet meant that we had to sail

out to the Atlantic Canyon, which is off Long Island, a distance of about one hundred nautical miles from West Harbor. Given good winds, it would take fifteen to twenty hours to get there and an equal amount of time to get back. That meant night sailing, limited sleep time, and two-hour watches. We'd be flirting with the big boys, freighters that could mow us down without knowing it. Two tired old men and a ninety-two year old lady as frail as a dried leaf.

Our sail plan called for heading to Montauk, then bearing southwest until the depth sounder registered six-hundred feet. I noticed on the chart that the Canyon was filled with unexploded ordinance; I hoped Ivan wouldn't wind up cuddling up to an old torpedo for eternity.

THURSDAY, JULY 12 –

MONDAY, JULY 16

The mortician, a guy named Gene Lechtenheimer, showed up at eight the next morning. Foregoing the casket entirely, Ivan, wrapped like a mummy, was loaded onto the swim platform. Doris showed up a half hour later dressed in widow weeds complete with a black veil. She was mightily upset that Ivan wasn't going to share her berth and she put up quite a fuss until Ernie calmed her down. My regret meter was tilting toward red.

We departed on schedule. Under full sail with clear skies and fair winds, we made Montauk at 1345 hours and headed southwest for the Atlantic Canyon, a distance of about sixty nautical miles. I pinned the ETA at 0400 hours the next morning. Doris slept most of the way in the aft quarters which included a fully appointed head. Ernie took care of Doris like she was a princess. Curmudgeon that he was, his softer side overflowed with tenderness. The Atlantic, balmy winds with soft swells, turned *That Good Night* into a cradle; a few lullabies and I could have slept through the entire passage. As it was, Ernie and I set up a two-hour watch, so I did manage to get a few hours of sleep. Commercial traffic was light. We spotted one freighter but it was far enough off to pose any threat. It was a great sail under starry skies with one dramatic exception.

I had relieved Ernie for the 0100 watch. He went down below to check on Doris while I curled up to the helm. A few minutes later, Ernie was back in the cockpit.

"We have a slight problem," he said much too calmly.

"What now!"

"Doris," he responded quietly. "She's dead."

"Doris is dead?"

"Dead. Broken heart."

I sat dumbfounded. Where the hell was I, in the Twilight Zone? Was I Charon ferrying the dead? One on the swim platform, another down below. My gorgeous vessel was becoming a transport to the great beyond.

"We need to make a decision," Ernie said.

"My decision is that I screwed up making this trip in the first place."

"Let's not get carried away. Why don't we just bury Doris along with Ivan? Seems pretty simple to me."

"Simple," I protested. "What the hell is so simple about burying two bodies at sea? And how do we explain the disappearance of Doris? We get back to port and no Doris. Explain that to her family!"

"What's to explain? She died, we buried her. That's that. Happens all the time."

"All the time! Yeah, who cares if people go sailing and come back less one or two? The Coast Guard understands those kinds of things. Oh, they died and we dumped them overboard. 'Good for you,' they say. What, do you expect to get a medal for this? We could have murdered the old lady. Maybe you did. Or she could have fallen overboard. Look, I'm the captain of this boat and what happens on it, *everything* that happens on it, is my responsibility. Somebody's going to ask questions."

"Of course there'll be an inquest. We stand before a judge, tell him what happened, and that's that. No big deal other than keeping you around for a few more days."

"An inquest? Damn it Ernie, that mean the Coast Guard gets involved!"

"Maybe, maybe not. I've never been in this situation before. But on land, when someone dies, the court usually likes to know why. In this case, it's a ninety-two year old in ill health. They'll understand."

"Understand! You know what the Coast Guard will understand? They'll want to know how I allowed a sick old woman to get on my boat in the first place. They'll inspect the vessel, examine my ships papers, question my judgment, and now that they're a part of Homeland Security, probably lay a charge of espionage on me."

Ernie was as cool as could be. He placed his hand on my shoulder and said, "Take it easy, Charlie. Look, I've been taking care of Doris for fifty years. Her chart will show that her days were numbered. The lady's vitals were battling each other for any milliliter of oxygen they could get. You name it and it was in failure: kidneys, liver, heart, lungs. Something had to give."

"So what about family? I guess they'll just thank us for taking sick old Mom out for a nice sail so she could die at sea. Are you nuts?"

"Charlie, calm down. There is no family. No friends. No church. I'm it. I'm the executor of the estate. Everything goes to the Claremont Elementary School. There's nothing to worry about here."

"You knew this, didn't you? That Doris was going to kick

the bucket on this trip and you didn't tell me. Maybe *you* did a Kevorkian. Jesus, Ernie, you put my whole world right between a rock and a hard place. There are things that you don't know."

"Care to explain?"

We sat down in the cockpit facing each other. For the next half hour, I told Ernie about escaping Sunset, leasing the yacht. Being tracked by an investigator. That any inquiry was going to sink my plans like a stone in water. That I wished to God almighty that my anchor never found bottom in West Harbor. That he was an unmitigated prick that used me.

"Let me think," Ernie said, not buffeted at all by my tirade. He stood and left the cockpit to go forward. I watched him saunter along the darkened deck. None of this was any good. When people die, it's all about inquests, post mortems, wakes, funerals, caskets, burials, flowers, processions. When people died at Sunset, more people went to the funeral than ever came to the home to visit. The vessel of death overflows with guilt. When Lori died, people came out of the woodwork. Some I never met before. Where were they when she needed them? I was convinced that coming back without Doris would raise a storm of accusations. My days of sailing bliss were in great jeopardy.

That Good Night sliced through the dark, leaving a hissing sound in its wake. The chart plotter's updated ETA had us arriving at the Atlantic Canyon at 0338 hours, an hour and a half to go. Ernie came back to the cockpit. "You want some coffee?" he asked. I nodded. He went below and soon returned with two steaming mugs.

"Sorry about all this," he said. "I promise that I didn't plan Doris's demise. I guess I should have left her back in town."

"Yeah, that would have been good," I said.

"But Charlie, what would have happened to her? I mean, let's get real here. She'd have been like those folks in the nursing home you left behind. I've known these two for a lot of years and to tell you the truth, while I'm sorry about all the crap this lays on your shoulders, I'm glad she'll be joining Ivan. They had been married for sixty-three years. Except for Ivan's wartime service, they were apart for maybe ten minutes. Joined at the hip is an apt description. They ran a candy shop in West Harbor where they lived above the store. No children, no family, no relatives. They shut down the store only after Ivan could no longer make it down the steps to open up. You know what Doris's last words were?"

I shook my head.

"She asked me if she could kiss Ivan goodnight. To put your mind at ease, Doris just died. I didn't do anything to hasten it and I didn't get in the way. She just died."

The depth meter stopped registering after five-hundred feet. We had reached the Atlantic Canyon. Thankfully, with the exception of a gentle swell, the sea was calm. Doris couldn't have weighed more than eighty pounds. We wrapped a bed sheet around her clothed body then spiral bound the sheet with a good length of line. I on one end and Ernie on the other, we struggled getting Doris up the companionway steps. Still pliable, she was nearly bent in half by the time we got her to the cockpit. From there, it was a matter of dragging the poor woman up onto the aft deck. It was my job to jump down onto the swim platform where Ivan was secured. We slid Doris off the aft deck, plopping her down next to Ivan.

"How about some weight, otherwise won't she just float?" I asked.

"Good point" Ernie responded. "Have any old chain on board?"

"No, I do not. I do have about forty feet of chain on my lunch hook. Never been used."

"That'll have to do," Ernie said. "I hope you don't mind."

"No choice, Ernie. It's just chain."

After busying ourselves for a half hour unshackling the chain from the small anchor and wrapping it tightly around Doris, she was ready to join Ivan for burial.

Bowing our heads, Ernie mumbled something under his breath that I couldn't understand except for the words *commit* and *deep*. With that we rolled both bodies off the platform into the sea where they disappeared forever.

The sail back to West Harbor was quiet and uneventful. On watch, I sat thinking about how death visits us all. When you're young, it's weddings and baptisms and birthday parties, anniversaries and celebrating the Red Sox or whatever team strikes your fancy. With age, it's wakes, funerals, and burials. Before Lori died, we had been to quite a few. Same old, same old: little kids darting around with death so remote that they couldn't care less. Grieving family members sniffling, wiping tears. Old people thinking about how it's going to be for them. Lori and I had planned our funerals down to the last detail. We laughed at how similar it was to planning our wedding. What to wear, selecting the pallbearers, the words to engrave on the tombstone, whether cremation was an option. Sometime during our sixties, we bought a double plot in Quiet Hills Cemetery, plopping down a good bit of money for perpetual care. Isn't that foolish? Making sure that our grave site would have its grass manicured, flowers on Memorial Day. We also paid a good chunk of money for a hunk of granite engraved by some machine. Crazy, huh? Lori didn't think so and God bless her soul, there she is today, resting peacefully in a dark box six feet underground. Her particulars are engraved on the left side of the stone: birth and death dates, as if what happened between those years were as common as dust. Is it that everyone in our overloaded cemeteries has essentially lived the same life over and over again? On my and Lori's stone, the right side has my name, my birth date and an empty space for the death date. So, what do I do with that? Maybe have them engrave *lost at sea*. I think not. Perhaps *went off to sea*. Maybe mention that I liked Bach or was a nut about baking the perfect molasses cookie. I'm sure as hell not going to make my way back to Northern New York to die. And I can't just die alone drifting around the Atlantic on a ghost ship, Ernie's right about that. A bit of a quandary.

As Ernie had suggested, the inquest was five minutes of reaffirming the death certificate, accepting Ernie as the executor. Case closed. The Coast Guard never entered the picture.

Leaving the courthouse, I asked Ernie "Why the Claremont Elementary School?"

"That's where they met," he answered. "Ivan and Doris fell in love in the fifth grade."

TUESDAY, JULY 17

I left West Harbor at 0430 just as eastern light was cutting through the fading night. Ernie and I had said our goodbyes the night before, after dinner—a sumptuous meal of roasted pork served with some chocolate sauce conjured up by Mildred. She said it was a secret recipe but admitted to hot sauce, maple syrup, and cinnamon as being a part of the ingredients. She gave me a cup of it to take on board. I never made a roast in my life and doubted that I would be using her wonderful sauce, but I couldn't refuse.

My plan was to get to Maine as soon as possible with a stopover in Boston. I figured that three easy days of good sailing would get me from West Harbor into Boston Harbor where I would spend a few days enjoying one of my favorite cities.

From West Harbor, my first stop on my cruise to Boston was Point Judith, a harbor of refuge located on the southern tip of Rhode Island. It was a rather miserable forgotten place, with deteriorating breakwaters and scenery that would make a moonscape look inviting. Just after setting the anchor, I heard a persistent ding-a-ling sound coming from somewhere down below. My heart pounded. Engine alarm? I checked the engine gauges. Dammit, I didn't even have the engine on. Shallow water alarm? Depth meter read seventeen feet. High water in the bilge alarm? I left the cockpit to go below, certain that I was going to step into a foot of water in the cabin. Bilge was dry as a bone. The alarm stopped. I checked for a propane leak, nope. Bewildered, I went back up to the cockpit.

Ding.

I wasn't even sure if I heard it.

Ding.

The damn thing, whatever it was, reminded me of some gadget that Mike Peterson had hung around his neck back in Sunset. I think it was some kind of pump that shot stuff into his bloodstream to keep him half alive. But poor old Mike wasn't on board. I was half way down the companionway when it I heard it again. I went below and stood on the cabin sole and waited. Aha! Whatever it was, it was coming from the forward stateroom. I moved forward.

When it dinged again, I narrowed it down to my bedside table where sat a carbon dioxide alarm with the screen blinking, *low battery.* I pulled out the dead batteries and stuck the gadget into my bedside table drawer, promising to get to it later. My eye caught my cell phone that I had turned off after the *Little Turnip* call. I flicked it on. It beeped once. A message on the screen read: Message.

What the hell ever happened to phones that rang? I had a a bunch of messages, all from Baxter with the same message: *Call me back ASAP.* I went topsides and hit *Send.*

"Not good news," Baxter said right off. "I've been trying to get you since you left."

I explained that I had turned the phone off.

Baxter went on to tell me about the insurance investigator's visit. "He's an idiot, Charlie. But this guy is dangerous. I tossed him out of my office, I mean literally tossed him like throwing

out the trash. I didn't tell him a thing. Remember Evan and Carol, your dock mates? Well, he tried them, too. They gave him nothing but a brush-off. But before telling them to go to hell, he yelled to them that he was going to Maine. That he didn't need their or anyone else's cooperation. He's a nutcase Charlie, and I would be very wary if I were you."

I took a moment to think, and then said, "I understand. Thanks for the heads-up."

"Where are you now?" Baxter asked.

"Am I in the clear to talk or is that prick still around?"

"He's gone and I told my security folks to nail him if gets near my place again."

"Maybe the less you know the better. Let's just say I'm on the water and having a hell of a time. Now, Baxter, go back to selling yachts and forget about this idiot. I owe you one and don't doubt for a minute that I'll be popping in on my way south. And thanks again for making it all work out."

I hung up and called Bob to give him the latest news.

"Like I said before, let him come. It might even be fun," he said without a hitch.

"Fun? What fun?" I asked Bob.

"I'll tell you when you get here. Where are you, anyway?"

I told Bob that I was heading for Boston by way of Point Judith and Sandwich.

"Point Judith? With all the great places on the North Shore why Point Judith? Didn't we stop there years ago? Run down place as I remember it."

"Nostalgia," I answered. "I have good memories of the place. Lori and I stopped there back too many years to count."

"Your call, but Newport's right around the corner. Sailors'

paradise with a bar on every corner."

"I'll give it some thought. Maybe for Emma."

"Who?"

"Emma," I repeated. "Didn't I tell you about her? The lady from back at Sunset?"

"If you did, I don't remember. Doesn't matter. Listen, with this guy on our trail, why don't you lay over in Boston until I deal with him."

"What are you going to do with him?"

"Just let me deal with it. I'll give you a call with the all-clear."

I decided to go along with whatever Bob had in mind. He was nuts in many ways, and I worried about what he might do, but I would have bet my life on it that he wasn't a killer.

I changed the subject. "How's the woodpile coming along?"

"I'll show you when you get here. Remember, don't come until I call."

WEDNESDAY, JULY 18

I stayed in Point Judith last night. Taking Bob's advice, I pulled anchor and headed to Newport, about ten nautical miles northwest. Taking advantage of a light breeze, I motor-sailed, flying the jib on a starboard tack. After securing the boat to a rental mooring, I called for a motor launch and headed to shore. The place was teeming with tourists. Whirly jigs, flags, discreet flashing lights (after all, this was Newport!), and hawkers in costumes added to a festive climate of capitalism at its best. I watched kids getting what they wanted from parents aiming to please, young couples walking arm in arm, retirees nestled together on any number of benches thoughtfully placed along the sidewalk. Amidst all this flurry of families on vacation and people enjoying each other, I had a stab of loneliness that I hadn't felt since the day Lori died. *What the hell am I doing here?*

I felt old. I was old. Maybe too old. How does one escape their life? Go sailing. Alone. At eighty-four years old? I walked over to an empty bench that looked out over the harbor. I have had these stabs before when I was on the road looking for business. I tried flying first class; buying attention was what it was. It didn't work. I can see why escort services are so popular, though I never used one. Here I was in vacationers' paradise with people all around and I didn't feel a part of any of it. I was less lonely sailing with me, myself, and I. I looked out over the harbor. It took a while for me to recognize *That Good Night* amidst hundreds of boats. My spirits gladdened. She might be fiberglass, cloth, and wood, but she was where I rested my soul. I had an urge to get back, but resisted it in favor of taking a good long walk. What a great privilege it is to take a walk. Ultimate freedom. That's what a walk is. Go where you want, at whatever speed, to anywhere or nowhere at all.

I missed Lori, feeling her warmth next to me. Hugging. Cuddling. There's this song from a show that Lori and I went to years back called "The Golden Apple." A musical based on the Iliad and the Odyssey, if you can believe it. We used to sing it duet style, like Ulysses and Penelope did in the show:

It's the going home together when your work is thru,
Someone asks you "howde" do and how'd it go today?
It's the knowing someone's there when you climb up the stair,
Who always seems to know all the things you're going to say.

Feeling wanted. Loved. If you've got that, you've got the world. Emma kept that feeling and that kept Emma alive. Her thoughts of Damon were not vague. For her, Damon was right there, everyday. Her thoughts of him gave her an aura. Every day she was on that lip-smacking voyage with her lover. And wore those earrings every June to memorialize the journey of body and mind. Emma spoke of nothing else, as if the rest of her life meant nothing. I wonder if she ever married Damon or had his children.

I wondered, too, that if I had a brain rewired like Emma's what it would be that played on my tape loop. All I could come up with is one terrible storm I had sailed through, or more accurately, how I felt pulling into a safe harbor. And I was alone through all of that. What the hell does that say about my life? I have to rethink this whole nostalgia-laden memory thing of my sailing alone while my family stayed shore side. Hell, I never even took my kids. Was sailing back then an escape from my real life —which actually wasn't all that bad? Before sailing, before kids, I was simply a machinist working on lathes and millers, precision machining steel to make prototypes for tool makers or some inventor. They were wonderful days. The smell of a machine shop sticks in my mind. Whenever I smell fat burning, I think of standing in front of a lathe watching lazy streams of smoke coming from lubricated steel. Can't imagine my endless tape loop being the daily grind of running a machine shop.

When I bought the machine shop from an old Dane named Gersten Myers, I had pictured myself working with a team of machinists, opening the shop at eight, closing at five. It didn't work out that way. As the owner, it was up to me to drum up enough business to keep things going. Of course during the war years—Korea and then Vietnam—business came to me. But after the war, competition was like weeds in a flower garden. I was away most of the time. Alone except for meetings with potential clients. I'd hit the road Sunday night, returning on Thursday with a bunch of orders, repeating that whirlwind week after week just to stay ahead of the curve. Not like Ivan and Doris and their beloved candy store.

I don't miss Sunset, but I do miss having people around who knew my name, although I must admit that it boiled down to a precious few. Some of the Sunset's more vacuous clients assigned names to people rather than try to remember them. For instance, in the eyes of Samuel Guttman, I was his son Isaac. I played along. I wasn't the only one lonely. We all were. The anticipation of visiting day helped to ameliorate loneliness. But when the day ended, loneliness came back with a vengeance.

I caught myself wallowing in self-pity, the precursor of depression. Why not just enjoy all the folderol around me instead of looking backward? Past is something we can't change so why live in it? I got up off that bench and joined the crowd. I smiled at people and they smiled back. My step quickened when I caught sight of an ice cream shop. A double dip of cherry vanilla and I was on my way, licking the glorious dripping of cream, dabbing a blob from my nose, as happy as a kid at a carnival. On the way back to the boat, I stopped in a toy store and bought a stuffed bear about the size of a small dog. The nose-studded teenaged clerk asked, "Is this, like, for one of your grandkids?"

I replied, "Actually, it's for me. I don't think that you can ever be too old to have a stuffie."

"I'll have to remember that," she said. "Have a nice day."

THURSDAY, JULY 19

I cast off the mooring at 0900 hours, heading for Cuttyhunk, the westernmost island of the Elizabeth Chain. The prevailing southwest wind at 15-plus knots didn't disappoint. Set to a broad reach and pulling on all sails, *That Good Night* moved along at a steady eight knots. The sea conditions were a bit choppy but that only added to the joy of feeling this yacht perform at its best. We sailors call it *having a bone in our teeth*.

I made Cuttyhunk Island before noon. I could have kept going, but Cuttyhunk has always been close to my heart and I'd be damned if I would pass it by. I anchored outside the harbor to avoid another crowded mooring field, using my dinghy to visit the island for lunch and a good walk around. When I returned to the boat, there was another boat anchored nearby. A young woman was sitting on the foredeck busily talking on a cell phone. I caught her saying, "I did it. I did it all by myself. My first solo voyage. Anchoring and everything."

I returned the dinghy to its davits and sat back in the cockpit with one of the books I had purchased in Annapolis, Robert Olmsted's *A Coal Black Horse*. I started reading it back in Henlopen Harbor and was more than halfway through. It was a remarkable novel set in the time of the Civil War. I looked up to see the young woman looking over my way. I waved. She waved back.

"Nice day," I said.

She answered, "It is, quite remarkable."

"What makes it remarkable?" I asked, wanting the conversation to grow.

"Oh," she said, "it just is. I solo sailed all the way from the Sakonnet River."

"Congratulations," I replied.

"My husband encouraged me to go off on my own," She said proudly.

"Good man," I said, giving thumbs up.

"Yes, he is," she said. A slight wind shift caused our boats to drift apart. "Have a good one," she said. I waved a goodbye.

A sailor's vignette. Actually, I had hoped to invite her over for dinner and some conversation, but decided that her solo sailing deserved a solo celebration.

FRIDAY, JULY 20

It's only been less than a month since I escaped Sunset and here I am leaving at sunrise, heading northeast through Buzzard Bay. How about a Sunrise Day Care Center as part of a Sunset Home. Why not?

Weather cooperated once again with steady winds out of the southwest. *That Good Night* could do well in eighteen to twenty knots without reefing, but as the wind piped up, I took in the jib, set the staysail and furled some main. I'm not into fighting with the wind. Whenever I did that I lost. Like the time I was hit broadside with a gust falling off the Palisades. I was heading north on the Hudson River, just south of the George Washington Bridge when I was slammed. If it wasn't for the lifeline encircling the cockpit, I'd have been pitched into the water, never to be seen again. As it turned out, my tiny boat and I survived. Lesson learned.

Entering the Cape Cod Canal, I was required to drop sail; motoring only is the rule for the canal. Cruising along at five knots I watched cyclists and folks walking along the path that ran the length of the canal. Here it was unfolding before me, the simple joy of doing simple things. As I see it, that's the essence of life. I watched people watching me.

Exiting the Canal I tied up at Sandwich Marina, a rather crowded nondescript harbor on the east end of the canal. I arrived at 1500 hours, went below, and took a long nap with Agatha, the name I had chosen for my stuffy. After my nap, I spent time with navigation. My plan was to head north to Boston, stay a few days then beeline it for Bob's place in Maine. I called Constitution Marina for reservations. The weather forecast was calling for deteriorating conditions with a cold front on the way. I'd like to make Boston before that. Enjoy some city comforts.

SATURDAY, JULY 21

The storm hit on my approach to Boston harbor. With darkening skies in the distance, I had already furled the jib and dropped the main. Torrential wind-driven rain cut visibility to near zero. Lightning bolts crackled and boomed. Bow to the wind, I throttled back with enough steerage to maintain position; entering this busy harbor in the midst of a storm would be shear madness. Buffeted by wind and slapped by water, *That Good Night* took it all in stride as the thunderstorm swept eastward leaving the delicious scent of cool fresh clean air. I throttled up and entered the harbor.

To my right, busy Logan International airport. To my left, a dramatic view of Boston's skyline. Water taxis zipping about. An outbound tug-escorted tanker lumbers by. Small recreational boats dart about. Our country's history glides beneath my keel.

At the far end of the harbor, I swung north and entered Constitution Marina. I was fortunate to get assigned to one of the last remaining slips which was located deep in the marina. It took a bit of maneuvering and some help from eager docking boys to get *That Good Night* tied up. My stern was sticking out three or more feet beyond the dock with just enough under my keel not to ground out. Old Ironsides, which was berthed next door to the marina, presented a stunning scene with her rigging back-dropped against a darkening sky. Maybe I could get tickets for a Red Sox game or whatever, but for now, I'm staying put. It's been a long day.

TUESDAY, JULY 24

I'm in Portsmouth, New Hampshire tied up to the town dock. I spent three days in Boston and took no time to keep up my writing. Actually, my three days was a lifetime. I am renewed. My soul is at peace. My head is lofty. My body is no longer eighty-four years old. I'm young at heart. The world is beautiful. You guessed: I met a wonderful woman. That's all I can report because I simply am not poetic enough to capture or convey what occurred. If you've ever been in love then you know what I'm talking about. If not, no words will attach themselves to what it's like.

I'll take time today to refresh my stores and refresh my water supply. Plenty of diesel fuel, so I'll not worry about that.

ABIGAIL'S INTERRUPTION

This is Abigail writing. Pardon my interruption, but Charlie's account of his time in Boston needs some explanation. I can understand his being awestruck by the entire episode because I'm feeling quite the same way. But perhaps his reticence is a bit unfair to you, the reader. What occurred in Boston is a slice of life that needs to be told. And so, I'll give it my best shot to describe what Charlie and I experienced.

I was on a photo assignment for the National Geographic trying to capture the comings and goings at Constitutional Marina, a recreational boat basin just south of the berth of the famous ship Constitution. *My objective for one of the shots was to place a ghostly image of Old Ironsides as backdrop for a stealthy French racer that was tied up at the marina. I had arrived at the marina just before dawn, hoping to capture the shot using first light to accentuate the silhouette of this famous Revolutionary War vessel. I had perched myself on the edge of a wobbly finger dock, snapped the photo, lost my balance, and wound up chest deep in water and ankle deep in mud. Luckily, with my right arm stretched high above my head, I saved my freakishly expensive camera. The bad news was I was stuck there. One false move and it was good-bye to my Hasselblad HeDII-50. That's when I met Charlie or better put, Charlie met me.*

"Don't move," a stern, gravelly commanding voice came from somewhere behind me. I couldn't turn around without losing my

balance. "I'll get you out of there. It'll just take a moment." I heard some grunting. "I'm getting my dinghy," the voice said. More grunting followed. "I just have to lower the damn thing, you just be patient." Of course, I had no choice other than to be patient and to trust that the spasms in my arm muscles would disappear before assigning my camera to a watery demise. To ease the strain, I fixed my index finger on the exposure button and, twisting my aching arm, took a series of random shots. I heard some soft splashing which I took to be oars. And then, there he was peering over the side of a bulky inflatable boat.

What hit me immediately were clear blue, spirited eyes; they will stay with me for the rest of my life. I lowered my arm slightly, handing my camera to Charlie. He took it as one might take a child. "Nice camera," he said, laying it gingerly on top of a life preserver in the dinghy's bow. Charlie said, "I think it would be easier if we walk you over to my boat and get you out from there."

"Thank you, sir," I responded, "but it would be easier if I just swam. Which is your boat?"

Charlie pointed to a high transom two docks down. "That Good Night," he said.

I reached the transom platform just as Charlie pulled up. He instructed me to hang on while he tied up the dinghy and got onboard which, with camera in hand, he did with practiced ease. After stowing my camera in the cockpit, Charlie returned to the transom platform to help me on board. As I struggled to climb a small ladder attached to the swim platform, his fingers wrapped around my wrists like vises and with a fast move, he had me on the swim platform in a snap. I weigh one-hundred-thirty pounds which, to Charlie, apparently seemed like nothing at all. Of course, I was soaking wet, embarrassingly so with a clinging T-shirt and *a translucent linen skirt. Once safely in the cockpit, Charlie disappeared down below, returning with a large thick terry towel—oh, for the time of gallantry. He suggested we go down below, offering me a warm shower, a cup of hot coffee and breakfast. "How do you take your eggs?" he asked.*

I'd been on a sailboat only once, thanks to a college boyfriend who thought sailing was the most wonderful thing after fraternity parties. I, on the other hand, felt like I was in prison with thoughts of drowning. But being in Charlie's boat was far from being in a prison. Coming aboard was like entering a different world, an elegant world with pricey woods, brilliant chrome and soft upholstery.

The shower, located in the captain's cabin, was full sized. I couldn't understand where all the hot water was coming from, but come it did and within minutes, Boston harbor grime swirled down the drain. As I was toweling off, I heard Charlie call out, "Use the robe, we need to wash your clothes." Wrapped in plush terry cloth, I left the captain's cabin, taking a few steps into the main salon. The table was neatly set with a pot of coffee, orange juice, china plates, solid flatware and colorful place mats. Charlie was at the stove, fussing. A destroyed egg was on the floor, another on the counter. "I keep breaking the yokes," Charlie declared. I eased up to his side and gently took over.

"Let me," I said. "You get the flour, I'll do the eggs." Charlie handed me the spatula.

"I can do scrambled, but sunny side up doesn't work with broken yokes. Damn eggs," Charlie said, grabbing a towel.

"Cabin sole," he said while bending to kneel and clean up the mess. "It's the cabin sole," he grunted, "not the floor."

We ate eggs, bacon, and toast. Drank cold orange juice and steaming coffee. Charlie answered my questions about sailing with a nomenclature that included halyards, sheets, mast and boom, self-tailing jib, port and starboard, aft, and a whole lot of stuff dealing with navigation. I talked about my work in photography, my degree in women's studies, to which Charlie laughed and said he'd been studying that for years and should have earned his PhD by now. I asked Charlie if his crew was off somewhere.

"No crew. I guess that surprises you, an old man alone on a boat?"

"Hemingway would've understood," I said.

"Maybe he would. But I don't plan to fish. Never did. I guess I just like to go places by boat. Everything looks different, more romantic than arriving by car."

Charlie went on for some time talking about his sailing adventures. He told me that he was on his last sail, but never mentioned, as you have read, about being in a nursing home and how he escaped and all that. To me, Charlie was a sailor whose life was full of romance and challenges. He was the kind of man I dreamed of meeting. Adventurous, full of moxie. I guessed his age to be mid to late seventies—isn't that today's sixties? I'm forty-three and sometimes I feel like I'm ninety. I didn't dare ask Charlie his age, so, when I read in his journal that he was eighty-four, I was really surprised. But pleasantly so. I mean how many women my age can claim to have had a wonderful and quite memorable romance with a man nearly twice her age?

It may be a bit shocking to some. But here was a sensitive, intelligent, witty man, strong in stature, eyes of crystal blue, tough but gentle hands, caring and, well...How can I put it other than I fell in love with Charlie? I just did. It's not all that complicated and maybe if we would have been together more than three days, things would have fallen apart. As it was, we enjoyed Boston, we counted stars through the hatch while lying on his bed, and we ate great meals— some on board, with me doing the cooking of course, and some on land. We drank wine and on our last night together, Charlie uncorked a great bottle of champagne. I must admit that I'm a little surprised that he didn't reveal his age or about his going through the ordeal of living in a nursing home. But I understand why he held back on that stuff. Knowing Charlie, he probably stuck that stuff back in his psyche; I mean, why carry that weight around when life can be so light and airy?

Could I imagine spending the rest of my life with Charlie, or should I say the rest of his? I'll give that a probability. I would have sailed off with him in a heartbeat, but he never extended the invitation.

PRIVATE INVESTIGATOR

Adapted from the digital recorder of Private Investigator, Justin Roberts recorded July 24, 2138 hours.

I'm catching up with my notes after having had to run home to see after the wife, who came down with some kind of nasty bug. I hate interrupting an investigation, especially when things get hot. And the insurance company wasn't happy either. To make matters worse, whatever infected the little woman got me, too. I arrived in Maine on the Wednesday night, July 20ᵗʰ, staying overnight at the Day's Inn in Portland.

This Bob Liscome guy lives on Bickles Island in Casco Bay. Finding the place was first on the list. Whenever I asked the locals for the location all I got was another question: "Why?" I tried looking at a chart, but there's no Bickles Island that I can see. There are so many damn islands in Casco Bay, it'd take a month of Sundays to check them all.

Next on the agenda was finding a charter to get me to Liscome's island. Tour boats are all over the place, each loaded with slack-jawed tourists dangling digital devices like they were jewelry. The answer was the same everywhere: "It's against regulations to disembark passengers on any of the islands."

I was directed more than once to visit Sebasco Lodge. "They might be able to help."

Now, it's not like there's a straight line along this coast; it zigzags around like a cornfield maze. Half my day was spent finding a bridge to cross the Meadow River to get to the damn lodge. When I got there, I was directed me to Sheila's Lobster Pound, which required me to backtrack about twenty miles on snaky roads. As it turned out it was worth it. Bill Ducksworth, a local lobsterman was willing to take me out to Liscome's place. "Two hundred fifty dollars should do it," he said, poker faced as a guy holding a royal flush.

"A bit much, isn't it?"

"You could always swim; tide turns in about three hours. Float you right out there. I'll even lend you a float if you want."

I peeled off two-fifty in bills.

"Welcome aboard. This here's Sonny," he said, directing attention to a scruffy looking lad dressed in yellow slickers. "Sonny's my first mate."

I had never been on a lobster boat before. Truth is the smallest boat I was ever on was a cruise ship for an overnight from Fort Lauderdale to Nassau. I puked most of the way and the seas were calm. "I get a little seasick," I warned Ducksworth.

"Pick whatever is leeward and let her go is the best I can do about that."

"What the hell is leeward?"

Ducksworth looked at me like I had the mind of a two year old. "Away from the wind. Got it?"

My visit to leeward began about a mile from the dock. Ducksworth had the boat's engine roaring like a jet fighter. Spray came at me like bullets. Yeah, I've heard all the tales about the striking beauty of Maine's coast, but all I got to see was my puke hitting the white foam spraying off the hull. Mate Sonny took pity on me. He came out on deck and handed me a weathered rain slicker. "Might want to put this on," he suggested, and then helped *me into the thing. It felt like I was being wrapped in oil cloth.*

It took a lot longer than I thought it should for us to get to Bickles Island which I understand to be no more than two miles from the mainland. But hell, I was in no shape to judge—heaving your guts out has a way of altering time. Ducksworth landed at a pier that was one good stiff fart away from collapsing. "Hop out," he commanded. "Don't have all day."

"How about getting back?" I asked, stepping cautiously onto the weathered dock.

"Bob's got a boat, ask him. Shouldn't take much." With that, Ducksworth backed away from the dock. "Keep the rain gear," he yelled over the growling engine. "Might need it."

I stood on the rickety dock waiting for my knees to stop banging into each other. The dock was more like some sinister catwalk designed for a carnival funhouse. A number of planks were missing and those that were still in place looked like rot had got the best of them. I figured that I was about twenty feet from land. The spot where I was standing was about three feet above the water which, at this point, looked about a foot deep. I took a few steps before the whole damned thing slowly tilted to left, dumping me into clear, cold Maine water. The depth of clear water is deceiving. Cold water was now hugging my waist. I waded ashore or maybe I should say dog-paddled to shore after losing an argument with slippery round rocks that covered the bottom. I was soaked, cold, and mad as a son-of-a-bitch. Adding insult to injury, my favorite Allan Edmond wingtips were ruined. I was beginning to think that this Bob character was some kind of nut case living out here. And I was even crazier looking for him. But as I discovered in due time, Bob didn't live out here. Nobody did. I'd been had.

In my heyday, none of this would have happened. First of all,

I'd be on the trail of some saboteur or organized crime boss or drug lord, not some old wacko who escaped from a nursing home. I must be getting old myself to be snookered by all this crap. It's downright disheartening. I took this job from the insurance company not because I needed the money; the government sees to that. What I need is to continue using my skills. Once FBI, always FBI.

The island has a few bare trees, some scrub brush and raucous rookery of skinny-necked black birds complete with a carpet of their stinking droppings. It took me less than a half hour to slosh around the place. The sun helped keep the shivers in check.

The place appeared to be solid rock with a dusting of top soil. I made my way up to the highest point to get a view and that's when I discovered a ramshackle hut that looked even less stable than the dock. Inside, there was a cardboard box with a note attached. It read:

Investigator From Away, welcome to the rock. Here's some provisions, water and a nice blanket to keep you warm and some matches for a fire. Some good eats. We won't let you die out here.

The note was signed: Maine Welcome Committee.

I spent three god-awful days and nights on that island before I was able to hail a passing motorboat, folks on vacation from Massachusetts. Nice folks with a furry white dog that barked incessantly. They thought it was cool that I had roughed it on such a demanding campsite. Seasickness came on almost immediately with no warning. Back to hanging over the side.

I thought about bringing the police into the matter of finding Lambert, but where would that get me? I decided to rent a boat and do it myself. It may seem odd for a seasoned FBI agent that frequently went up against almost impossible odds nailing murderers, bank robbers, and other slime of the world—but the idea of getting on another boat and driving it myself had me as nervous as I've ever been.

I found my car sitting just where I left it. I called AAA to come out and tow me to a nearby garage to replace the two slashed tires, after which I grabbed a motel room, showered and shaved, slept for eight hours, woke with a headache and an empty stomach, had a meal and went shopping. First on the list was buying two cell phones, one of which I secreted in a pouch in the small of my back—a little more comfortable than the Glock I used to carry. My second stop was a Rite Aid for a chat with the pharmacist. When I mentioned seasickness, she smiled and went on to tell me not to be ashamed, that it is quite normal, that it had to do with the inner ear, that I should look at the horizon—yeah, try that when you're puking overboard—and that she was going to get me all fixed up. I left the store with Dramamine, a wrist thing that's supposed to stop the madness, some ginger candy, and a quart of Gatorade just in case, as the pharmacist said, I lose too much fluid.

My next stop was an EMS store where I bought a pair of sturdy boat shoes, two pair of shorts, a sun hat, a compass, a quart water bottle, sunscreen, Deep Woods Off, and after trying on a few backpacks, one that was comfortable and big enough to carry all my stuff. I spent the night back at the Day's Inn.

WEDNESDAY, JULY 25

Portsmouth is a laid-back city with good restaurants and lots of goings-on. I was berthed at the city dock which was directly across from the Navy Yard, a busy place with bustling cranes and enough Homeland Security personnel to ward off even a hint of disturbance. The Piscataqua River rushes through the place with enough current to bury the buoys. To protect *That Good Night's* hull, I had laid out every fender I had on board. The experience of Boston and Abigail had me renewed, but for the moment, twice as lonely. I talked earlier about building new memories, that old folks rely too much on the past because there isn't a lot of future. At Sunset, there was really nothing to build memories on; the patchwork quilt was already sewn. Too much *used to*. Meeting Abigail added another patch to my growing quilt. I had left room for a lot more.

With just a day away from Bob's place, Portsmouth put me in position to get to his place with relaxed sailing or motoring if needed. I haven't heard another word about the insurance investigator. Maybe he gave up. I spent the day onboard reading and listening to music. Just after a great seafood dinner at Jumpin' Jay's Fish Café, Bob called.

"Coast is clear. Where are you?"

"What do you mean by *clear*?"

"Just come. I'll tell you about it all later. So, where are you?"

"Portsmouth," I answered. "I have your place on the plotter."

"What's your ETA?"

"Can't say but it looks like maybe five hours or so. I haven't plotted a course yet. I can't leave Portsmouth until an hour or so before ebb and I haven't checked the tables yet."

"Well, call me when you get closer. I won't be leaving the island any time soon." Bob hung up.

THURSDAY, JULY 26

I called Bob at 1512 hours. "Where are you?" he asked.

"Just past Portland," I answered. "I should be at your place in an hour or so."

Bob said, "Maybe as the crow flies. Better add about a half-hour for the twists and turns. Give these islands some room; lot of outcroppings out there." He added, "Be waiting. See ya."

"Hey, wait." I yelled into the phone.

"What?"

"My boat's forty-six feet. I draw five feet. You have room?"

"To spare." The phone went dead.

With islands sprinkled like snowflakes on a bare lawn, navigating through Casco Bay requires serious diligence. The chart plotter gave me Bob's location but I hadn't entered a route in the electronic wonder. I guess I was too excited to take the time before departing. I had taken the time to prepare for docking which meant attaching the fenders and laying out the docking lines. Anyway, I'm of the old school of following a paper chart. It's more fun and gives much more perspective on surroundings. I started the engine and dropped the sails. Beating a zigzag course around a bunch of close-knit islands with uncertain wind and a flood tide was not my idea of fun, at least at my age. There was a time when the challenge would have been normal procedure, but not now. Besides, I was pretty anxious to get to

Bob's place, so motoring it was.

Actually, Bob's suggestion to add a half-hour to the EPA was only off by ten minutes. As I approached his dock, there he was, waving a welcome like there was no tomorrow. He gave me a circling motion indicating that I should approach the dock starboard to. Once I turned, current grabbed the bow. I backed the throttle to dead ahead. I left the helm, readied the docking lines, kicked over the fenders that I had previously lashed to the guard rails and was back in the cockpit in no time flat. With a few bursts of the thrusters, I eased *That Good Night* dockside. I handed the breast line to Bob, who quickly chocked it down. As I slid down to his dock, I retrieved the stern line while Bob went forward to grab the bow line which I had coiled along the life line. With a few turns around the chocks, *That Good Night* was fast and secure. This was all done without a word. Like old times—there is nothing a sailor likes more than to work in sync with a knowing mate.

"So, you went for the bigger one, huh? Hell of a boat," he added before walking along her length tapping the hull and caressing the toe rail. "Thirty-amp okay?" he asked.

"Yup," I answered, stealing Bob's answer for nearly everything

I jumped back on board, killed the engine, went below and flicked off a few electronics and reappeared to see Bob holding a sturdy electrical cord. "This ought to fit. Where's the onshore hook-up?" I directed him aft. Once plugged in, I went below and flicked a few more switches to tie in the shore power. I poured us two hefty glasses of scotch before going topside. I sat to port, Bob starboard.

I looked past Bob, my eyes landing on a neat brick path bordered by flowers of various sorts. Grass spread from the flowered edges to wooded land where to my right, a path reached back into a stand of pines. Crowning the path, about twenty yards from the dock, was a sturdy cedar-shake roofed log cabin. This was a slice of heaven. Spruce, fir, some oak and maple covered the island.

Bob quietly let me take it all in before saying, "Welcome to Maine."

"My pleasure," I said. We sat quietly sipping our scotch. Words would come later. For now, it was enough to enjoy the sweet aroma of fir trees and the soft sounds of lapping water.

Finished with our scotch, we set our empty glasses in a cup holder attached to the helm. Bob led the way.

Reaching the cabin we went up three steps to a porch that ran the width of the cabin. Adirondack style furniture sat invitingly on a shiny enameled dark green painted floor. Chairs, rockers, side tables, and a neat coffee table topped with live edged boards. Bob directed me to a rocker, went inside the cabin and reappeared with two cold cans of Miller Genuine Draft.

"Your favorite, as I recall," he said, handing me the sweating can.

"Pretty good memory you got going there," I said.

"Yup," Bob replied as he sat in the rocker next to mine. "Some things are more worth remembering than others."

A few gulps of beer later, I asked, "So where's that wood pile?"

Bob didn't answer. Instead, he rose from his chair declaring, "I need to go inside a bit. Enjoy the scenery."

I put my can of beer on the coffee table next to Bob's. I walked around the porch noticing how every board and every rafter was perfectly fitted. His craftsmanship was akin to fine machining. The cabin itself was constructed with untreated cedar logs that had mellowed into a shimmering grey. Bob had told me many times how he had built the place from ground up using timber that he had harvested from the island. I was admiring the view of some of the many islands dotting Casco when he returned carrying two more beers. "Just in case one isn't enough," he said, lifting the shiny black-labeled cans in the air as if they were trophies. He set them on the table separating our chairs as we slipped back into the comfortable Adirondacks. I filled him in about buying the boat, some stuff about people I met along the way, briefly mentioned meeting Abigail in Boston, leaving out most of the details. I then asked what ever happened to the investigator.

"Vacationing on Stone Island," he replied matter of factly.

"Stone Island? Sounds like a rather desolate place."

"Yup, unless you're a cormorant."

"How did you manage getting him out there?"

"Made a phone call. Forget about him. He's a storm gone by."

"Any chance that he'll show up here?"

"Well, he can't swim here from there, can he? If he makes it, well, we'll just deal with that when the time comes."

"My guess is that you have things covered?"

"Charlie, I've lived here all my life. My parents and grandparents were Mainers. There are things that people From Away will never understand about what it is to be of real Maine stock. So, yes, things are covered. Now, how about a tour of that boat of yours?"

Ever the mechanic, he spent a lot of time sticking his head into the engine compartment, looking under access hatches in the cabin sole, examining the futuristic electric panel, studying the generator like he never saw one in his life and marveling at all the comforts akin to a swanky hotel suite. When I invited him to take a voyage Down East, he readily agreed with the comment: "Can't pass that up, but we're going to have to do that pretty soon."

"We have all summer," I commented.

"Maybe you do, but I have things to do," he said, getting up and leaving the boat. I followed.

On our walk back to his house, I again asked to see the woodpile. After all, it was his reason for abandoning me in Annapolis. He took me around to the back of the cabin. A shed stood about fifty feet away, the construction similar to the cabin. The wood pile or where the wood pile should be was next to an access door at the rear of the cabin.

"Not much to show," Bob said flatly. Motioning to a few rows of split logs, he added, "That's it."

"So, you've decided to head to the Caribbean with me?"

"Nope. I'm dying."

"Jesus, Bob, aren't we all?"

I had a sinking feeling. Quite honestly, since arriving, Bob seemed, well, not like himself. I figured that he had lost a bit of weight because of endless physical chores. And there was something lacking in his eyes, maybe a bit of jolly gone out of them. He directed me to the porch where I sat while he went inside for more beer. When he returned, we sat in silence for a good ten minutes before he opened up.

"Sailor's disease," he said calmly. "Skin cancer. Too much sun and not enough brains, I guess. Spread all over the place like spilled stew. They want to put me on chemo, but at best that would buy me maybe a few months and who the hell wants to spend their last few moments puking their guts out? Can you imagine going through that just to buy a little more time? It's not for me. I'd much prefer to be looking up at my own ceiling, the one I put there, than one in some hospital. I'll die right here, in my own creation."

I struggle to get out a somber, "How long?"

"Three months, maybe. I don't know. I haven't told any of my family and I don't plan to. It is what it is." Bob's voice had a tinge of anger laced to it.

"Now look," I said, with as much as I could put behind it, "there's no way you can tough it out alone. Somebody needs to be here to help."

Bob bristled. "Why? I've taken care of myself all my life. When the time comes, I prefer to be alone and not slobbered over."

"Pretty tough talk. But I understand. Back at the nursing home the best death was when somebody just faded away. Alive at night, dead in the morning. But that's not going to happen here."

"You're being a good friend, Charlie, but this doesn't concern you. Not really. So let's put it aside, do a bit of sailing and let it go at that. Maybe I won't wait for the end."

"Ridiculous and damn right contradictory." I found my voice and used it like a club to try to knock some sense into him. "How can you call me a 'good friend,' then dismiss me just when a good friend is exactly what you need, just like what I needed to get the hell out of Sunset. Am I crazy or did you save me from a slow death? So let's cut the bullshit and come up with a plan. Suicide? That's another kettle of fish."

We sat silently for what felt like an eternity. I was turning it over in my mind. What to do? What to say next? Should I try to find his kids and let them in on what's going on? I concluded that Bob was not going to die alone and that I'd stay right here for as long as it takes. I broke the silence. "You don't seem to fear death, Bob. Am I right?"

Eyeballing me with furrowed brow, Bob answered, "Afraid? Do I sound afraid? What should I be afraid of? Going to hell? Are trees afraid? Flowers? Bees? Deer? You know, living on the island I see life and death all the time. People need to be in nature to appreciate the cycle. Life and death, why that's the way of nature and nature looks at things with a wide angle lens. The human race is not going to go extinct because I die. And if it did, I'm sure nature would get on just fine. It sure did pretty good before we ever showed up on this planet. So, no, I'm not afraid. I can't say I'm looking forward to it but when it comes, it comes. That's just the way it is."

"I admire you, Bob. I must say, I wish I had your courage. Where does it come from?"

"How the hell do I know? I live. Can't we just let it go at that?"

Again, we turned to silence before Bob slipped into the comfort of nostalgia. "Remember the time we took on water? Damn boat turned into a bathtub and there we were somewhere from nowhere. You fixed the bilge pump while I pumped my ass off. We got through that one."

I countered with other occasions like the time Bob challenged me at pool then proceeded to run the table. Like two kids we laughed our way through memories from meeting other sailors to dealing with lines caught on the prop, from being calmed to roaring through thirty knot winds. The beer flowed until our conversation melted into sentence fragments slovenly delivered, nonsensical, all punctuated with frequent calls of nature and bouts of laughter. Dinner that night consisted of some kind of fish cooked somehow, and eaten only as two drunks could. I retired to my boat, Bob to his bed. The question of Bob's call to death went unanswered.

PRIVATE INVESTIGATOR

Adapted from the digital recorder of Private Investigator, Justin Roberts recorded July 27, 1104 hours.

Trying to keep up with my notes. I'm closing in. I rented a boat from Dinger's Rentals and am on my way to finally nab my quarry. The last time I steered a motor boat was at some county fair back when I was a kid. So Martha Dinger was a bit wary about letting me out on my own. "No more than ten-horsepower. Can't hurt much with that," she said.

The best thing that I can say about the boat is that it floated. But, from what I could tell, Bickles Island was not much over a mile away with a few tiny islands separating it from the mainland. Here the odd thing: On the chart, Bickles Island is identified as Ruby Island. Back at the Days Inn I googled Bickles and it told me it was really Ruby Island and that the name was changed to Bickles Island during World War II in honor of General Bickles, who was born in a tent on Ruby Island, when his mom went into labor while camping there with her husband, back in the early twenties. Unfortunately, the name was never changed on the chart.

Minutes after leaving Dinger's Rentals, I watched fog rolling toward me and there wasn't a damn thing I could do about it. I took a compass heading on the third island, crossed my fingers and held a steady course. In a matter of minutes I was wrapped in a cloak of fog so thick I could barely see the front of the boat. What the hell was I doing here? I throttled back just far enough to just keep moving, knowing full well that making Bickle Island was only a matter of luck. Feeling like the boat was just sitting there, I goosed the throttle and plowed onward.

In a few minutes the boat made an awful crunching sound then stopped so suddenly that I was nearly tossed overboard. The engine made a terrible metallic sound and died. I looked over the side to see floating flecks of fiberglass amidst the seaweed that surrounded the boat. I'd found a rock and the damn boat was taking on water. I was livid, but what the hell was I supposed to do. I wasn't going to drown, especially with an outgoing tide, which in a matter of ten minutes had me and the boat sitting solidly aground, surrounded by a garden of rocks covered with seaweed or algae or something. The fog lifted for a minute, enough for me to see that I was on the rim of an island. What island was the big question. I jammed the chart into my back pack and headed ashore.

Getting off the boat was like trying to ice skate for the first time: flailing arms, gyrating hips, falling, while slipping and sliding my way to the shoreline. I looked back at the wretched boat sitting catawampus on a bed of rocks.

Covered in green slime, I pushed through a mosquito-laden forest with undergrowth thick enough to challenge a groundhog. Thank God for the insect repellant, otherwise I'd need a blood transfusion. In the distance, I heard music, changed direction and headed for what accounted for civilization on an island in Maine. Clearing a patch of thorny wet brambles, I walked into a clearing with small cabins placed here and there. "Hello there," came from my left, where a fellow in coveralls was coming my way. "Name's Fabinham, Hibernian Fabinham. People call me Hi," he said, "Mother was Irish, but I suppose you guessed that already," he giggled.

"What brings you to True?"

"True what?" I asked.

"This here island. That's what we call it, True. Me and the wife rent out cabins. Island Vacations, we call it. If you're looking for one, well, that's too bad because we don't open up for another week. Awful late this year, but me and the wife, well, we had life get in the way." Fabinham stepped back eying me from head to toe. "How'd you get here anyway? You sure didn't walk although you look like maybe you tried. Those thorn apples are nothing to fool with lest you're a rabbit."

"Of course I didn't walk. My boat's over there," I said with a flick of my hand.

"Well, there it is then," is all he said to that. "How can I help you?"

"I'm looking for Bickle Island."

"Bickle Island's the next one down. Go west. Just a stone's throw. Got a row boat at the dock. Use it if you want. No sense traipsing back to yours. Just follow the path," he said, pointing to a well trodden path. Curiously enough he didn't ask who I was or where I came from or why I was covered in green slime. Maine hospitality, I guess. Or was I expected?

I figured that this Fabinham guy might be pulling a fast one, so I warily followed his directions. A short walk led me to a grassy picnic area at water's edge. The fog had lifted enough for me to make out what was supposedly Bickle Island, about which was about two-hundred yards due west. A well used wooden row boat sat at what appeared to be a well kept dock. Low tide showed a sandbar about half way across.

At this point, I had given up trusting anybody, especially anybody living in or near Maine. Ginger back at the boat rental seemed *innocent enough and consulting the chart, her advice seemed right on. But this Fabinham guy seemed as slippery as those rocks I just climbed over. I sat down on the picnic bench, spread out my chart and opened up my compass; it was time to do some orientation. The FBI gave us solid training in land navigation and while the charts are quite different, it was an easy transition to chart a course over water, especially given all the islands around here. Taking a bearing on the Portland fog signal and another on Bickle Island, I drew intersecting lines on the chart. If the bearings were correct, I should be on the western edge of True Island. It felt wrong. I knew the fog horn was spot-on. I checked out the plaque on the row boat which indicated that I was indeed on True Island. But according to my bearings, I was not looking at Bickle Island, but rather Base Island. Bickle was not west but almost due south. I'd had enough of these Mainers playing me for an idiot.*

I took a bearing of 180 degrees and headed into the lifting fog.

FRIDAY, JULY 27

A hangover can be a terrible thing and that's just what I had when I awoke to a rocking boat accompanied by claps of thunder and a deluge that sounded like my decks were being attacked by thousands of marbles, rain drops as big as fists. It was late morning. Bob was probably up and at it. Sipping coffee, I sat in the salon thinking about Bob. He was so damn stoic it hurt. For sure, I just couldn't cast off to head out to sea. No, I would stick it out until his family made me redundant or until I'd nursed him to the end.

That wasn't something I'd ever done before. When Lori died, it came quickly. Her heart gave out and that was that. I found her sitting on the couch and I knew right away that I had lost her. It was like she just sat down and died. It was a quiet affair. I sat down next to her and put my arm around her shoulder, nestling her still warm body in the crook of my shoulder, like we used to do at the movies. Tears came, of course, but softly. I remembered small things like when Lori dropped a whole roasted turkey on the kitchen floor and how we laughed about it all. Skinny dipping in a pond years back when the boys were just toddlers. Small stuff that added up to a lifetime. Our quilt of life. I have little recollection of how long I sat there before getting up from the couch and placing an afghan around Lori's body for no reason other than just because. My first call was to Jeff Mason, our lifelong doctor. Jeff took it from there. But who would I call for Bob? His wife was gone, I had never met his kids, and I had no idea about his friends or anything else.

My headache seemed to diminish right along with the cloudburst. I dressed and went up on deck. Bob was sitting on his porch. "Good morning, Rip. Enjoy your slumber? Coffee's on." I motioned that I was on my way. I admired the flowers bordering the brick path and the thick grass beyond. I eyed the darkened path that led into the damp pines. The rain accentuated the smell of evergreens, the kind that seemed to just love the islands of Maine. As I approached the porch I asked Bob if he had neighbors. "Yup, a few on the other islands around here."

"So," I asked, "you're the only one on this island?"

"Yup, it's my island. Why would I want anybody else on it? That's what an island's for, isn't it?"

Taking the three steps up onto the porch with a good grip on the handrail, I said, "I guess so, but isn't Manhattan also an island?"

"People that live there have as much sense as a bag of hammers. I was there once when I was in the navy and I never wanted to go back. This is where I belong and this is where I'll stay. Built this place fifty years ago." Bob went on and on about how he lived with no electricity until a cable was run out to the islands. How he had to conserve water, how it took him umpteen boat rides hauling building supplies, building a house with hand tools only, on and on with a lot of details that I heard before. I sat listening through the aftershock of that nasty hangover.

Bob, seemingly cured of any such aftershocks, decided that the best cure for mine was to take a tour of the island. Mugs of coffee in hand, we strolled onto the darkened path that led through the evergreens. Rain dripped on my head and shoulders as we meandered through dense aromatic growth, accompanied by a chorus of birdsong and chattering insects. I had to stop now and then just to take it all in. I wished I could share this with Abigail. There's some sad and sweet irony here. Had I not met Abigail, I would not be missing her. Missing her was the sorrow part; the sweet part was having met her in the first place.

I think those incompetent administration and staff back at Sunset would profit by knowing that romanticism doesn't decrease with age, it actually grows with age. There they were, squeaking around in their rubbery clogs, talking to us like we were toddlers, never once considering that we still had passion, could still fall in love, could still have sex, could still, even with all the ailments of aging, embrace fantasy, could still have a future. If that goddamn investigator tried to take me back to Sunset, I'd kill the son-of-a-bitch or he'd have to kill me.

"Are you coming?" Bob yelled from some place around the bend. I threw a kiss into the pines and headed on my way.

Bob was right; a good walk with nature had my mind clearing, my body returning to its steady course. We followed the path through the evergreens, across a grassy field laden with wildflowers and grazing deer. We climbed up a rocky slope until we came to an outcropping of granite that overlooked Casco Bay. The air was fresh and clear, the placid water below glimmering blue in eastern light. Bob and I found a smooth spot and sat down.

After a few meditative minutes, Bob said, "I've been thinking."

PRIVATE INVESTIGATOR

Adapted from the digital recorder of Private Investigator, Justin Roberts recorded July 27, 1206 hours.

I pulled the row boat up on a rocky shore. A cloudburst caught me halfway between the two islands. I was soaked through. Again. At least most of the green slime washed off my clothes. I slid the rowboat up onto shore enough to hold it there. Slippery rocks, jagged rocks, rocks hidden under seaweed. Getting my bearings I headed into the island. Thick undergrowth clawed at my clothes. After 20 yards or so, I came upon a curvy path, turned right and ascended a slight slop. The fog was lifting. Around the second turn I spotted a cabin. Blurred by lingering fog, it had a ghostly appearance. With the exception of a few high chirps from some unknown bird, the place was dead quiet. I was certain that I had found Liscome's place. That certainty was underscored once I caught sight of a sizable yacht tied up at the dock. Chalk up another one for good ol' agent Roberts! Maybe it's not nailing one of the top ten or busting up a drug ring, but these two geezers were a slippery pair. I went up on the porch and rapped hard on the door. No answer. I sat down on a porch chair and waited.

FRIDAY, JULY 27 (CONTINUED)

Bob and I sat quietly as our world got smaller and smaller. We became the center of a small peaceful orb, fog slowly closing off our world. Below, the ebbing tide lapped softly against the rocky shore. In the distance, the sound of Portland Harbor's fog horn echoed its reassuring commentary.

"What is it you were thinking?" I asked Bob.

"About all this. Here we are, two old men staring death in the eye. Numbered days. Never gave it much thought. Death, I mean. Comes on a person like this fog: one day, everything's clear, the next, gray and cloudy. Never been lonely on this island, even after Maggie died. Just went about the business of living. Now I'm lonely. Least I was before you came. That depression? Wouldn't know, never been there before. When the doc said I was doomed, I came home and started splitting logs for winter. Did that for a few days until it dawned on me that it was a waste of time and time for me was getting pretty pricey. Left the maul stuck in the block and there it sits. Maybe that's when the depression hit. Like whatever I did till I died meant nothing at all. I gave some serious consideration to doing myself in, even loaded my gun, but something, I don't know what, wouldn't let me do it. Maybe it was knowing you were on your way, something to look forward to, I guess. Anyway, wouldn't be very hospitable of me to welcome you with my stiff corpse."

I remained quiet. Encapsulated in cottony fog, our world had become safe and quiet. What lived or happened beyond us at that moment was of no consequence. The only thing that mattered was the two of us sharing the uncertainties of our truncated future. Bob would die and I would most certainly follow.

I broke the silence. "Was it worth it?"

"What do you mean by it?" he asked.

"Being alive. Having lived?"

Bob turned to look me in the eyes. "Well, now, what choice did I have? Mom and Dad did their thing. Sperm met egg. Bingo, me. The rest was up to me. And if you're asking me if I have any regrets. The answer is no. We do what we have to do. Get by. Then it's over. We do, or at least we should, have a say in how to end it. Just suppose I started to go downhill really fast, the cancer knocks me down. And just say that you're dumb enough to call 911. What would happen? I mean it, what would happen?"

"I guess an ambulance or boat full of EMT's would come out here?"

"Then what? Don't answer that! Let me tell you. I'd be shipped off to the hospital and have tubes stuffed in every opening, get all drugged up. Hell, they would know I was dying but that's not acceptable, is it. Keep us alive. That's their job. Nobody's going to say, 'Hey, this guy's loaded with cancer. Let's just make him comfortable and let him die.' What hospital emergency room would do that? Okay, let's say I pull through. Know where I'm going? To your good old nursing home. Hell, you know more about that than me. I sure as hell didn't have a say on being born, but I sure as hell do have a say how and when and where I'm going to die. And that's going to happen right here. If you're hell-bent to stay, I won't argue with you." Bob leaned forward placing his elbows on his knees and looked down at the ground.

"I'm staying, then," I said quietly.

The sounds of Maine swirled back on us as we became lost in our own thoughts.

After a while, Bob perked up and said, "Got to thinking, why not one last go of it? Sail up to Grand Manan, hit a few of the harbors along the way. I sure would like to jump into the Cows and maybe visit Roque Island. Then head back here. Doc suggested that I look into hospice—you know, where people go to live out the final days without care or worry. That's what I've been thinking."

"I couldn't agree more. Why we might…"

Bob's cell rang, interrupting me. He took the call.

"That was Hi," he told me after hanging up. Over on True Island. Said he sent the investigator over to Base Island. He's sending the guy on a circle tour of Casco Bay in a row boat. The change of tide'll have him drifting into Portland by night-fall. Hi told me that he alerted the others to keep him busy for awhile. So, back to what I was saying. How about taking me on my final voyage?"

I responded with a high five slap. I commented, "Cat would be proud." In the back of my mind, I was thinking about Ivan and Doris sleeping peacefully in the deep blue sea. I decided to give Ernie a call later on, maybe he could shed some light on what I might expect.

Illuminating the thinning fog, the sun's soft light turned Casco Bay into a world of golden splendor. Bob led me on a slow walk back to the cabin on a circuitous route around the island. If there was a Garden of Eden, it must have been like this: lupine-filled glades with butterflies enjoying easy access to pollen; osprey screeching overhead; rabbits frolicking, deer doing whatever it is deer do, and three groundhogs. Hardwoods and evergreens defined the open fields. Our way back took over two hours and my stomach was in full protest.

We came at the cabin from the rear where I caught sight of the diminished woodpile and the heavy maul driven deep into a thick tree stump. We walked around the cabin to the front porch where a man sat silently looking out over the water. He was a sorry looking specimen, soaking wet with dried green algae stuck in his hair, covering his shorts and legs. Sneakers muddy. Bob didn't hesitate. He just walked over to the guy and asked, "You want lunch?" Startled, the man stood staring at us. "Lunch," Bob repeated. "You hungry?" The man nodded. I took this fellow to be a local with bad brain, but that wasn't the case. Bob walked past him and went to the cabin door where he stopped and turned to me. "Meet Justin Roberts," he said. "He's the guy that's been on your trail." Bob went into the cabin.

"Enjoying Maine?" I was trying to be nonchalant about it on the outside, but inside I was swirling. No matter what this idiot said or did, I was going to take Bob on that sailing trip and the sooner the better.

Roberts stared back at me with wolf eyes and said, "I'm just beginning to."

Enjoying sarcasm, I asked, "Stone Island's a nice place, isn't it? Did you swim over from there or are you in the dulse trade, harvesting the local seaweed?"

"Look Lambert, I'm here for *you*. And it looks like I've

found you alive and well, so as far as I'm concerned, mission accomplished."

"Go screw yourself," I said. "Don't count your damn chickens just yet."

Roberts gave me a smirk and fell silent.

Bob came back onto the porch with three paper plates, each with a ham sandwich, two gherkins, a paper napkin, and a few slices of cucumber. He handed one to Roberts then to me, set his on a small side table and went back inside. He reappeared. "Hope you like Coke," he said, handing me and Roberts each a cold can. We sat silently, not a word said. After lunch, Bob gathered up the plates and cans, stepped off the porch and went around to the back of the cabin. Roberts commented on the fog lifting so suddenly as if it was some mysterious quirk of nature. I remained silent.

In due time, Bob reappeared, his hand clutching the maul, half sledge hammer and half axe. Without a word, he stepped up onto the porch, set the maul down next to his chair, sat down, looked at Roberts and asked, "What are you doing here?"

"You know why I'm here," Roberts responded. "I must commend you guys for making it a bit of a challenge."

"The challenge has just begun. You're on my island uninvited. Trespassing on private land. Maine land. And we don't take that lightly up here. Got a warrant?"

"You know I don't. I'm not here to arrest Mr. Lambert. I'm not a cop. This is a private affair. No need for the law, unless, that is…" Roberts said eyeing the heavy maul sitting to Bob's left. Roberts turned toward me. "Mr. Lambert, people are worried about you. Your sons don't know whether you're dead or alive. The folks at the nursing home, as you must know, are responsible for all this, and believe me, they are very concerned."

"Well you can call my sons and tell them that the insurance folks can go to hell. As far as the nursing home goes, well, screw them, too. You can leave; we're done here."

Roberts stood. "If that's the way you want it, then that's fine with me. My report will have you back at Sunset and the insurance company off the hook."

"Tide's comin' in," Bob interrupted. "I suppose you tied that row boat up?"

A frown crossed Roberts's brow. "I pulled it up on shore, a good three feet. Hey, how did you know that?"

Ignoring his question, Bob exclaimed, "Three feet!" He gave a short, barking laugh. "Now there you go. Tide'll never get at it so high up on shore. This here is Maine. We have real tides here, not some piss creek that overflows when it rains. From Away folks just don't understand the ocean: it taketh and it giveth. Might try swimming. Maybe clean some of that slime off. Considering that you're going to get wet stem to stern, I'll take that phone in your hip pocket for safe keeping."

"The phone will stay where it is. I'll be going now, and don't worry; I'll make my way back."

Bob stood up. He was about to blow. It's rare, but I've seen it before and it is *not* pleasant. Sinewy, heavy boned, and muscular, Bob is of gentle character unless he reaches his Mount Etna point. I could feel the rumbling. If he got that maul raised shoulder high it would come down and there'd be no stopping it. Bob hefted the maul. "You have a choice. I smash that gadget of yours on a rock or I smash it while it's still in your pocket."

"Easy Bob," I said like I was talking down a growling German Shepherd. "Let's work this out."

"Phone first," Bob commanded.

I nodded to Roberts who reluctantly tossed his phone to Bob. "Now lift your shirt and drop your pants." When Roberts hesitated, Bob started to raise the maul. The shirt went up and the pants went down and out fell another cell phone. Phones in hand, Bob left the porch to go around back to the chopping block.

Roberts pulled down his shirt and pulled up his pants. I motioned to Roberts to take a seat but he appeared more comfortable pacing the porch deck. "What is it with this guy? Is he nuts?" Roberts asked shaking his head.

"Nope, just being a friend," I said.

"Look, I'm trying to do a job here. I might not like tracking down an old man, but that's what I'm paid to do."

When you've lived as long as I and Bob have, you learn over time not to lose your cool. Roberts is an idiot, that's plain to see. I don't think it's dawned on the nitwit that he's on an island. He has no place to go, no one to call. He's screwed and doesn't even know it.

"You're a damn bounty hunter, that's what you are," I said. "What the hell did I ever do to become a wanted man? Ironic, isn't it, going from being unwanted to being wanted in what, a little over a month. As far as I'm concerned you can leave now. Swim! Whatever! Do you think for one moment that Sunset or my kids care one flame in hell whether I'm dead or alive? They don't give a crap. You don't give a crap. Bob, *he* cares. You've been to Sunset. You've met the guests. Guests, my ass. Prisoners is what they are. How old are you? In your sixties? You better get your ass in gear because unless you're damned lucky, Sunset's in your future. But it's not in mine. You screwed up here, buddy.

You're trespassing on an island in Maine owned and guarded over by a tough son-of-a-bitch that could eat the likes of you for lunch. You called me an old man? Just what does that mean? That my brain has holes in it? Just what do you have in mind?"

A couple of heavy thuds interrupted my lecture. "You hear that!" I warned Roberts. "That's your phones being smashed to smithereens. Keep your *old man* bullshit going and the next thing on that chopping block will be your empty head."

Bob returned from around back, leaving the maul behind. "You might as well sit down," he said to Roberts. "Tide doesn't turn for six hours or so. Try swimming now and you'll look like driftwood out there." Roberts sulked his way back to the Adirondack. Bob continued, "I don't like your trespassing, but as long as you're here, I'll treat you guest-like and I expect the return courtesy; it's the way it is here. I'm not saying you're welcomed here because you're not. But as long as you're here as I said I'll treat you like a guest. Abuse the courtesy and you'll come to regret it." Eyeballing Roberts, Bob added, "Do you understand?"

Roberts nodded with an "I do."

Bob walked to the other side of the porch and with his back still to Roberts, he asked, "You like the Red Sox?"

The non sequitur caught Roberts unaware. "Damned if I do, damned if I don't?" questioned Roberts.

"The maul's out back," laughed Bob. "Just say the way it is."

"I do," answered Roberts. "And, I hate the Yankees." Bob came over to me and gave me a high five. He swung around to high-five Roberts. Roberts shied away.

"Cat would've enjoyed that one," Bob chortled.

With the mention of Cat, Roberts commented, "I've got to

admire you guys. In all the years I've worked for the FBI—don't worry, I'm retired—I've seldom come across the likes of two ol…ahhh…seasoned men pulling off something like this. I met Cat and he's destined to be successful in anything from crime to commerce."

"Cat's a good kid," I chimed in. "Smart. Finding his way."

The three of us bantered about for the rest of the afternoon. Roberts wasn't such a bad guy; typical but not bad. He got a little close with questions about me buying the boat, but I simply said it was none of his damn business where I got the money. My guess is once FBI, always FBI. I could see the idiot turning me in for fraud the minute he had the opportunity, which would come eventually unless he pissed off Bob again. Bob convinced Roberts that he stank enough like seaweed to warrant a good shower, which Roberts welcomed. While he was showering, Bob and I talked about what we were going to do with him. Bob said, "Minute we let this guy loose, he'll be reporting in like a good little investigator. Can't keep him here forever. Like to make Grand Manan sooner than later; not good for me to be sitting here waiting for the pain to start. Sure as hell don't want to take him along, unless we deep six the son-of-a-bitch."

That night the three of us ate fresh mackerel with boiled potatoes and just-picked asparagus. We washed it down with rum and Cokes. Roberts regaled us with his FBI exploits of tracking down wanted criminals and even terrorists. Bob and I listened with feigned interest. By ten o'clock, yawning out-paced conversation. Bob didn't mince words about sleeping arrangements. "You're welcome on the island, but not to sleep in my cabin," he said to Roberts. "And should you have ideas of sneaking away at night, I have a stout chain that says you'll be right here in the morning."

"That won't be necessary," Roberts said. "I give you my word."

"Your word is about as good as a dog turd in a rain storm. I'll lend you a pillow and a blanket; you can bed down right here with a nice chain to keep you comfortable."

During dinner, I had noticed Roberts seemed to enjoy being in the company of two *old* men. He struck me as a man confused with how to spend the rest of his life; going from FBI intrigue to tracking down nursing home escapees must have been deflating. Roberts was not ready to retire because, like a lot of retired people, his identity was still tied to his work. He had yet to find out who or what he really was. The assisted living section of Sunset and nursing were full of men like Roberts—all they could talk about was what *was*, not *is* or *what might be* but what *was*. Their lives were past-tense.

Roberts was by no means trustworthy, but I couldn't see chaining him on the porch like a dog so I offered the alternative of having Roberts join me on *That Good Night* for a good night's sleep. Perhaps, we could come to terms. With a stern warning to Roberts, Bob said, "Try to leave the island and you'll be crab meat."

"From kidnapping to murder. That's a life sentence," Roberts said.

"What the hell do you know about life!" Bob said. Then he turned to me, "Take this guy to your boat, save me from getting the chain, but be careful." Bob turned and retired into the cabin. Roberts and I walked down to the boat, climbed aboard and went below. I offered to toss Roberts' still damp clothes into the dryer. He agreed with the exception of his underwear and his leather belt which he wasn't willing to give up. I wasn't about to lend him my robe.

"I don't mean to sound disrespectful, Charlie, but this is a lot of boat to handle alone," Roberts said while we sat in the salon sipping Black Grouse whisky.

"No, it's a fair observation, get it all the time. The fact is I'm in great shape. Before they slapped me in the nursing home, I was living in a senior suite. I went to the exercise room every day, sometimes twice a day. I did what most prisoners do, built muscle. Once they stuck me in the nursing home, it was a matter of just push-ups and calisthenics. When you sail a boat, your muscles are under constant use trying to stay upright. Some old men just sit down and melt. I'm not one of them"

"Understood," Roberts said. "What about Bob?"

"What about him? He's lived this way all his life. He's the real thing: hunter/gatherer. He bought this island when he was in his early twenties. Spent his life at sea. Anything you see here, he built. There are still men like that around, but they're getting rarer."

"I must admit, I kind of envy you two. I retired four years ago when the government offered a buyout for early retirement. It's how they cut overhead without having to fire anybody. I snapped it up, a bit too quickly perhaps. One day I was investigating serious crimes, the next I was twiddling my thumbs. I hoped they'd call me back to duty, but the call never came. I found out pretty soon that I didn't really have any hobbies. It drove me nuts sitting at home with the wife. She didn't like it either. Said she'd married me for better or for worse, but not for lunch. So, here I am working for an insurance company. Not what I had in mind for retirement."

"Well, this is my choice, drinking scotch on my very own yacht and this is where I'm going to stay. So, now that you found me, what's next? Handcuff me to a wheelchair? I'm going to make this abundantly clear; there is no way on God's green earth that I'll be going back to that maggot farm."

"So what's your suggestion?"

"Give me some choices."

"There are none!"

"What the hell are you talking about? There are always choices."

"Not in this case. I've found you and that's that. I'm not the judge here, only the investigator. We leave the island together. What Sunset or the insurance company does with that information is up to them. And this business of buying the boat! You and that yacht broker Baxter could be looking at serious jail time. Look, my job is upholding the law. I take you in, the wheels of justice do the rest. That's my job."

"No, your job is to make a report. You found me. I'm alive. No life insurance gets paid out. You don't need to take me in for that. But you just can't give it up, can you? You still think you're in the FBI! You're driving a car by looking through the rear view mirror. How dumb is that? You can't face the harsh reality that those days are over. Poor little old Roberts sent out to pasture to end his days playing golf or some other inane pastime. Big block headline: RETIRED FBI AGENT CAPTURES NURSING HOME RUNAWAY. Just who did I hurt by trying to live out my life my own way? My kids? Sunset? My kids will be disappointed that I'm not dead because they'll have to wait that much longer to get the insurance. And Sunset, they're going to get sued no matter what. Maybe *I'll* sue them for endangering my life by not protecting me against myself. Time to face up to it, Roberts. This is not about me or Baxter or Cat or Bob. It's about you. About your inflated ego. Grow a pair before it's too late. Why don't you just declare me dead and go home to your empty life?"

"My life isn't the issue here. It's you and your inability to accept old age. Give it up, Lambert. You've caused enough trouble."

"I've caused enough trouble getting old! Is that what you're saying? That's just it, isn't it? Keep us alive at any cost, and then toss us to the wolves! Let me tell you what trouble is. You're here in my boat. You're on an island with no way to contact the outside. Bob wants to chain you to the porch and I'm getting close to agreeing with him. You see, Bob and I are past the point where we run our lives by some oath to uphold the law or anything else. We do what we have to do and want to do and that's that."

"You're threatening me? Do you think for one minute that you could stop me? I'd have you down on the floor crying uncle in the blink of an eye. Listen Lambert, here's the deal: we're going to sail out of here right now. I'll toss the lines, you drive. And don't try something stupid."

With that, Roberts reached into the back of his underwear and pulled out the tiniest pistol I've ever seen. I almost laughed. Some new gadget cooked up by the FBI is my guess. And a special pocket in his underwear to boot. But it looked like a real gun and hell if I wanted to get shot by such a puny firearm.

Roberts directed me on deck where I started the engine. He jumped off the boat. I directed him to cast off the bow first, and toss the lines on deck, then come and get the stern line and toss it to me before climbing aboard. Just as Roberts' feet left the dock, I gave the thrusters and a good hit which sent the boat skittering away from the dock. Roberts missed the boat and ended up treading water. A blast of the horn alerted Bob, who was dockside in no time flat. Roberts was clinging to the dock like a wet lab, his pea-shooter deep sixed. I had a good mind to bring the boat alongside and crush the bastard.

By the time I got the boat tied up and helped Bob chain Roberts to the porch and toss him an old army blanket, it was time for bed. Tomorrow was another day.

Tired as I was, I lay awake wondering what the next step was going to be. Killing Roberts was not really an option and I was fairly certain that Bob was a bit blustery with all his talk on that subject. Nor was it an option taking Roberts along on Bob's twilight cruise. I tossed and turned with little to show for it. I cuddled up to my stuffy which had now become a Lori-, and sometimes an Abigail-substitute. I wanted more than anything to see Abigail again and maybe, when all this was over, I'd make my way back to Boston. Why not dream?

PRIVATE INVESTIGATOR

Adapted from the digital recorder of Private Investigator, Justin Roberts recorded July 28, 0215 hours.

It's damn humbling to be chained to a porch railing on an island in Maine by two men at least twenty years my senior. And forget about sleeping. One of the old guys has threatened to kill me. The other is on the verge of letting him do it. They're sleeping as I dictate this. At least if something bad happens there will be a record of it, thanks to the BBDRD. I've never been so humiliated in my life. It all began with that damn Sunset Senior Citizen Village and Nursing Home. Finding a tracking device in a dog turd should have been a sign that this was not going to be good. Now I'm chained to a porch railing. I've really lost my edge.

This Bob guy has this heavy rusty chain tight around my waist and padlocked behind my back. He called it an anchor rode, whatever the hell that is. Every time I move, the damn chain bites into my gut and clanks like something out of Ghostbusters. *Doesn't fit in with the sounds of a night in Maine. Escaping this is not an option. Even Houdini couldn't get out of this. But maybe coming to my senses is. Outwit these guys. How hard could that be? I'm not so sure of this Bob character, but Lambert has a soft side. I'll work on it.*

Last night Lambert lambasted me for hanging on to my career, or trying to. He's got a point, but one doesn't just walk away from thirty years of service. I had awards and citations for bringing down some pretty rough characters. But capturing rapists and murderers is one thing, tracking an old man is quite another. After retiring, Mary and I bought a motor home and for six months drove around the good old US of A. Once I got back home I went crazy with boredom. I tried golf and hated it. Bought a canoe and left it in the backyard. Watched Judge Judy *for crying out loud! The wife, she kept making lists of what I could be doing. Guess I was driving her crazy too. I tried a stint as a security guard at the local mall. I was fired after I slapped some teenager for shoplifting. Then this job working for an insurance company came along. It got me away from the house, the pay's good. And now I'm here.*

SATURDAY, JULY 28

With my stuffy still cradled in my arms, I awoke to a soft light filtering through the hatch, the same hatch that Abigail and I counted stars through. Savoring the afterglow of pleasant dreams, I lingered in bed before rising to face so many unanswered questions.

Before going up to the cabin, I called Ernie. From the grogginess in his voice, I suspected that I woke him up.

"This better be good, waking me up so damn early," he said. I apologized for calling before noon. After briefly catching him up on my travels, I told him about Bob having cancer, specifically asking him how I can help Bob deal with the pain. When. I mentioned morphine. Ernie was very clear that he would not risk trying to send me any morphine. "You think I want to spend my waning years in prison?" was his response.

"I wouldn't ask you to do that," I said. "Just suppose I got my hands on some, tell me how much to give him and how."

Ernie settled into straight doctor talk. "First of all, I'm not prescribing anything, just giving you some facts. Are we talking about injection or pills?"

I answered that I wasn't sure.

"Well in that case, I'll go with injection, but call me if you wind up using pills. Of course, you'll need a syringe. Anyway, I suggest starting with a low dose, say 4 mg every three to six hours. If that doesn't work, increase the dosage a little, but 15 mg is the limit. At that dose, expect your friend to get some pretty deep sleep. Okay, that's it. I don't want to know anything else. Like I said before, you can call me back. One more thing, I strongly advise you to get your friend to his doctor for any treatment. You're nuts if you try it on your own. Understand?" I told him that I did. He offered to talk to an oncologist friend of his for any other ideas and said that he would call me back.

Roberts was in miserable shape all scrunched up against the porch railing with a heavy chain showing itself like a snake slithering out from under the old army blanket which was wrapped snuggly around him. I took no pity. Neither did Bob, who was laid back on an Adirondack drinking coffee. I tossed Roberts his now-dry clothes. He squirmed from underneath the blanket. The unforgiving heavy chain wrapped around his waist clunked and clanked as he pulled himself up, using the porch railing as leverage. He struggled to dress, finishing with putting his belt back on. "Mug's waiting," Bob said, gesturing to a steaming cup sitting on an end table. "Sleep well, did you?"

"Probably the best sleep I've ever had," I answered. "How about you?"

"To tell you the truth, that crap last night gave me a hell of a headache. It's getting so I'm just not up to all that much excitement anymore. This numbskull," he said looking over to Roberts "is getting in the way of some good sailing." Roberts grunted.

"So what are we going to do?"

"Let's hike up to the lookout and talk it out."

Before we left, Bob gave Roberts a cup of coffee with two

pieces of buttered toast. And an empty coffee can with the warning, "Piss on my flowers and you'll be eating them." Bob's soft spot has a few barbs.

We sat overlooking Casco Bay. The air was sweet with a slight ocean breeze, the sky a clear powder blue. An osprey glided by, its high chirps cutting through the still morning light. I began the conversation with an abrupt, "We can't kill him."

"No, we can't," Bob readily agreed. "Sometimes I talk a bit too much. But, damn it, we both know that my days are precious and I don't want to give them over to nurse-maiding that son-of-a-bitch. Any chance of reasoning with him? I mean, is he so damn thick-headed to think that you are going to go back to that place and just give all this up?"

"I could do that if I have to," I said. "Maybe I make a deal that we go sailing, come back here and then I go back with him."

"Over my dead body," Bob shot back. "Maybe we ship him back to Stone Island with a few of my buddies to keep him comfy. I can arrange that with one phone call." Catching himself, he said, "Did I just say *over my dead body?*"

"Yes, you did, Bob. It's not a cliché anymore and we need to talk about it." I told Bob about my call to Ernie, about his suggestion that we see his doctor for pain killers. Maybe get some morphine and have it ready just in case. Bob argued that he wanted to fight to the bitter end and that taking painkillers would only dull his mind. I countered that pain would do that, too, and there was no sense to it. Bob quieted then looked up into the tree tops. Lowering his head, almost bowing, he said, "No more doctors. No more much of anything. I'm not trying to be stoic here, I just want to go sailing and get on with whatever life I have left. The morphine? Maybe, but not until we get back from sailing."

He was adamant that he would not leave his island and would not set foot on the mainland ever again. The lone exception to leaving his island was to jump on the boat. Regarding Roberts, we agreed that leaving him on Stone Island while we went sailing was the best option. Worst case scenario was me being hauled off; best case was Roberts dying of some rare disease while we enjoyed wind and wave.

On our way back to the cabin my phone rang. It was Ernie. He reported that his talk with an oncologist suggested that, since the cancer has metastasized, it is likely that the brain is involved. Piercing headaches would be a clear sign. In any event, death was certain and it could come at any time. Hold off with the morphine as long as possible. Once you start that stuff, your friend's life will get pretty foggy. Hospice would be the best place when the time comes." Ernie ended the call with, "Be sure to look after yourself. What you're into here can take its toll."

I asked Bob to hold up so we could talk. He directed me to a bench that overlooked the same clearing where I saw deer the day before. I talked with Bob about the possibility of hospice, but he was adamant that he would be in charge, no one else. I promised that I would be with him to the end and he seemed to accept that. We sat for some time looking over the field. Bob pointed out three deer that emerged from the woods. Watching them graze he began to cry. I put my arms around him and we wept together.

When we came out of the woods, Roberts was stooped over in the unmistakable posture of a man taking a leak, his left hand holding the coffee can. Seizing the moment, Bob yelled, "Shake

it more than three times and you're playing with yourself."
Startled, Roberts swung around, giving Bob a full frontal. Bob
finished the harangue with, "Not much to work with, I see."
Roberts uttered some indiscernible remark. We walked up to
the porch. Bob was sweating like he'd just run the quarter mile.
He went into the cabin, leaving me alone with Roberts who
had sat down on the porch floor, his back against the railing. I
remained standing.

"Chasing you all over the place has put a crimp in my plans
and I'm not sure what I can do about it. Last night I could have
crushed you against the dock like a ripe tomato and that'd be
that, a bad accident. Bob could have smashed your head with
the maul, but he didn't. I guess what I'm saying is we're not
cut out to be murderers. All Bob and I want to do is go sailing.
We could take you along but that'd ruin the trip. Besides, we
hate babysitting. We could just leave you chained to the porch
for a few weeks. Would you like that?" Roberts shook his head.
"I didn't think so. That leaves the only one other option, which
is to let you go. But that means we're going to have to trust you
and after you pulled that shitty little gun on me last night, that's
going to be a very hard thing to do."

"I apologize for that," Roberts said. "It's just that in training
we were told when in doubt, show your weapon. Way overboard,
I admit. So, I'll just promise to you right now that if you release
me, I'll go on my way. As far as I'm concerned I was never here.
You're missing and that's that. How about it?"

This patronizing bastard really pissed me off. "You're not
in junior high school, you pathetic son-of-a-bitch, and I am
certainly not your principal. You sound like some kid who's
been caught playing with himself in a stairwell. *How about it,*

my ass. It doesn't go like that. We just don't shake your hand and send you on your way. And you know why, because as long as you're still playing G-Man, you're going to continue to bird dog us. Or worst yet, invite the local sheriff to haul us in. No sir, letting you go means taking you back to Stone Island, at least until we get back. Is that clear?"

"Yes sir!" Roberts barked like he was a private in basic training speaking to an officer. Bob reappeared on the porch, steaming coffee mug in hand.

"Another thing," Bob chimed in. "If you are not there when we return, it'll only mean you're lobster bait. A few of my acquaintances will be enjoying some R&R on the island to keep you company. You'll be picked up tomorrow morning to begin your exile while we go for a sail. When we get back, we'll decide what to do with you. How about it?"

Clanking the chain as he struggled to stand, Roberts shot back, "This is beyond ridiculous. You're talking federal offense here. Kidnapping, holding a person against his will. Threatening murder. You guys will spend the rest of your life behind bars."

Bob began to laugh, a chuckle at first, then a hearty guttural laugh that tore off into the surrounding woods. He was still laughing when he turned and went back into the cabin. I stood for a moment staring at Roberts with utter contempt. I had a good mind to kick him in the teeth.

PRIVATE INVESTIGATOR

Adapted from the digital recorder of Private Investigator, Justin Roberts recorded July 28, 1155 hours.

They went into the woods. I've got to think through this. Lambert has a point. What good would it do to drag him back to Sunset? But that's my sworn duty. You see, there I go. I'm not sworn to do anything other than to help the nursing home and the insurance company save a few bucks. Besides, Lambert's got me thinking. Why am I doing this? I don't need the money, I'm still healthy enough to do whatever I want to do. I've got grandkids. I shouldn't have pulled the gun. I knew the minute I pointed it at Lambert that I was play acting. It didn't feel real anymore. But this chain? That feels real. Still, being chained up like a dog, humiliated like some school kid, somebody's got to pay for that.

So what if I don't return Lambert to Sunset. His sons certainly don't seem to give a damn, except for the money. I wonder what the story is behind that relationship. Anyway, I need to make a decision. Either I let Lambert off the hook, or I get him back to Sunset..

I've come to respect Lambert. I feel somewhat the same way about Bob, although he is unpredictable, headstrong and, I'm afraid, capable of carrying out his threats. After all, he chained me to the porch. Then again, he did feed me and just this morning gave me a cup of coffee and two slices of toast. Damn! I'm losing it. Can't let my personal feelings get the better of me. That's dangerous. First lesson at Quantico. I don't have much time. Gotta think! Gotta think how to get to Lambert's soft side!

SATURDAY, JULY 28 (CONTINUED)

Bob was sitting stooped at the table, head in hands. I put my hand on his shoulder.

"What's going on?" I asked. Bob shrugged his shoulder. "Pain?"

"Yeah."

"Should I call your doctor or anybody else?"

"No. And don't let my friends know. I don't want anybody to know. Promise me. The pain'll pass. It usually does. I've got some pills; they're in the cabinet above the sink. Get me three and screw the label."

I gave him my word and I did what he asked. The label read *take two tablets every 3–4 hours when needed, not to exceed 8 tablets in 24 hours*. I poured a glass of water and returned to Bob.

He swallowed all three with a few sips of water. "I need to go to bed," he said. "These should knock me out for awhile."

Once he was in bed, I returned to the kitchen. Without morphine, there'd be no sailing. No question that the pain would increase. But where to get it? I couldn't leave him alone. And that idiot on the porch, what the hell would I do with him? Bob's friends would take care of him in the morning, but then what? Maybe Bob's buddies would know what to do. I heard Bob moan and went to his side. He was in a fetal position. Soft moans came with each breath, interspersed now and then with groans. Oh God, how helpless I felt.

As I paced, I was hailed by Roberts. "Mr. Lambert, is everything okay in there?"

That put me over the top. Maybe I should get the maul and finish this pathetic bastard. I came out of the door like a bull ready to gore. Roberts cowered.

"Easy," he said. "I didn't mean to pry, but…"

"But what?" I asked, trying hard to control myself.

"Something's wrong. I heard moaning."

"Mind your own fucking business," I said.

"Wait," Roberts said. "I know what you think of me, but let me try to explain. Let me just try to turn the clock back with all this. I'm wrong. I've been wrong. I screwed up, I know it. You're right. I can't seem to let the past be the past. I want to, believe me. Pulling a gun on you, my God, I regretted it the moment I did it. I'm amazed you didn't squash me against the dock. I'll go to Stone Island, willingly. But right now, I give you my word: I will not try to return you to Sunset. As far as I'm concerned, you're missing and that's that. I'm sorry."

"All this because you heard a moan? You think I'm nuts enough to believe anything you say?"

A heavy groan came from the cabin. I reached over and closed the door.

"There," Roberts said. "That's what I'm talking about. I know what that sound is. I know it because that's how my grandfather sounded when he was dying. Come on, what's going on here? Can I help? I'm no good to you chained up. How can I gain your trust?"

I remained silent for some time. Roberts had been in his *I'll help* mode before. I admit, his tone was different, but trust him? That was asking a lot. The thing of it is, with Bob suddenly going downhill, letting Roberts go might be a blessing. He'd rat me out, of that I was certain. But so what? If he showed up with the law, at least Bob might get some help and I would've kept my promise not to tell anyone. I wouldn't go back to Sunset, I promised myself that much, but I'd figure it out. I've always been able to figure it out.

"Years ago," Roberts said calmly, "I tracked down this kid accused of killing his aunt and uncle along with two cousins. He was sixteen years old. I found him in Dubuque, Iowa working as a dishwasher at a local resort. He was living under an overpass. During my investigation, I became convinced that this kid was innocent. All of the evidence pointed to a vagrant who had wandered by this farmhouse in the middle of a Kansas cornfield. The district attorney, though, was not to be convinced. No matter what evidence I threw at him, he held fast. Get the kid, he told me. Let justice do its work. Well, I did. I took the kid in and you know what? He was convicted. I still wake up with that one. The kid was tried as an adult and executed. I should have let him go."

"Why are you telling me this?" I asked.

"I'm not sure, except that letting you off might somehow ease my guilt over that case. You know, watching you and Bob do your thing, I'm a bit jealous. You're so damn free. Maybe it's time for me to look out of the windshield instead of through the rearview mirror, as you said. Maybe things would go better. Do you remember saying that to me?" I nodded. "Well, it struck home. So did your comments about me someday being in a nursing home. Look, what I'm trying to say is, just let me help."

"Let me think about it," I said.

I went inside. Bob looked relaxed now. I stroked his brow. It felt like he had a slight fever. His breathing was labored. Now and then he gave a moan, but they were soft, almost purrs. The bedroom was sparsely furnished with what appeared to be home-made furniture. His dresser top was covered with photographs. His wife, kids in various stages of life, Bob standing on his boat with a large lobster in each hand, a yellowed photo of a couple, maybe his parents. I pulled a chair up alongside his bed and sat down. I nodded off. When I awoke, Bob was still fast asleep. He was snoring, which made me smile. Whenever he and I had gone cruising, his snoring nearly drove me crazy. I'd taken to carrying earplugs whenever he came aboard. But not now, his snoring was the best music I'd heard in some time.

I rummaged through the kitchen and came up with some lunch meat and a few slices of bread. I made two crude sand-wiches and went back to the porch. I gave one to Roberts and, taking the other with me, walked down to my boat. I climbed aboard and ate my lunch in the cockpit. My first and only concern at this point was helping Bob get through the pain and that meant getting my hands on some morphine. I went back to the porch.

"Morphine," I said to Roberts

"What about it?"

"Can you get your hands on morphine?"

"That's not easy to do."

"Yeah, you think I don't know that? Can you get it?" I repeated.

Roberts took a deep breath and nodded, "Maybe."

"I need more than that."

"Portland. If I could get to Portland, I'd probably find some on the streets."

"Just how do you do that?"

"FBI does it all the time. Find drugs, I mean. Once you get onto it, dealers are easy to spot. The problem is that dealers are as good at spotting agents as we are at spotting them."

"What are you telling me?"

"I'll need some cash; a couple grand would do it. I've been down this route before. Of course, I was wearing a wire back then. Tricky stuff, but with luck, I could be back here tomorrow. The question is, how do I get to Portland?"

"I'd give you my tender. A Zodiac with a thirty-horse power motor. Goes like hell. But could you find your way?"

"Without fog, I could. How about I use the inflatable to run back to the boat rental place, get my rental car, and go from there."

"What boat rental place?"

Roberts told me the story about wrecking the Boston Whaler.

"It seems to me that the boat rental people are going to be asking a lot of questions if you come sauntering up to their dock in a Zodiac."

"Not if I land the boat and just go get the car. There's an abandoned lighthouse just around the corner from the rental. I could land there, get the car and be on my way. Can you find my keys? Your partner put them somewhere."

"Yeah, I saw your keys on the kitchen counter. I'll get them when I go back inside. Are you sure that you can be back here early tomorrow morning?"

"If things go well, maybe even tonight."

His plan seemed plausible. He even sounded enthusiastic,

a chance to practice the profession he'd never mentally left. I went back into the cabin, picked up Roberts' car keys and went into Bob's bedroom. He was sleeping like a baby. I checked in his pants pocket, found the padlock key, and went back to unchain Roberts.

Free of the chain, Roberts went through a series of stretching exercises, deep knee bends, back twists, swinging arms, neck bobs, the whole gambit. He wound up the routine with a bunch of push-ups, ending by flipping over on his back to pull one knee then the other up to chin and back down. About to get up, he asked, "How about a hand?"

I reached out to him and in a split second, I was on *my* back with Roberts on top of me. His eyes shot darts. He grabbed my wrists and twisted my arms above my head. Pain shot through my shoulders and down the length of my back. "Listen, you creep," Roberts said, his spittle spraying my face, "You mess with the FBI, this is what you get." He let go of my left arm and slapped me hard across the face. I grabbed his hair, tried to knee his back, yelled as loudly as I could, but it was of no use. His hands grasped my throat. "Resisting arrest," he hissed, bearing down. "You don't do that to a federal officer." His hands tightened.

I was on the verge of passing out when felt something warm splashed over my face. Roberts' grip eased. I gasped for air. His body slumped forward, twisting and writhing on top of me. I was caught in a nightmarish tangle of snakes. I struggled to breath. I tasted blood as a gush of viscous fluid cascaded over my face and neck. Roberts' shuddering body fell to the side. Vomiting, I twisted away from it, grabbing long, noisy breaths before settling into steady inhales and exhales.

When I looked up, there was Bob standing over Roberts' body, a blood-covered maul in his right hand, an odd look in his eye. It was a look I hoped never to see again and one I knew I'd never forget.

Bob looked at me. A long silence passed between us before he finally said, "Let's get you cleaned up. We have some work to do."

Setting the maul aside, Bob leaned down and helped me to my feet. Now still, Roberts's body lay face down. A jagged crater the depth of the maul's head had been chopped in the center of his shoulder blades. Bits of exposed vertebrae were embedded in bloody flesh and torn cloth. I turned to the porch rail and threw up again. Never in my life had I seen such gore, such absolute destruction of the human body. I wiped my mouth. "My God Bob, we just killed a man. Wasn't there another way?"

"*I* just killed a man," Bob shot back. "Not you. But, I'd rather look at it like I was saving your life, not taking his."

"Self-defense?"

"Yeah, you could say that." Bob moved to cover the corpse with the old army blanket. "Let it go, Charlie. Let's go inside and get you cleaned up."

I said, "Wait, Bob. I've never been involved in a killing before. Shouldn't we at least call the police, I mean let somebody know about this?"

Bob walked to the far end of the porch, as far as he could go from Robert's body. He turned, staring me in the eye.

"You say that like I enjoyed myself—like I'm a serial killer or something. For the record, this is a first for me and I don't enjoy being treated like I'm some deranged murderer. Can't you ever just understand that life is something that happens, that we're not in charge of every goddamn thing under the sun? Roberts was a nutcase, pure and simple. He couldn't get over growing old. For Christ sake, the bastard would've killed you!"

Poking his finger at me, he raged on, "Suppose I was the one being choked to death, what would you've done? Asked Roberts to please stop hurting your friend? Call for Mommy? What the hell was I supposed to do, tap him on the shoulder? If you haven't noticed, I'm a bit weak these days. If I didn't take him out with one blow, he could have killed us both.

"So, go ahead," Bob said sarcastically, "make the call. But before you do, here's some facts. First, the police will come out here, ask all sorts of questions. Forget the sailing trip; we'll be tied up with inquests, district attorneys, lawyers, detectives. Newspaper folk will descend on my island like hungry black flies. Second, you'll be back in Sunset faster than a cat shot in the ass. Third, I'll be dead before the legal wheel turns half-way. So, go ahead and make your call if makes you feel better." Bob side-armed me out of the way, grabbed the screen door, and disappeared inside.

Stunned, I moved to the side of the porch away from Roberts' corpse. I looked down at *That Good Night*. My first impulse was to jump aboard. Hide myself from myself. I want life to be simple. I've always wanted that. But life isn't simple, is it? All I wanted was to get out of Sunset and enjoy my remaining days sailing. But no, my kids abandon me, my best friend is dying, I was just nearly killed. And now instead of praising Bob for saving my life, I challenge him. Life is a series of decisions. We have choices to make right up to the end, that is if we still have the guts or wherewithal to make them. Back at Sunset, we were denied choice. We ate what they gave us, didn't get to go shopping, went to bed and woke up according to a schedule. Hell, life without choice is no life at all. Bob's right of course, calling the police or anyone else about killing Roberts would be the end of it.

I caught a whiff of myself. Vomit, the coppery smell of blood, and God knows what else. My shirt looked like it was tie-dyed by a butcher.

I went into the cabin. Bob was sitting with his elbows on the table, his head bowed and cupped in his hands.

Without moving, he said, "Sorry about all that. Caught up in it, I guess."

"You did the right thing, Bob. There was no alternative. And as far as calling the police, I was way off base. Can we go on from here?"

"Yup," was all Bob had to say.

"So," I asked, "how did you know I was in trouble out there? You were sound asleep when I left your bedroom."

"You wake a dead man when you go through his pockets," he answered.

"The key?" I asked.

"Yup," Bob said, slowly getting up from his chair, and giving me a grin that made everything seem as right as rain. "Why don't you get cleaned up," he said. "Those clothes will have to go into the burn barrel. While you're in the shower, I'll go down to your boat and get some fresh stuff. There's a bottle of mouthwash in the medicine chest. I suggest that you use it."

I went through a half bottle of Listerine before my mouth felt even close to being clean. Hearing my gargling, Bob popped into the bathroom to hand me a tall glass of Black Grouse. "You need this," he said, leaving. I took a few healthy swigs. I stayed in the shower until the hot water gave out. I could have used another half hour, and knew that I wouldn't feel clean for a long time. Bob called to me that he had my change of clothes, which he had brought up from the boat. "Found these," he said dangling up a sexy red thong through the partially opened bathroom door. "Pretty good time in Boston, huh?" he teased. I grabbed them and let it go at that. How Bob was able to joke after going from abject pain to a snooze to killing a man was beyond me, but Bob is Bob and may he never change. Washed and dressed, I joined him at the table.

"I guess that we better clean up," I suggested, gesturing toward the porch.

"No need right now, Charlie. Friends are on the way. We've had enough struggles for one day. Go down to that boat of yours and take a nap, maybe snuggle up with that thong, slip it over your head for all I care," he laughed. I just shook my head and left. On my way out, I focused my eyes straight ahead. One look at *That Good Night* with her promise of safety and solace was all I needed.

I woke up from my nap to the heavy throbbing of a turbo diesel and looked out of the companionway. A lobster boat was tying up behind *That Good Night*. Three men hopped off the boat. Though the weather was clear, they were dressed in yellow foul weather gear. They headed up to Bob's cabin. I gave a thought to joining them, but the thought of the gruesome act of cleaning up the porch killed that idea.

About an hour later once the mess was taken care of, Bob called down to me to come up and meet his friends: Francis Jensen, Earl Honauer, and Dustin Adams, all retired lobstermen, each hitting their mid-seventies. I was the interloper as they exchanged one fishing story after another: traps wrecked after storms; the idiots that moved in on their territories only to find their traps destroyed; the varying price of lobster, the big four pounders. They talked of boats and engines and stories of wives and children, families stretching back generations. They were shocked over Maine property value reaching unimaginable heights and didn't like the idea that our government was ungovernable. But not once in all this conversation did talk of the disposal of Roberts' body cross their lips. The porch was as clean as a pin; all signs of Roberts having been there were gone. When I asked about it, I got cold stares. Bob offered that Roberts must have died at sea. His battered rental from Dinger's Rentals was already reported to the coast guard. Martha Dinger confirmed that Roberts had rented the boat. The rowboat was returned to Hi Fabinham as if it had never left his property. A search was on. Maybe Roberts' body would wash up, maybe not. That's the way it goes in tidal Bay of Fundy.

I could sense that Bob was experiencing the onset of pain. He affirmed my suspicion when he got up and, excusing himself, went inside. I followed, letting the lobstermen get back to storytelling. Bob took three more pills and headed to his bedroom.

"Tell the guys I have a stomach virus and went to bed. They'll understand." I nodded and told him that I'd check in on him later. I left his room and returned to the porch.

The lobstermen were standing at the sturdy railing peering down at *That Good Night*. "Pretty fancy boat you got there," Earl commented. "Draw a lot?"

"Five feet," I said.

"Pretty good for such a big boat. How long is she anyway?"

Francis asked.

"She's forty-six feet overall," I answered.

"Bob says you single-hand. A bit of a chore, I'd say," he said.

"Not bad once you get used to it. She has a lot of extras that make it doable."

Conversation bogged down and the four us just stared straight ahead. There just wasn't a lot we had in common.

Francis broke the silence with a bit of sarcasm: "I guess we better be on our way. I hope the Coast Guard finds that guy. It can get pretty lonely floating around Fundy." Muffled chuckles all around. I ignored the macabre banter.

I joined the three guys for the walk down to the dock. About ready to climb aboard their boat, Dustin paused and asked, "So tell me, what's going on with Bob? Doesn't seem himself. Hasn't for some time."

"I think he has some kind of virus," I lied.

The three men looked at each other, then Dustin continued, "Look, Charlie, we don't mean to pry, but that's no virus. We've known Bob since grammar school, fished with him, our families grew up together. Why, we're as close as twins in a womb. Now, Bob's always been the quiet sort, keeps his cards pretty close to his chest. If you know something that we don't know that would help that stubborn mule, why not just come out and say it."

Here I was being stared at by three of the most honest, hardworking men on this earth—albeit now involved in a conspiracy to dispose of a corpse—and lying to them. Well, I just couldn't do it. Breaking the promise I made to Bob was a serious matter, but watching him suffer was worse. "Cancer," I said hoarsely. "Bob has cancer."

"How far along?" Francis asked matter-of-factly.

"I'm not sure. He said it's spread and that he doesn't have much time left. He asked me take him on one last sailing cruise. That's all I really know."

Of course, you can imagine how somber all this was, the four of us standing on Bob's dock realizing that each of us in our way was about to lose a dear friend. Earl had turned away to dab his eyes, not willing to let his friends see his tears.

"There's got to be something we can do. Hell, we just can't let the man suffer," he said.

I said, "Bob made me promise that I wouldn't tell a soul, so whatever you do, you've got to act like you've come upon this on your own."

"Oh hell, that's Bob all right, stoic as a terrier meeting a grizzly," Francis said.

"There is one thing you might help with, but it's a long shot," I said. "Morphine. If I could get some morphine, it would ease Bob's pain, which is going to get a lot worse."

Earl rejoined us. His eyes were red and swollen. "Morphine?" he said. "They gave that to my mother during her last days. It works with the pain, but it sure put her down."

"More than the pain?" I asked.

"Well now," Earl came back, "You got a point there. Let's just say she was better off being in another world."

"How soon do we need to get it?" Francis asked

"As soon as possible," I said. "With the investigator 'lost at sea,' we're free to go on that last voyage. I'd like to depart tomorrow if we could."

Dustin jumped in, "We can get some. There's always ways." The others nodded their head in agreement.

"It'll be expensive," I said.

"You let us worry about that, Charlie. We'll take care of that. You take care of Bob," Francis said.

"Bob can't know where I got it. How do you plan to get it to me before we leave?"

"What time you casting off?" Francis asked.

"I'll take the tide out; I think it's around ten."

"We'll be here to send you off. We can get it to you then."

Before jumping aboard the lobster boat, Earl approached me.

"Hey Charlie," he said, "when we were getting that guy ready, you know up on the porch, I had to, well, uh, lift him up some. Oh, the looks of that fella wasn't something to talk about in church, I'll tell you that. I used his belt, well, like he was a suitcase and his belt was a handle and the dang buckle snapped open and came right off in my hand. Now, I think this here buckle is some strange gizmo because when I fiddled with the flicker thing, a teensy light on the back lit up green.

"Here, I'll show you." With that Earl flipped the post back and forth, and sure enough, a pinhole sized light flickered green.

"Thanks, Earl. You did good work. I'll have to check it out," I said, pocketing the device. Thinking of the tiny FBI gun Roberts pulled on me, my guess is that this new find had something to do with his investigation. I made a mental note to examine it once I had a moment.

Without another word, Earl undid the bow line and jumped aboard. Francis cranked the engine, and in a plume of diesel exhaust, they were off.

I climbed aboard *That Good Night* and went below to cook up some soup for Bob. Cook? Hell, I heated up a can of Campbell's and headed back to the cabin. Bob was sleeping. I put the heated soup on the cold stove, and then went to his side.

His snoring let me know that pain was not an issue. I returned to the kitchen and stuck a note on the pot that he should just heat and eat. As I was about to leave, Bob called my name. He was sitting up when I reentered his bedroom. "Good sleep?" I asked.

"Slept more in the last three days than I did during my entire lifetime. Don't like it. There's work to be done." The minute he stood, he teetered and plopped back down on the edge of the bed. "Do me a favor, he said. "In the third drawer in the dresser is a yellow envelope. Can you get it for me?" I did as he asked and handed the envelope over to him. "This," he said, "is important." For the next half hour, Bob explained that the envelope contained his last will and testament. "All signed and legal," he said proudly. "Giving some of my stuff to the kids and the church, but this here island is going to The Nature Conservancy. Those deer out there are the real owners, but they sure as hell can't hold a deed. Folks at the Conservancy, they'll do right by these creatures. Lawyer has the originals; he'll handle everything. All I need is for you to call him when the time comes, his number's on the front of the envelope, right here," he pointed. It read Arden Schmidt, Esq., followed by an address and phone number. I asked Bob why he was giving me the envelope. "You never know. If old Arden dies or gets killed before I do, you have the back up."

"And what's the likelihood of that happening?" I asked.

"Snowball's chance." Bob snorted.

I took the envelope. "How about some soup?"

"Yup, that'd be good."

"Let me heat it up for you before I head back to the boat."

"No, Charlie, you did enough for one day. I can get by."

Hoping that the lobstermen would show up with the

morphine in time for us to depart, I said. "We can leave on the voyage tomorrow if you're up to it."

"Yup," he said. "We can."

We said goodnight and I returned to my boat. Before turning in, I grabbed a can of tuna and ate it right out of the can. That night, I slept the sleep of the dead, Abigail's thong tucked under my pillow, stuffy cradled in my arms.

SUNDAY, JULY 29

The weather report couldn't be better. High pressure centered over Northern New York would probably keep Maine sunny for at least three or four days. The sailplan that I laid out would take us to Boothbay Harbor then up into Penobscot Bay. From there we would sail the wind. Since Grand Manan Island was in Canadian waters, I couldn't go there with an outdated passport. Maine, though, is good enough, it being one of, if not the best sailing waters in the world. I had a cup of coffee onboard before going to check on Bob, hoping that the boys would show up with the goods. I wouldn't leave without the morphine.

On approaching the cabin, I was relieved to see Bob's old sea bag sitting on the porch. That raggedy bag has been with Bob since I first met him.

Because the lobstermen hadn't shown up yet, I suggested that we might want to take a stroll around the island before leaving, but Bob refused, itching to get to sea. He grabbed his sea bag and started heading for the boat. About halfway down the path, I heard the unmistakable sound of a lobster boat running full tilt. "What are they doing here?" Bob asked.

"Come to see us off," I answered which seemed to please Bob to no end.

We grabbed their lines as Francis shut down the engine.

"We're here to give you a going away present. Two

three-pounders we pulled just this morning." He gave me a wink as he handed me the bag.

"What do I owe you?" I asked.

"On the house," he said.

Francis walked over to Bob and handed him a piece of paper. "My cell phone just in case you need it."

Bob stuck it in his shirt pocket and closed the button. "We won't, unless we send this crate of Charlie's onto the rocks. But thanks."

Earl came off the boat and gave Bob a big hug. "Have a good time, old man," he said, near tears.

"Whoa, what's all that? Be gone a bit, but not much more, Earl. Tell the missus I send my regards."

Earl steeled himself, "You guys get set and we'll cast you off. Go on now.

Bob and I got on board. "I'll go below and take care of the shore power switches then you can disconnect," I said to Bob.

"I know the drill," he answered back.

After I turned off the shore power panel, I looked in the bag that Francis had given me. Besides two good-sized lobsters there was a small Tupperware box with four vials of morphine and a half dozen or so needles. I secreted the Tupperware in my dresser drawer in the stateroom, and then put the lobster in the refrigerator. Before going topside, I flicked on the appropriate switches and yelled up to Bob, "Fire it up." He started the engine. I came topside, the lobstermen tossed me the docking lines and we were on our way.

With Bob at the helm, I raised the sails. Bob cut the engine and the sails filled.

I hadn't sailed with Bob in fifteen years or so, but that space collapsed the minute we were on the boat. Bob had a grin on his face like a kid out for his first solo around the marks. Islands notwithstanding, we had the sails set shortly after leaving Bob's dock. His tacit knowledge of the area had us close-hauled one minute, reaching the next, as we soared around this and that island like a flitting dragonfly. Forty-six feet of boat, full keel and all, flying a 150 Genoa, and full main, *That Good Night* might as well have been a sleek sailing dinghy in the hands of teenagers. I busily tended sheets to Bob's calls of *hard-a lee, falling off, coming-up, prepare to jibe, jibe-ho*. We rounded Cape Small and to avoid a running tide sweeping out of the Kennebec River, we reached on a Southwest wind to the southern tip of Seguin Island then ran our way eastward to Boothbay Harbor.

The hearty set of sail accompanied by the frothy white hissing from the boat's bow has been the sailors' song from time immemorial. We talked of olden times, compared notes on the marvels of sailing such a responsive vessel, and busted our guts laughing over the escape from Sunset. Nearing Boothbay, we decided to forego the business of being tourists in favor of anchoring. Slipping east past Squirrel Island we made for Linekin Bay, a stone's throw from Boothbay. With practiced ease Bob sailed to one of his favored anchoring spots, a cove tucked into the northeastern corner of the Bay. "Prepare to anchor," he called out, adding "under sail." I furled the genoa before switching on the anchor winch. Rounding up, the main centered on the wind, the boat lost headway and Bob gave the order to drop anchor, which I did with the flick of a switch. Anchor set, I furled the fluttering main with yet another button. We patted each other on the back with congratulations all around for anchoring the way it used to be.

Secure, we had our traditional drinks of scotch for me, and rum for Bob. For dinner we boiled the lobster, served it with canned potatoes and canned peas and washed it down with a bottle of Chardonnay. Bob commented on the luxury of *That Good Night*, with both of us agreeing that we damned well deserved it. Near bedtime, Bob complained of a mild headache, but other than that, he seemed fine. Holding to our tradition, Bob told me that coffee would be ready when I woke up, which was usually about an hour or more after Bob.

MONDAY, JULY 30

I awoke early to the sounds of gulls and the squeaky chirp of osprey. A wake from a passing boat had *That Good Night* gently swaying like a rocking cradle. The stillness was a luxury after the tension of the past few days. I amazed myself how easy it was to put Roberts somewhere in the wake of the boat. I'm not one for killing anybody, but I guess sometimes it's kill or be killed, and then it just has to be done. I thought about Emma and hoped that she was doing well. And Cat? I would love to see that kid grow to adulthood!

Just before getting out of bed, as had become my morning ritual, I said Lori's name softly as if she just might answer.

I was washing my face when it dawned on me that there was no smell of coffee, no one prodding me to *get the hell out of bed*. Bob was going to get the full brunt of my teasing for having slept longer than I did. A first, I assure you. After toweling off, I headed aft. The aft cabin door was closed. No snoring came through the louvered door and I knew right then and there that I had lost the best friend a man could ever want. Gently, I opened the door, hoping against hope that I was wrong, that Bob would be grinning his shit eating grin of *gotcha*. But no. Bob was lying on his back, eyes closed, relaxed in everlasting slumber. I searched for a pulse. I put my ear next to his nose listening for even the smallest breath. I held his still-warm hand. And I cried.

In time, I covered Bob with a sheet, made a pot of coffee, and went up on deck, the steaming mug in hand. Everything seemed changed for me. Where was I going with this boat of mine? Was my ship the Flying Dutchman, doomed to sail alone forever, never to make port? Bob was hope for me. He was my destination. My port-of-call. All gone. Losing Bob was losing a part of me. I guess when you live too long, there's no one left to visit, to think about, to hope for. Now I can see why some old people just give up.

I finished my coffee and shook my head to undo the cobwebs left over from deep-felt grief. I thought of calling the Coast Guard and letting them handle the details. Maybe going back to Sunset wouldn't be all that bad. Grief can twist reality that way, letting false hope in where there is no hope to find. I needed time to gather my wits about myself. I walked around the deck. The sun was already full up. A new day had dawned, a sad one, but one to be reckoned with nonetheless. I went down below and carefully undid Bob's shirt pocket. I retrieved Francis' phone number and called him on my cell.

Francis took the bad news as if it were no surprise. "Maybe best," he said. "Bob deserved to die at sea." He asked for my lat/lon and suggested that I head back to Bob's island, that he'd meet me somewhere along the way. We agreed to stay in contact by cell phone and not to use VHF.

I was about ten nautical miles west of Boothbay when a lobster boat headed my way. Francis pulled alongside and motioned that he'd stay behind me on my port side. Dustin and Earl waved a somber greeting. A few miles further along, two other lobster boats joined us, then another two, then three more, and more yet until I had some twenty rumbling lobster boats all flying black flags motoring behind me. Bob was being celebrated not for some heroic act. He wasn't a firefighter, or a soldier, he didn't jump off a bridge to save a drowning child. Bob was just Bob, an honest, hardworking, tough Mainer who lived his life the way he wanted to. Now, I'm not a religious person. I don't believe in heaven as a place, and if there is a place, Bob wouldn't like it very much. He certainly wouldn't like flying around and being nice to everyone. But, looking back on those lobster boats, I automatically looked up in the sky hoping Bob was seeing all this. To cover all my bases, I hollered down below, "Hey, Bob what do you think of this?"

My VHF came to life as lobstermen chatted from boat to boat with stories about Bob, *remember the time he did this* or *remember when he did that.* It was a wake creating a wake. This time, I was proud to be the hearse.

As we neared Bob's island, one by one the boats peeled off, sounding their air horns as they left in a mournful salute to one of their own. Men stood on deck saluting.

I brought *That Good Night* dockside. Francis followed. Dustin and Earl jumped ashore. Earl took my dock lines as Dustin tied off Francis' boat.

"This is just terrible," Earl said, "Terrible is what it is. I've known Bob forever. I just don't know what to do. Terrible."

"It's all of that," I agreed.

Francis left his boat and came aboard *That Good Night.* I said to him, "That was some display of boats out there. I wonder how they knew about Bob's passing? We were on radio silence, or so I thought."

With a sheepish grin, Francis gave a slight shrug of his shoulder's. "Beat's me," he said, evading the question.

After securing my dock lines, Dustin and Earl joined me and Francis on my boat for a chat.

We sat in the cockpit to discuss things. Francis began, "Bob filled us in about your needing to lay low, so let's make sure we keep it that way. The way we figure it, it'd be probably best to put Bob in his bed and just say that's where he died. That way we avoid the Coast Guard and a lot of red tape. Do you agree?"

I nodded my approval.

"Well, then," Francis added, "I think we need to move Bob's body and be done with it."

"He's in the aft cabin," I said. "Let me go down below for a few minutes, and then it's all up to you."

"Take all the time you need," Francis said quietly.

Seeing Bob the second time was more devastating than when I first discovered him dead. Tears came immediately. Sobs followed. It had been an unusual friendship. He didn't live down the street from me; we weren't members of the same club or church. We didn't talk sports or exchange books or hunt together or fish. Our families never met; they were outside our circle of friendship. When we sailed together, it was as if the entire world spun around our boat. There was never a call for giving orders. When the sails needed trimming, it happened. The same with anchoring or with all the little things required of sailors. In storms that would make a man's knees shake, there was calm onboard. No drinking underway, always a scotch or rum when the anchor was set.

We lost contact with each other for more than a decade, and then, with my call for help, those vacuous years disappeared in an instant. He came to my aid without hesitation.

"Remember Cat?" I said to Bob's lingering spirit. "You two

made quite a couple." From there I reminisced: The time we first met. That storm just off Grand Manan Island. The times we went aground, caught lines in our props, dragged anchors and a whole lot more.

I kissed his forehead before going topside. "He's ready," I said to Francis. One by one the men descended the companionway, hats removed.

Soft murmurings came from below accompanied by quiet weeping and a few bursts of "Oh, Bob," from Earl, I guessed. I was standing looking out on the Bay when Francis called, "We're bringing him up." I stood aside and remained on board as the three men solemnly carried Bob up to his cabin. A chapter of my life was closed. One more, I told myself, one last chapter left of Charley Lambert's life.

I went back down below, retrieved the envelope that Bob had given me and called Arden Schmitt, Esq. A crusty voice answered the call.

"Arden Schmitt here. Who's calling?"

I introduced myself as Charlie, Bob Liscome's friend.

"Unfortunately, I was expecting your call. I assume that your call is to tell me that Bob's gone. Right?" Before I could answer, he jumped in demanding, "Hold the fort. You understand that. Hold the fort. Don't for one holy minute let any of Bob's family on that island. Dead man's relatives can smell inheritance like a dog smells you know what. Anybody with you?" I told him about Francis and his boys. "That's as good as having a pack of Dobermans. Tell them to keep the place tied up until I get there. Not one person more on that island until I get there, you got that?"

I answered with a simple, "Yes sir."

"Good. I should be on the island early tomorrow morning. We'll go from there." Arden hung up.

"Good going, Bob," I said, looking over at the empty quarter berth.

Walking up the path to the cabin, I saw Francis, Earl, and Dylan sitting on the porch, feet on the railing, each drinking a beer. I stepped up on the porch and took a seat. Earl handed me a can. "Damn," he said, "that was about the hardest thing I ever did, putting Bob to rest." He wiped away a tear. "We've been friends since Miss Potter's class back in the third grade. Clammed, fished, drank, and pissed together since forever."

I raised my can of beer. "Here's to Bob," I offered.

"Damn right," Dylan chimed in. Our toast was followed by reverent silence.

I told the lobstermen about my call to Arden Schmitt and they agreed to guard the island, Francis assigning each of us to various posts. I was assigned to the dock. "See something, do something," Francis commanded. "We'll lock this place up tighter than a bullfrog's ass."

It was now getting late in the day and my stomach was in a full blown protest. Dylan and I went into the cabin and boiled up some potatoes, cut raw carrots, and grilled whatever fish it was that Bob had in the refrigerator.

During dinner on the porch, I asked, "Where does Bob keep his boat? I haven't seen it anywhere. There must be one." The boys looked at each other with sadness all around.

"Nope, and you won't see none neither," Earl said.

"Why's that?" I asked.

"Because he gave it away," Earl said, a look of disappointment crossing his weather-beaten brow. "It was a Beale! Know anything about lobster boats, Charlie?" I shook my head. He went on to explain in one hell of a long story about the famous boat builder, its design features, the turbo diesel, special handling characteristics, how it's the envy of all the lobstermen and a few stories about Bob and his boat. "There was that time he was hauling up traps and found a bag of *marijuana* hanging from one of the traps. Kept us all pretty happy for a month or so."

Francis took over. "Just so you know, Charlie, a good lobster boat up here is a matter of pride. You folks From Away might like your fancy cars or McMansions, but around here we take to boats, and a Beale is status. Now don't get me wrong, it's not like wearing diamonds or Rolex watches. The status here comes from power, grace, reliability, and safety. I must admit, when Bob gave that boat away, I suspected that he was on the edge of craziness. And I felt a real disappointment because I wanted that boat more than a good shade tree on a hot summer's day."

"So, who did he give it to?" I asked.

"That's the craziness behind it all. He gave it to the bird people. The Audubon folks up to Hog Island. Why? He never said. One day it was here. The next it was gone." Francis hung his head like a kid who lost his last quarter down a sewer drain.

"When did he do that?" I asked.

"Maybe two weeks ago," Francis answered.

Each of us became lost in our own thoughts. Our quiet was filled in with the now familiar sounds of an island in Maine: birds, buzzing insects, croaks with a background of tidal swishes and lapping saltwater.

Francis broke our collective reverie by reviewing our guard assignment. "We'll spot anyone nearing the place and that'll be that," Francis assured me before walking off. "You can stay here and relax, we've got things covered."

I slumped down on an Adirondack. Soon enough a deer meandered its way across the lawn. A light sea breeze stirred the branches and brambles which framed both sides of the mown grass. It was quiet and peaceful, but empty now that Bob was gone. Things were not the same, would never be the same for me and I just wanted to leave, get off this island. But to where? I've never sailed to nowhere before.

In time, Francis wandered back to the cabin for insect repellent, the perfume of dusk in Maine. I said my good night and headed down the brick path to my boat. I sat up for a long time that night thinking about where to go or what to do. I wasn't one to take to the deep blue sea without having a clue of where to go. I thought of calling Cat, see if he was interested in sailing. I scrapped that idea. Three scotches later, I decided to just head south along the coast putting in here and there. Perhaps things would become clearer if I just gave myself some time. A good sleep would help.

TUESDAY, JULY 31

Arden Schmitt stood all of five feet, four inches tall with an equator for a waistline. Tufts of wiry gray hair jutted at strange angles from his balding head. Thick bushy eyebrows shaded deep-set brown eyes that were solid and focused. He was dressed in an off-white linen jacket, wrinkled and unkempt. No tie. Thick kakis and leather boat shoes. We were having breakfast when we heard his launch approach the dock and met him halfway up the path. He greeted Francis, Dylan, and Earl like they were old friends before turning to me. "You must be Charlie," he said, proffering his puffy hand which once around mine, squeezed the bejesus out of it. "Hell of a boat you've got there," he said, casting his eye toward the dock. I was about to say something when he continued, "So boys, we have some work to do. Coffee?"

We filled Arden in on Bob dying on my boat, the sail back to the cabin, putting him into his bed, and making the call.

"Given the circumstances of your needing anonymity, Charlie, I'd prefer to keep you clear of all this, but that's not going to happen, given that word of Bob's demise has already reached shore. A parade of lobster boats and all that VHF chatter saw to that. What I'm saying is that the medical examiner who got word of all the chatter wants to come over here and be sure everything's on the up and up. Expect him to be here by noon. I've got Bob's medical file in my briefcase, so cause of death won't be an issue."

"So, what's the problem?" I asked.

"Well, you see, Charlie, when somebody dies on a boat, the Coast Guard gets involved and when the Coast Guard gets involved it's a matter of homeland security. And since that's the case these days, who knows what the hell they're going to do. They might want to see your papers, you know, bill of sale, documentation, and all that crap. From what Bob told me, that might be a problem. Is it?"

"Not really," I answered. "I'm leasing the boat." I didn't tell Arden about the demise of poor old Doris Heller. That was none of his business. I did say nonchalantly, "I'm not worried about it," which caused the lawyer to frown an unspoken question. I let it go.

Arden continued. "From the look of things, your boat should pass inspection without a hitch. I've already got Bob's will ready for probate, so once the Coasties leave, we'll have to get Bob to the funeral home before I contact the family. The island here gets locked up until the Nature Conservancy takes over. As far as Bob's stuff is concerned, it'll have to sit here until the will's settled." Arden turned to me. "Exception of course, Charlie. Stay as long as you like, just leave things as they are." I thanked him with a nod.

As it turned out, the medical examiner only asked a few questions, glanced at Bob's medical report, and declared everything on the up and up. As the ME was leaving, three Coasties showed up in one of those inflatable fast-boats outfitted with two 150 HP Mercs, flashing lights aplenty. A machine gun was mounted forward. Arden walked up to the cabin, leaving the four of us to deal with the ritual of boat inspection.

The Coasties were all business. "Permission to board your vessel, sir," Chief Coastie asked.

"Permission granted," I answered.

I was asked for my ships papers: lease, insurance, documentation, personal identification (the out-of-date passport was acceptable). On to safety: life jackets, fire extinguishers, flares. They checked the bilge for oil.

Back on the dock, the Coastie that seemed to be in-charge asked me, "Did you transport a dead body, sir?"

"No, I did not," I stated.

"Your radio transmissions seemed to indicate otherwise."

"What you heard, officer, was a memorial parade honoring a dead sailor whose body is in his bed up there," I said, pointing toward the cabin.

Francis chimed in, "That's right, sir. Old Bob died in bed. We came to pay our respects. Care to take a look?"

The Coastie shook his head. "Well, I guess nothing can be proven. As long as everything is in order, we'll be on our way." He turned to leave but hesitated. Looking around at us, he asked, "You know about the missing person, suspected drowning?"

"Yes sir, we do," answered Francis.

"Any signs of him?" the Coastie asked.

We all looked at each other like truant kids standing before a principal.

"Nope."

"Nary a hair."

"Couldn't say I saw any."

"Not on my watch."

"Well, keep your eyes out," the Coastie said before turning to me. "And you, Mr. Lambert, take care of yourself and good luck out there. Need anything, give us a call."

With that, the Coast Guardsmen returned to their speedboat and roared off toward Portland.

Officials out of the way, Arden prepared to leave. "Some folks from a Portland funeral home will be by soon to claim the body. Can you guys handle that?"

"Well," Francis offered, "if it's all the same to you, we need to tend our traps before those lobsters start eating each other. We can't be letting that happen, can we, boys?" Earl and Dylan shook their heads.

I offered to stay until the funeral folks come for the body. After all, I really wasn't in a rush to go anywhere. Following in short order, Francis, Dylan, and Earl bid farewell, headed to their boat and cast off with a smoking stack and the roar of their diesel.

I walked Arden to his boat.

After handing him the now redundant envelope Bob gave me *just in case*, I said to Arden, "I have a favor to ask," I said.

"Go ahead," he replied.

"I want to retain you for some unfinished business."

"Consider it done," he said. "What business?"

I explained the whole nine yards, escaping Sunset, leasing the boat, having a bag of warm money and that I would never under any circumstances return to a nursing home.

"I'll probably head south," I told him, "maybe end my days in the Caribbean somewhere. I need to get my affairs in order and I need to do something with my money."

"Where is it now?" he asked.

"On my boat."

"A lot?"

"A lot," I answered.

"Traceable to anything other than you own it clear and free? In other words, did you steal it?"

I answered, "No, I didn't steal it. It's mine free and clear. I earned it, Arden; that's where I got it, blood, sweat, and tears. So?"

"I could set up an account at the firm, an escrow account. We can send you a check whenever you ask for it. There'll be a fee, of course."

"That works for me. Another thing, I want to name you as executor."

"Like I did with Bob?"

"Yes, like you did with Bob."

"Can do," he said.

"When?"

"Well, not here. Not this minute. Any way you can get to Portland?"

Glancing over to *That Good Night*, I said, "I think I can handle that."

Handing me his card, he said, "Call me and we'll set up a time. We can take care of the money when we meet."

"How about tomorrow?" I asked.

"Tomorrow morning's fine. Can you make it by, say 10:30?"

"I'll be there," I said. We shook hands, Arden jumped aboard his launch, I tossed him his docking lines and he was off.

I climbed aboard *That Good Night*, sat down in the cockpit and watched his boat until an island took him out of sight. The roaring sound of the engine lingered a bit longer. Then silence. I went below, poured a scotch, and then made my way back to the porch to wait for the folks from the funeral home. The subtle rustling of a breeze soughing through the trees. A chattering squirrel. Bird song. Lapping water. The distant sound of a bell buoy. An unseen osprey chirping to its young. I looked down the flower-edged path to *That Good Night* bobbing softly to the rhythm of the tidal flow. The water was sunlit blue. Without Bob's care, I figured the flowers might have a few weeks before the weeds start crowding them out. The grass was already getting a bit long. Death of one is the death of many, I suppose. My eye caught the flit of a butterfly, then moved to watch a spider on a porch roof rafter dash quickly along its web to capture a fly. Bob's lingering presence was all around me. I closed my eyes and drifted off. I woke to the soft clatter of a diesel.

Two men from the funeral home tied up their grey cruiser to the dock, right behind *That Good Night*. It was all rather formal: They came, bagged Bob's body, wheeled it on a gurney to their boat and left. We said only a few words. I had to sign a paper. And that was that.

I had lost my best friend. The last one alive. I was alone. Very much alone. It was too late in the day to sail down to Portland. I felt myself giving in to inertia but was suddenly jolted when my mind scooped up an image of Sunset's television room: Booming from its squeaky speaker was *The Price is Right*, around me sat huddled figures, some nodding off, some watching the screen, some sound asleep under hand-knitted blankets.

I stood, gathered my thoughts and headed off the porch to give Bob's plantings a final shot at a good life. I found an old gas mower in his shed and dragged it to the lawn. It started on the first pull. When I finished mowing, I put the mower back in the shed, grabbed a weeding hoe and cleaned up the flower beds. I put the tools back in the shed, knowing that they might just sit for a long, long time. The grass and flowers lining the walkway beamed contentment. A little tending was all they needed. Don't we all? I retrieved my empty scotch glass from the porch and retreated to *That Good Night*. I thawed some frozen lasagna, ate what I could, put on a recording of Glenn Gould playing Bach, crawled into my berth and, to end the longest day in my life, fell fast asleep.

WEDNESDAY, AUGUST 1

I didn't bother with sails; it was too busy with all the islands about. Slow ahead, it took a bit more than two hours before I was tied up at Portland Marine. A short cab ride had me at Arden's office. It was 1015 hours.

I tipped the cabbie and, being the old tar that I was, slung my duffle bag of money over my right shoulder, and walked briskly. The storefront office could easily pass for a 19th-century movie set: electrified gas lights, a pot-bellied stove, an oak wall clock with roman numerals and swinging pendulum. Green felt covered the receptionist desk. The computer was disguised behind an oak paneled screen. Miss Ethanridge, Arden's secretary, greeted me with bright hazel eyes behind cute wire-rimmed glasses. Her grey hair was pulled tightly into a pinned bun on the back of her head. She led me along a short hallway to a quaint waiting room just outside of Arden's office.

Directing me to a dark burgundy high winged-back leather chair complete with tufts and the wrinkles of age, she asked, "May I take your bag, Mr. Lambert?"

I answered, "No thank you, ma'am, I'll just hold onto her."

She gave me a quiet smile. "Will you be having tea or coffee, Mr. Lambert?" she asked politely.

"Coffee, black please."

"My pleasure. Please make yourself comfortable," she said,

turning and leaving the room.

I placed my duffle to the left of my chair and sat down. On wood-paneled walls hung oil paintings of ships and commerce, portraits and renderings of old Portland, each painting with its own focused light. The floor was covered with a thick, fringed Sarouk carpet. To my right, separated by a leather topped end-table was a matching wing-backed chair. A damask covered sofa was across the room. Above it was a large gold-framed abstract seascape which reminded me of approaches to Bass Harbor Light.

Miss Ethanridge returned with coffee in a bone china cup and saucer, which she set on the table next to me. "Mr. Schmitt will be with you momentarily," she said before exiting.

I hadn't sipped coffee from a china cup in…hell, I can't remember such formality. My lawyer back in upstate New York ran his business out of a scruffy office with a secretary dressed in a man's flannel shirt and blue jeans. Jackson Catrini was his name. He handled all the crap associated with running a business and let me tell you, he was one tough son-of-a-bitch. Once when I was being sued by a client for *disregarding the explicit tenets of the contract*, Jackson went at him with such fury that we settled out of court with the client giving me two grand just to dump the counter suit. Jackson died right around the time I lost Lori. Hell, everybody I knew is dead or has disappeared from my life. And here I am in Portland, Maine sitting amidst law office splendor, wondering what the hell I'm doing here. But what's the alternative? If Arden Schmitt was good enough for Bob then he's good enough for me. I've got to trust somebody.

Arden appeared from behind a heavy paneled door just to the right of the sofa. White shirt, striped red, gold and blue tie, dark blue suspenders, perfectly pressed charcoal gray pinstripe trousers and cordovan wingtips were in complete contrast to what he had worn yesterday. Here I was in wrinkled kakis, an equally wrinkled blue short sleeved shirt, and worn Docksiders an army surplus duffle bag at my side.

"Good to see you again, Charlie," Arden said, coming over. I stood and we shook hand. "I trust that Bob's place is all set. The funeral home called and reported that everything was in order for the arrangements."

"Arrangements?" I asked softly.

"Bob's wishes are for his ashes to be spread around the island."

"That sounds like Bob." I was glad now that I tended to the lawn and flowers.

Arden's office carried on the décor of old New England prosperity. His antique mahogany desk sat in front of a large window overlooking Portland Harbor. Out there somewhere was *That Good Night,* waiting. That boat had become my home, my refuge, my future. Whatever I was or have become was tied to that vessel. She was my partner, my friend, protector, guardian of my soul. I was damn antsy to get back to her, to finish my voyage wherever it might take me.

Arden positioned himself behind his desk. I sat down in a comfortable chair facing him, clutching my duffle on my lap. "So, let's get down to business." Sliding a paper my way, he said, "This is a bill of retainer. Sign it and we're all set. Our retainer charge is $10,000. Is that okay?"

I nodded my approval and signed the form.

"First of all, I need to deposit most of this," I said, tapping my duffle. "My preference is that I can contact you for any amount I need. We'll need to figure out how you can get it to me. I have no address other than my boat and sending funds to a Lat/Lon will probably not work." Arden chuckled. "My guess is using a post office wherever I happen to be. Secondly, I want to write a will.

We spent a good part of two hours getting everything in order. Miss Ethanridge was charged with counting the money while Arden and I dealt with the will. I left his office just past noon with $25,000 dollars in cash stuffed in my pockets and a certified check in the amount of $10,000 as backup, which I had neatly folded in my buttoned shirt pocket. I decided to walk back to the marina dock even though it was hot and muggy. On my way, I stopped in at a sandwich shop, had a quick lunch, then bee-lined it back to *That Good Night*.

With the help of an experienced dock attendant, I moved *That Good Night* to the fuel dock to top off her tanks with diesel fuel and water. I took some extra time to run down my check list and found everything to be in order. I could have spent the night in Portland but, antsy to get underway, I decided to head down the coast, maybe stop in at Biddeford Pool or go further down to Portsmouth. The sky was clear blue, the barometer steady. I cast off from the fuel dock at 1310 hours.

Once clear of Portland Light, I raised the main, set the jib, trimmed to twelve knots of west-south-west wind, engaged the auto helm, and sat back to a glorious sail at a steady seven knots. What a beautiful day, a celebration, actually. The cool sea air was a welcomed relief. I went below, slipped a disc into the stereo, pushed the external speaker button and returned topside to listen to Bach's Brandenburg Concerto # 5. I grabbed a cushion, sat down on the starboard side and just listened: Bach accompanied by swishing saltwater flung aside by a slicing bow. There are few words to describe the feeling that enters a sailor's soul when all the elements are working in favor of a great sail. One might think that these moments occur frequently in a sailor's life, but not so. More often than not, winds are on the nose, or there's no wind at all, or it's blowing snot or gusting all over the place. Absolute contentment is rare and needs to be savored. Sort of like life, huh?

Biddeford Pool was soon off to starboard but there was no way that I was going to put in, not sailing like this. The wind had shifted a bit north. I eased the sails to a reach picking up another knot and a half. Sunset was late this time of year, probably around nine or so. I could probably make Portsmouth by nightfall, especially at this rate.

Luckily, I hit the Piscataqua near slack ebb. This river has one of the nastiest currents in North America and hitting it at the wrong time is no fun. With the wind now nearly on my nose, I furled both main and jib, favoring motoring up river, Maine to starboard, New Hampshire to port. There's enough eye candy on both banks to make this harbor entrance one of my favorites. After rounding a few bends, I spotted the Portsmouth Naval Shipyard, actually a misnomer considering that the installation is really in Kittery, Maine. I swung *That Good Night* to port and tied up at the Portsmouth City Dock.

I took a brief walk in the lush gardens surrounding the landing. Sitting on a bench, I watched children play, couples holding hands, folks meandering, stopping here and there to witness the simple beauty of blooming flowers. The antsy feeling I had about getting back to my boat, the feeling I had in Newport, was simply gone. I'm not sure what it was that came over me. All I can say is that I felt peaceful, happy to be alive. I suspect that Arden's words had something to do with it.

Yesterday when I was with Arden, talking about my will, I had made it clear that I didn't want my sons to have anything. When I told Arden that, his only comment was, "A bit harsh, isn't it?" At first, I blustered, carried on how they were ingrates, took my things, put me in a home.

To which Arden said, "But you're here, aren't you?"

"In spite of them!" I answered.

"Perhaps," Arden said to me quietly. "But, you're here," he repeated, and then went on, "I've written a lot of wills and believe me, rancor never works. Maybe your sons were a bit hasty, but maybe they were just trying to do their best. I'm your lawyer, not your spiritual advisor, so what I have to say on the subject of you and your relationship with your sons comes only from personal and professional experience. Maybe if you let your anger ease a bit, things will look different."

"I doubt it," I said, "but I'm willing to give it a try." At that, we both decided that I should write my will at another time, a time when I had thought things over. He gave me the necessary papers with the warning that I would have to have my signature witnessed by two persons and notarized before sending them to his office. His advice was echoing in my head since leaving Portland. Maybe just the thought of those words brought on this feeling of peace. Damn, could he be right?

With daylight slipping away, I returned to *That Good Night*. I ate some leftover lasagna and retired for the night.

THURSDAY, AUGUST 2

I awoke to the slaps of water against the hull. The Piscataqua was on the ebb which I'd have to catch if I wanted a fast ride out of there. I ate a hasty breakfast and with the help of the dock boy, cast off into the maniacal sluice at 0705 hours. *That Good Night's* propeller bit into the rushing water like nobody's business. The excitement of casting off in such waters is akin to parachuting where there is no chance of returning to safety if you make a mistake; it's do or die. Clear of the dock, I slung the wheel starboard, took the ebb on port and turned eastward toward the Atlantic. I was on my way, but I really wasn't sure where I was sailing to. There was no final destination, no schedule, only the notion that I was going to head for the Caribbean. I had broken my hard and fast rule of doing my navigation before leaving but this was of no concern. Once clear of the Piscataqua, I would be heading south in waters that I knew well. Take my pick: Cape Ann, Gloucester, Boston, Plymouth. I'll decide later. Right then I was enjoying a carnival ride.

Serendipitous sailing might not be a bad idea. My life had boiled down to that. It was not like I was running a business, meeting deadlines, putting food on the table, or meeting payroll. I was free of that now. In fact, I was free of everything, accountable to no one, no address, no mail, no identity. I don't know why, but I wondered what the folks back at Sunset were doing.

Enjoying what life they had left, I hoped. My guess is that with Roberts out of the picture, I'd be declared dead, the insurance company would iron out a settlement and my two boys would be in for a windfall. With no body, there'd probably have to be an inquest. Who knows? This was all bittersweet of course. On one hand I had only myself to be concerned about. On the other hand, I only had myself to be concerned about. Catch twenty-two.

With the wild push of an ebbing Piscataqua, I cleared Portsmouth Harbor motoring toward the Atlantic. With calm winds and seas, I left the sails furled until, nearing Cape Ann, I picked up a light land breeze of about eight knots. Unfurling all sails, I ghosted along the coast on my way to Gloucester Harbor, and here and there I was tied to a city mooring in one of the busiest fishing ports in New England. Of all the commercial ports I have visited, this is my favorite. With the hustle and bustle of fishing vessels and all the services that support the industry, the no-nonsense feel of this fisherman's paradise is in stark contrast to boat-packed marinas. You'll find no white painted rocks or yacht burgee laden yardarms dotting the busy shores of this harbor.

Now it may not seem all that exciting to a landlubber, but heading ashore after a day's sail is one of the great pleasures of cruising. You could cut the romance with a knife, not at all like visiting a place by car. Harbors like Gloucester are lined with history, of fishermen and adventurers coming and going. Swooping gulls; large and small vessels chugging in and out; their throaty diesels set on idle to obey no-wake rules; men busy loading and unloading stores or their catch. All with a backdrop of weathered shore side buildings dating back centuries.

I visited the famous fishermen's *Man at the Wheel* memorial. *Down to the Seas in Ships* is inscribed at the granite base of the iconic bronze oilskin-clad fisherman at the helm. Surrounding the memorial are small bronze plaques inscribed with the names of approximately 5,400 sailors lost at sea dating from 1715 to present day. Think of that when you eat fish!

I ended my visit by having a few beers at the Crow's Nest Bar, made famous by the Sebastian Junger's bestseller, *The Perfect Storm*, before grabbing a delicious fish dinner at a dockside restaurant.

Returning to *That Good Night*, I laid out a float plan for the next few days: Gloucester to Provincetown; Provincetown to Nantucket. I'd plan the rest of my southerly voyage in Nantucket. I pumped waypoints into the chart plotter, had my third scotch of the evening and went to bed with thoughts of the Caribbean Islands dancing merrily in my head. It was time to move on with what the rest of my life had in store.

FRIDAY, AUGUST 3

I was now moored in Provincetown Harbor. The forty nautical mile jaunt from Gloucester to Provincetown took me through Stellwagen Bank and with it the sighting of a mammoth humpback. I was close enough to catch the fishy smell of the whale's exhale and was glad that he didn't see *That Good Night* as a possible mate or as distant relative of the whaler *Essex*.

It's a stark contrast sailing from commercial Gloucester to the tourist Mecca of P-town. Instead of fish fresh off the docks, here there's trendy restaurants, more antique dealers than *Antiques Road Show* and galleries galore.

Lori and I had pictures on our walls, family photos. The boys covered their walls with posters ranging from athletes to rock stars. But art, no! Our home was devoid of anything challenging or even resembling art. At the machine shop we displayed posters of machinery with scantily clad beauties holding micrometers or depth gauges, all gifts of machinery salesmen. Rigid Pipe Company had the best posters. The truth is I have never walked into an art gallery in my long life before being lured into one in P-Town. Catching my eye in the window of a small gallery was a small oil seascape. I wandered into the store and bought the thing—$900 worth of art. The artist, a Nova Scotian named Leonard Lane, captured the sea the way I felt about it. I mean there is nothing stable about the ocean;

it's constantly changing and that's what this painting said to me. I hung it on the bulkhead forward of the port settee. I'm very proud of myself for buying it. Good for me.

I finished reading *A Coal Black Horse* last night. Tonight I'm starting *Last Stand at Saber River* by Elmore Leonard. An oldie but a goodie.

SATURDAY, AUGUST 4

I'm writing this from crowded Nantucket Harbor. The anchorage is boat on top of boat with little room to lay out a proper scope. I'm hooked in all right, but I don't know about everybody around me. If a blow comes up, I'll just hope that a slew of boats don't come bearing down on me.

I have no desire to go ashore except, perhaps, to buy some orange juice, which I can do without if need be. Provincetown was quite enough of the tourist trade for me. I'll take time to inventory my stores and plan the next leg of my voyage south.

Bob stays in my mind with more good memories than sad thoughts of his death. And Lori, as well. I'm feeling younger, freer to think ahead. More open. I'm not sure why and quite frankly, I don't care to analyze the feeling of freedom that's come over me. I will say that putting the past in the past is just where the past ought to stay. Of course that means having an eye for the future. The further ahead you can think the younger you become.

In Provincetown, I met a young couple who were anchored just off my port side. When I was zipping back from shore, I passed close astern to their boat. Peering over they hailed me over to compliment me on *That Good Night*. Always nice to receive compliments, and she gets a lot of them. I invited them over and we decided to have dinner together. I offered the main course of fresh haddock, which I purchased in Gloucester with the proviso that they do the cooking. Gene and Cheryl Breckenridge were their names. They also brought salad and a dessert. We had a wonderful time with Gene doing the cooking, Cheryl doing the clean-up and yours truly pouring the wine. I didn't discuss anything dealing with my past, sticking strictly to jawing on about happenings at sea and saying that I was heading south. Gene and Cheryl were on their maiden voyage, having just purchased a used sturdy thirty-two foot Saber. Full of piss and vinegar they were. Hopes and dreams of sailing ventures flowed like the wine. Hailing from Boston, they had planned to return the next day. "Are you on Facebook?" Cheryl asked me. I had heard of it but really didn't have a clue how to use it. And I had no email address either, or land address for that matter. She was a bit amazed at all of that.

After Gene and Cheryl left, I sat down and wrote my will. The writing wasn't as difficult as I thought it might be. Actually, I took stock of things rather quickly, surprising myself that in less than hour, I was finished. Writing the will was cathartic. Who and what was important to me became clear. I thanked *That Good Night* as if it was she that had sent me off on a journey of self discovery, a voyage into the unknown regions of my soul. A sailboat can do that. I'll get it witnessed and notarized before sending it off to Arden tomorrow.

More Elmore Leonard then to bed.

SUNDAY, AUGUST 5

Not much to write about today. I spent most of the day giving thought to where I wanted to go, settling on St. Thomas or maybe just Florida for the winter. It's only early August and to rush my way south doesn't seem like a good idea. I had given thought of heading to the Chesapeake but August there would mean hot, humid conditions; the one thing *That Good Night* doesn't have is air conditioning. Any further south than that only invites troubling hurricane watches.

I decided to head back up north, maybe Boston, maybe Portsmouth. Either would work well for me given I could get a dock space close enough to the city that I wouldn't need a car or have to rely too much on public transportation. Of course, Boston had the extra attraction of perhaps seeing Abigail again.

I decided on Portsmouth—a 120-nautical-mile voyage was just about right for an overnight sail. The whole Abigail thing helped tip the scale—best to leave that good memory undisturbed. Based on averaging six knots, twenty or so hours should do it. I'd use Boston as a place to jump into if needed. My sailplan called for departing Nantucket at around noon with an ETA at Portsmouth somewhere around eight o'clock the next morning. I would have to keep a good watch crossing the Boston shipping lanes.

MONDAY, AUGUST 6 –

THURSDAY, AUGUST 9

Disaster. I'm writing this after days of just trying to stay alive. I'll do my best to give an accurate accounting, but to be honest, the three days I'm covering here seemed to blend into one unending stretch of time. One minute, the sun was out, the next it was dark.

Sixty-nautical miles into the voyage north, I was hit with a squall. With the autohelm on, I had dozed off for probably a half hour or so before being awakened by a rather unhappy *That Good Night*. The wind indicator showed wind coming from all over the place with gusts to 25 knots. The barometer was falling. Air temperature cooling. I've been in squalls before; they're no big deal if you handle them right. It was about 1730 hours and I was sailing with a reefed main and jib. On my way topsides, I flicked on the running lights. Once on deck, I kicked off the auto-helm, brought her about and furled the jib and main, opting to go bare pole; let the boat deal with it. The wind was now topping 20, gusting to 30 knots. I was far enough from land and shipping lanes not to worry too much. Besides these storms usually blow through in half an hour or so.

As I was descending the ship ladder, *That Good Night* took a wave on her starboard quarter. I was tossed like an old beanbag onto the cabin sole. The pain in my back was immediate. With the boat being whacked from all directions, I couldn't get up if I wanted to. I was a loose cannon, moving around wherever momentum decided to take me. On one roll, I was able to wedge my way into the galley area, and held on for dear life. Every movement brought pain soaring into my lower back. I nearly passed out.

Maybe a half-hour later, maybe an eternity, the wind abated. The sea state took a while longer to settle. My right leg was akimbo, my hip swollen. This was Sunset revisited. Broken hips were death notices. But I wasn't some debilitated old lady who took a spill on the slick lunchroom linoleum. I was a sailor, dammit! Maybe it was just a little crack. Give it some time, I said to myself. A few days and I'll be hobbling around. In the meanwhile I'll just lay low. Maybe just heave-to for a bit.

The boat finally steadying, I crawled along the cabin sole to the starboard settee, clawed my way upward, rolled onto the soft cushion and passed out.

It was pitch black when I awoke. My right leg was stiff as a baseball bat. Any movement brought severe pain. So what, grin and bear it! When I was a kid, my dad took me to a dentist who didn't believe in using an anesthetic. He had this sadistic philosophy that the pain of getting a tooth drilled without a painkiller would encourage kids to brush their teeth. Well, I brushed like hell and it didn't help all that much. We didn't have fluoride back then. That was what was running through my mind: grip the black arms of the dentist chair and squeeze like a son-of-a bitch. What the hell choice did I have? Single-handed drifting on the ocean blue. Call the coast guard? And then what, wind up in a hospital. Not on your life. No, make that not on *my* life.

I reached up and grabbed the handrail. Yelling like a stuck pig and running through my rather extensive repertoire of expletives, I hobbled over to the navigation station. It was 0120 hours. I flicked on the cabin lights. I had been drifting for over five hours. W 42 20.02; N 69 10.08. Depth 126 fathoms. *That Good Night* was drifting almost due east—next stop Falmouth, England. I was about fifty nautical miles off course. So what? I had a lot of food, water, and fuel. If I wasn't run over by a tanker or fishing boat, if I didn't hit some floating whatever-the-hell-it-might-be, I'd just drift and take it easy. I'd heal slowly, but I was most confident that I'd make out somehow. A few days and I'd be up and about. The boat was as solid as a boat can be. Hell, she might even enjoy being on her own for awhile.

Going handrail to handrail, I made my way to the head. Taking a piss was another torture. It dribbled out in drops—so much for pissing a steady stream. But I could deal with that; old men do all the time. But I couldn't deal with rose colored piss. I was bleeding inside. My bravado burst like a pricked balloon. Goddammit!

At the vanity, I reached into my medical kit and pocketed a vial of Hydrocodone, 500MG. Back at the starboard settee, I reached into the hanging locker, retrieved a bottle of scotch and washed down three pills. Before falling to sleep, I knew that there was no way out of this. Either I called the Coast Guard and I submitted myself to the indignities of another Sunset, or I call it a day. My final sunset. I slept on and off, drank orange juice, ate slices of bread and a can of sardines. I took more pills.

FRIDAY, AUGUST 10

The sun was peeking over the horizon when I awoke. *That Good Night* was resting on calm seas. The swelling in my right hip has increased. Streaks of pain are racing across my groin. I feel weak and a little light headed. My piss is redder. All I want to do is sleep. I'm dying and I know it.

Call the Coast Guard or take morphine? I choose morphine. It's not much of a choice, really. I can't get on deck to manage the sails or start the engine. If I called the Coast Guard, well, that would be the end of my future. I know where I would wind up and that's not going to happen.

When I add it all up, I'd say that I did pretty well for myself. I've cleared my head of bitterness—better late than never. I got to live my final days the way I chose. Cleared my decks to use a worn out phrase. I enjoyed the romance of a last love.

I've made inner peace with my sons. Charles Jr. and Thomas will live a better life because of me. I hope they can forgive their dear old dad. I think business was as much a mistress as it was a way of making money. It sure kept me away from family.

My plan is to fill two syringes of morphine, more than enough to cause my death. Go topsides, open the lifeline gate, sit on the rail, and inject myself. I'll fetch my lunch hook out of the port locker and tie it on. That ought to sink old Charlie just as its chain took care of Ivan and Doris. When I pass out,

I'll fall into the water and let the sea claim what she will.

I crawled to my dresser and retrieved the morphine. I injected 4mg, a sort of test. The pain eased considerably. So did the twirling in my head. I hobbled around making sure that the boat was presentable before filling two syringes with morphine which I put into my shirt pocket.

I'm putting these writings into an envelope along with Robert's tricky belt buckle, and addressing it to Abigail and leaving another envelope for Arden. Add to the list a note to the Coast Guard. Then I'll pour a big glass of Scotch and toast my life and everyone who helped me define who I am. Before going topside, I'll click on the EPIRB.

I'm ready to go topside this one last time. It's amazing how good I feel and it's not just the morphine. It's more like I'm relieved, the game is over, and I won. This has been a wonderful adventure but it's over. Thank God that I'm still in command, that I have the right to make my own decision about life and death. I choose death not as the dark side. But, as a place to go. A port in a storm. Perhaps like Henlopen Harbor or Point Judith. I heard it said once that anyone committing suicide is insane. Well, I'm not anywhere near insane. I'm a man who luckily was able to spend my final days doing what I wanted to do. And, by God, that's just what I did. Like I mentioned earlier, I'm not religious, but there is a little bit of comfort in thinking that I might see Lori again. That's what I want to be my last thought, of seeing Lori in the dress she wore on our first date. The one with flowers and short puffy sleeves.

POSTSCRIPT

The Will:

I, Charles Lambert, being of sound mind do hereby bequeath my estate as follows:

To Catlin Giffords I leave the sum of $50,000 dollars to be held in trust by Attorney Arden Schmidt until Catlin reaches the age of 18. My hopes are that he will use the money to advance his education but it is not required that he do so.

To Abigail Tennera, I leave the sum of $35,000.

To Sunset Nursing Home, I leave the sum of $25,000 to establish an endowment for a dog-in-residence program.

The remainder of my funds will be equally shared by my two sons, Charles Lambert Jr. and Thomas Lambert. Be happy, boys. Play as hard as you work.

ACKNOWLEDGMENTS

Writing a book is akin to solo voyaging. While there are many hours spent alone, perils to overcome, and bouts of waning courage, the knowing that concerned friends await in ports-of-call is a propelling force to complete the journey. And so as *That Good Night* reaches shore, I take this opportunity to thank those who helped make for a safe passage.

Dan Van Tassel, a retired Literature Professor and college dean gave me the go ahead without, thankfully, assigning a grade. Claudia Hornby, a friend and sailor was eager to help from day one. Steve McPherson, a yacht-broker, gave me a reality check on how the business works. Andy McPherson, golf partner—need I say more? Mary Kaskan, a newspaper editor who, bless her heart, forsook the blue pencil in favor of asking a lot of *who, what, when, where and whys*. John and Betty Probert, brother and sister-in-law for their suggestions and constant encouragement. James Chingos, MD for his advice and counsel which, hopefully, I got right. Then there is Karen Kaderavak, superb cellist and profound thinker who helped me tremendously with the flow of Charlie's tale. Bill Bolin of Island Packet Yachts and Edward Massey of Massey Yacht Sales for being sure I knew the wonders of the Island Packet 46. Dave Harrison, a Mainer through and through and one hell of a sailing buddy, helped me understand—if that's possible—what it's like to be born and bred Downeast.

Thanks turns into deep appreciation for my wife and dear friend, Carmelita Britton for everything she had to deal with in shepherding me through the process of writing a book. From first draft to tenth draft, from rejections to publisher's acceptance, from edits to finished product, Carmelita was the lighthouse that guided me from the storm-tossed seas of creativity to the calm waters of a voyage ended.

Many thanks to my editor, Megan Trank and her crew at Beaufort Books for their collective patience, advice, and encouragement. That goes as well for my agent Doug Grad whose tenacity and boundless energy made sure that I'd reach shore in one piece.